CW00493469

THE SILVER CANYON: A TALE
PLAINS
BY
George Manville Fenn

THE SILVER CANYON: A TALE OF THE WESTERN PLAINS

Published by Lasso Press

New York City, NY

First published circa 1909

Copyright © Lasso Press, 2015

All rights reserved

Except in the United States of America, this book is sold subject to the condition that it shall not, by way of trade or otherwise, be lent, re-sold, hired out, or otherwise circulated without the publisher's prior consent in any form of binding or cover other than that in which it is published and without a similar condition including this condition being imposed on the subsequent purchaser.

ABOUT LASSO PRESS

Lasso Press brings the Wild West back to life with the greatest Western classics ever put to paper.

Chapter One.: How they decided to run the Risk.

"Well, Joses," said Dr Lascelles, "if you feel afraid, you had better go back to the city."

There was a dead silence here, and the little party grouped about between a small umbrella-shaped tent and the dying embers of the fire, at which a meal of savoury antelope steaks had lately been cooked, carefully avoided glancing one at the other.

Just inside the entrance of the tent, a pretty, slightly-made girl of about seventeen was seated, busily plying her needle in the repair of some rents in a pair of ornamented loose leather leggings that had evidently been making acquaintance with some of the thorns of the rugged land. She was very simply dressed, and, though wearing the high comb and depending veil of a Spanish woman, her complexion, tanned is it was, and features, suggested that she was English, as did also the speech of the fine athletic middle-aged man who had just been speaking.

His appearance, too, was decidedly Spanish, for he wore the short jacket with embroidered sleeves, tight trousers—made very wide about the leg and ankle-sash, and broad sombrero of the Mexican-Spanish inhabitant of the south-western regions of the great American continent.

The man addressed was a swarthy-looking half-breed, who lay upon the parched earth, his brow rugged, his eyes half-closed, and lips pouted out in a surly, resentful way, as if he were just about to speak and say something nasty.

Three more men of a similar type were lying beside and behind, all smoking cigarettes, which from time to time they softly rolled up and lighted with a brand at the fire, as they seemed to listen to the conversation going on between the bronzed Englishman and him who had been addressed as Joses.

They were all half-breeds, and boasted of their English blood, but always omitted to say anything about the Indian fluid that coursed through their veins; while they followed neither the fashion of Englishman nor Indian in costume, but, like the first speaker, were dressed as Spaniards, each also wearing a handkerchief of bright colour tied round his head and beneath his soft hat, just as if a wound had been received, with a long showy blanket depending from the shoulder, and upon which they now half lay.

There was another present, however, also an anxious watcher of the scene, and that was a well-built youth of about the same age as the girl. For the last five minutes he had been busily cleaning his rifle and oiling the lock; and this task done, he let the weapon rest with its butt upon the rocky earth, its sling-strap hanging loose, and its muzzle lying in his hand as he leaned against a rock and looked sharply from face to face, waiting to hear the result of the conversation.

His appearance was different to that of his companions, for he wore a closely fitting tunic and loose breeches of what at the first glance seemed to be dark tan-coloured velvet, but a second look showed to be very soft, well-prepared deerskin; stout gaiters of a hard leather protected his legs; a belt, looped so as to form a cartridge-holder, and a natty little felt hat, completed his costume.

Like the half-breeds, he wore a formidable knife in his belt, while on their part each had near him a rifle.

"Well," said the speaker, after a long pause, "you do not speak; I say, are you afraid?"

"I dunno, master," said the man addressed. "I don't feel afraid now, but if a lot of Injuns come whooping and swooping down upon us full gallop, I dessay I should feel a bit queer."

There was a growl of acquiescence here from the other men, and the first speaker went on.

"Well," he said, "let us understand our position at once. I would rather go on alone than with men I could not trust."

"Always did trust us, master," said the man surlily.

"Allays," said the one nearest to him, a swarthier, more surly, and fiercer-looking fellow than his companion.

"I always did, Joses; I always did, Juan; and you too, Harry and Sam," said the first speaker. "I was always proud of the way in which my ranche was protected and my cattle cared for."

"We could not help the Injuns stampeding the lot, master, time after time."

"And ruining me at last, my lads? No; it was no fault of yours. I suppose it was my own."

"No, master, it was setting up so close to the hunting-grounds, and the Injun being so near."

"Ah well, we need not consider how all that came to pass, my lads: we know they ruined me."

"And you never killed one o' them for it, master," growled Joses.

"Nor wished to, my lad. They did not take our lives."

"But they would if they could have broken in and burnt us out, master," growled Joses.

"Perhaps so; well, let us understand one another. Are you afraid?"

"Suppose we all are, master," said the man.

"And you want to go back?"

"No, not one of us, master."

Here there was a growl of satisfaction.

"But you object to going forward, my men?"

"Well, you see it's like this, master: the boys here all want to work for you, and young Master Bart, and Miss Maude there; but they think you ought to go where it's safe-like, and not where we're 'most sure to be tortured and scalped. There's lots o' places where the whites are in plenty."

"And where every gully and mountain has been ransacked for metals, my lad. I want to go where white men have never been before, and search the mountains there."

"For gold and silver and that sort of thing, master?"

"Yes, my lads."

"All right, master; then we suppose you must go."

"And you will go back because it is dangerous?"

"I never said such a word, master. I only said it warn't safe."

"And for answer to that, Joses, I say that, danger or no danger, I must try and make up for my past losses by some good venture in one of these unknown regions. Now then, have you made up your minds? If not, make them up quickly, and let me know what you mean to do."

Joses did not turn round to his companions, whose spokesman he was, but said quietly, as he rolled up a fresh cigarette:

"Mind's made up, master."

"And you will go back?"

"Yes, master."

"All of you?"

"All of us, master," said Joses slowly. "When you do," he added after a pause.

"I knew he would say that, sir," cried the youth who had been looking on and listening attentively; "I knew Joses would not leave us, nor any of the others."

"Stop a moment," interposed the first speaker. "What about your companions, my lad?"

"What, them?" said Joses quietly. "Why, they do as I do."

"Are you sure?"

"Course I am, master. They told me what to do."

"Then thank you, my lad. I felt and knew I could trust you. Believe me, I will take you into no greater danger than I can help; but we must be a little venturesome in penetrating into new lands, and the Indians may not prove our enemies after all."

"Ha, ha, ha! Haw, haw, haw, haw!" laughed Joses hoarsely. "You wait and see, master. They stampeded your cattle when you had any. Now look out or they'll stampede you."

"Well, we'll risk it," said the other. "Now let's be ready for any danger that comes. Saddle the horses, and tether them close to the waggon. I will have the first watch to-night; you take the second, Joses; and you, Bart, take the third. Get to sleep early, my lads, for I want to be off before sunrise in the morning."

The men nodded their willingness to obey orders, and soon after all were hushed in sleep, the ever-wakeful stars only looking down upon one erect figure, and that was the form of Dr Lascelles, as he stood near the faintly glowing fire, leaning upon his rifle, and listening intently for the faintest sound of danger that might be on its way to work them harm.

Chapter Two.: What went before.

As Dr Lascelles stood watching there, his thoughts naturally went back to the events of the past day, the sixth since they had bidden good-bye to civilisation and started upon their expedition. He thought of the remonstrance offered by his men to their proceeding farther; then of the satisfactory way in which the difficulty had been settled; and later on of the troubles brought up by his man's remarks. He recalled the weary years he had spent upon his cattle farm, in which he had invested after the death of his wife in England; how he had come out to New Mexico, and settled down to form a cattle-breeding establishment with his young daughter Maude for companion.

Then he thought of how everything had gone wrong, not only with him, but with his neighbours, one of the nearest being killed by an onslaught of a savage tribe of Indians, the news being brought to him by the son of the slaughtered man. The result had been that the Doctor had determined to flee at once; but the day was put off, and as no more troubles presented themselves just then, he once more settled down. Young Bart became by degrees almost as it were a son, and the fight was continued till herd after herd had been swept away by the Indians; and at last Dr Lascelles, the clever physician who had wearied of England and his practice after his terrible loss, and who had come out to the West to seek rest and make money for his child, found himself a beggar, and obliged to begin life again.

Earlier in life he had been a great lover of geology, and was something of a metallurgist; and though he had of late devoted himself to the wild, rough life of a western cattle farmer, he had now and then spent a few hours in exploring the mountainous parts of the country near: so that when he had once more to look the world in the face, and decide whether he should settle down as some more successful cattle-breeder's man, the idea occurred to him that his knowledge of geology might prove useful in this painful strait.

He jumped at the idea.

Of course: why not? Scores of men had made discoveries of gold, silver, and other valuable metals, and the result had been fortune. Why should not he do something of the kind?

He mentioned the idea to young Bartholomew Woodlaw, who jumped at the prospect, but looked grave directly after.

"I should like it, Mr Lascelles," he said, "but there is Maude."

"What of her?" said the Doctor.

"How could we take her into the wilds?"

"It would be safer to take her into the deserts and mountains, than to leave her here," said the Doctor bitterly. "I should at least always have her under my eye."

He went out and told his men, who were hanging about the old ranche although there was no work for them to do.

One minute they were looking dull and gloomy, the next they were waving their hats and blankets in the air, and the result of it all was that in less than a month Dr Lascelles had well stored a waggon with the wreck of his fortune, purchased a small tent for his daughter's use, and, all well-armed, the little party had started off into the wilds of New Mexico, bound for the mountain region, where the Doctor hoped to make some discovery of mineral treasure sufficient to recompense him for all his risk, as well as for the losses of the past.

They were, then, six days out when there was what had seemed to be a sort of mutiny among his men—a trouble that he was in the act of quelling when we made his acquaintance in the last chapter—though, as we have seen, it proved to be no mutiny at all, but merely a remonstrance on the part of the rough, honest fellows who had decided to share his fortunes, against running into what they esteemed to be unnecessary risks.

Joses and his three fellows were about as brigandish and wild-looking a set of half savages as a traveller could light upon in a day's journey even in these uncivilised parts. In fact, no stranger would have been ready to trust his life or property in their keeping, if he could have gone farther. If he had, though, he would most probably have fared worse; for it is not always your pleasantest outside that proves to hide the best within.

These few lines, then, will place the reader au courant, as the French say, with the reason of the discussion at the beginning of the last chapter, and show him as well why it was that Dr Lascelles, Bart Woodlaw, and Maud Lascelles were out there in the desert with such rough companions. This being then the case, we will at once proceed to deal with their adventurous career.

Chapter Three.: The First Apachés.

Evening was closing in, and the ruddy, horizontal rays of the sun were casting long grotesque shadows of the tall-branched plants of the cactus family that stood up, some like great fleshy leaves, rudely stuck one upon the other, and some like strangely rugged and prickly fluted columns, a body of Indians, about a hundred strong, rode over the plain towards the rocks where Dr Lascelles and his little party were encamped.

The appearance of the Indians denoted that they were on the war-path. Each wore a rude tiara of feathers around his head, beneath which hung wild his long black hair; and saving their fringed and ornamented leggings, the men rode for the most part naked, and with their breasts and arms painted in a coarse and extravagant style. Some had a rude representation of a Death's head and bones in the centre of the chest; others were streaked and spotted; while again others wore a livery of a curiously mottled fashion, that seemed to resemble the markings of a tortoise, but was intended to imitate the changing aspect of a snake.

All were fully armed, some carrying rifles, others bows and arrows, while a few bore spears, from the top of whose shafts below the blades hung tufts of feathers. Saddles they had none, but each sturdy, well-built Indian pony was girt with its rider's blanket or buffalo robe, folded into a pad, and secured tightly with a broad band of raw hide. Bits and bridles too, of the regular fashion, were wanting, the swift pony having a halter of horse-hair hitched round its lower jaw, this being sufficient to enable the rider to guide the docile little animal where he pleased; while for tethering purposes, during a halt, there was a stout long peg, and the rider's plaited hide lariat or lasso, ready for a variety of uses in the time of need.

The rugged nature of the ground separated the party of Indians from the Doctor's little camp, so that the approach of the war party was quite unobserved, and apparently, from their movements, they were equally unaware of the presence of a camp of the hated whites so near at hand.

They were very quiet, riding slowly and in regular order, as if moved by one impulse; and when the foremost men halted, all drew rein by some tolerably verdant patches of the plain, blankets and robes were unstrapped, the horses allowed to graze, and in an incredibly short time the band had half a dozen fires burning of wood that had been hastily collected, and they were ravenously devouring the strips of dried buffalo meat that had been hanging all day in the hot sun, to be peppered with dust from the plain, and flavoured by emanations from the horse against whose flank it had been beaten.

This, however, did not trouble the savages, whom one learned in the lore of the plains would have immediately set down as belonging to a powerful tribe of horse Indians—the Apachés, well-known for their prowess in war and their skill as wild-horsemen of the plains. They feasted on, like men whose appetites had become furious from long fasting, until at last they had satisfied their hunger, and the evening shadows were making the great plants of cactus stand up, weird and strange, against the fast-darkening evening sky; then, while the embers of the fire grew more ruddy and bright, each Indian, save those deputed to look after the horses and keep on the watch for danger, drew his blanket or buffalo robe over his naked shoulders, filled and lit his long pipe, and began silently and thoughtfully to smoke.

Meanwhile, in utter unconsciousness of the nearness of danger, Dr Lascelles continued his watch thus far into the night. From time to time he examined the tethering of the horses, and glanced inside the tent to stand and listen to the regular low breathing of his child, and then walk to where, rolled in his blanket, Bart Woodlaw lay sleeping in full confidence that a good watch was being kept over the camp as he slept.

Then the Doctor tried to pierce the gloom around.

Away towards the open plains it was clear and transparent, but towards the rocks that stretched there on one side all seemed black. Not a sound fell upon his ear, and so great was the stillness that the dull crackle of a piece of smouldering wood sounded painfully loud and strange.

At last the time had come for arousing some one to take his place, and walking, after a few moments' thought, to where Bart lay, he bent down and touched him lightly on the arm.

In an instant, rifle in hand, the lad was upon his feet.

"Is there danger?" he said in a low, quiet whisper.

"I hope not, Bart," said the Doctor quietly, "everything is perfectly still. I shall lie down in front of the tent; wake me if you hear a sound."

The lad nodded, and then stood trying to shake off the drowsiness that still remained after his deep sleep while he watched the Doctor's figure grow indistinct as he walked towards the dimly seen tent. He could just make out that the Doctor bent down, and then he seemed to disappear.

Bart Woodlaw remained motionless for a few moments, and then, as he more fully realised his duties, he walked slowly to where the horses were tethered, patted each in turn, the gentle animals responding with a low sigh as they pressed their heads closely to the caressing hand. Satisfied that the tethering ropes were safe, and dreading no hostile visit that might result in a stampede, the guardian of the little camp walked slowly to where the fire emitted a faint glow; and, feeling chilly, he was about to throw on more wood, when it occurred to him that if he did so, the fire would show out plainly for a distance of many miles, and that it would serve as a sign to invite enemies if any were within eyeshot, so he preferred to suffer from the cold, and, drawing his blanket round him, he left the fire to go out.

Bart had been watching the stars for about an hour, staring at the distant plain, and trying to make out what was the real shape of a pile of rock that sheltered them on the north, and which seemed to stand out peculiarly clear against the dark sky, when, turning sharply, he brought his rifle to the ready, and stood, with beating heart, staring at a tall dark figure that remained motionless about a dozen yards away.

It was so dark that he could make out nothing more, only that it was a man, and that he did not move.

The position was so new, and it was so startling to be out there in the wilds alone as it were—for the others were asleep—and then to turn round suddenly and become aware of the fact that a tall dark figure was standing where there was nothing only a few minutes before, that in spite of a strong effort to master himself, Bart Woodlaw felt alarmed in no slight degree.

His first idea was that this must be an enemy, and that he ought to fire. If an enemy, it must be an Indian; but then it did not look like an Indian; and Bart knew that it was his duty to walk boldly up to the figure, and see what the danger was; and in this spirit he took one step forward, and then stopped,—for it was not an easy thing to do.

The night seemed to have grown blacker, but there was the dark figure all the same, and it seemed to stand out more plainly than before, but it did not move, and this gave it an uncanny aspect that sent something of a chill through the watcher's frame.

At last he mastered himself, and, with rifle held ready, walked boldly towards the figure, believing that it was some specimen of the fleshy growth of the region to which the darkness had added a weirdness all its own.

No. It was a man undoubtedly, and as, nerving himself more and more, Bart walked close up, the figure turned, and said slowly:—

"I can't quite make that out, Master Bart."

"You, Joses!" exclaimed Bart, whose heart seemed to give a bound of delight.

"Yes, sir; I thought I'd get up and watch for a bit; and just as I looked round before coming to you, that rock took my fancy."

"Yes, it does look quaint and strange," said Bart; "I had been watching it."

"Yes, but why do it look quaint and strange?" said Joses in a low, quiet whisper, speaking as if a dozen savages were at his elbow.

"Because we can see it against the sky," replied Bart, who felt half amused at the importance placed by his companion upon such a trifle.

"And why can you see it against the sky?" said Joses again. "Strikes me there's a fire over yonder."

Bart was about to exclaim, "What nonsense!" but he recalled the times when out hunting up stray cattle Joses had displayed a perception that had seemed almost marvellous, and so he held his tongue.

"I'll take a turn out yonder, my lad," he said quietly; "I won't be very long."

"Shall I wake up the Doctor?"

"No, not yet. Let him get a good rest," replied Joses. "Perhaps it's nothing to mind; but coming out here we must be always ready to find danger, and danger must be ready to find us on the look-out."

"I'll go with you," said Bart eagerly.

"No, that won't do," said the rough fellow sturdily. "You've got to keep watch like they tell me the sailors do out at sea. Who's to take care of the camp if you go away?"

"I'll stay then," said Bart, with a sigh of dissatisfaction, and the next minute he was alone. For Joses had thrown down his blanket, and laid his rifle upon it carefully, while over the lock he had placed his broad Spanish hat to keep off the moisture of the night air. Then he had gone silently off at a trot over the short and scrubby growth near at hand.

One moment he was near; the next he had grown as it were misty in the darkness, and disappeared, leaving Bart, fretting at the inaction, and thinking that the task of doing duty in watching as sentry was the hardest he had been called upon to perform.

Meanwhile the rough cattle driver and plainsman had continued his trot till the broken nature of the ground compelled him to proceed cautiously, threading his way in and out amongst the masses of rock, and forcing him to make a considerable détour before he passed the ridge of stones.

His first act was to drop down on hands and knees; his next to lie flat, and drag himself slowly forward a couple of hundred yards, and then stop.

It was quite time that he had, for on either hand, as well as in front, lay groups of Indians, while just beyond he could distinguish the horses calmly cropping the grass and other herbage near. So still was it, and so closely had he approached, that every mouthful seized by the horses sounded quite plainly upon his ear, while more than once came the mutterings of some heavy sleeper, with an occasional hasty movement on the part of some one who was restless.

Joses had found out all he wanted, and the next thing was to get back and give the alarm. But as is often the case in such matters, it was easier to come than to return. It had to be done though, for the position of those in the little camp was one full of peril, and turning softly, he had begun his retrograde movement, when a figure he had not seen suddenly uttered an impatient "ugh!" and started to his feet.

Joses' hand went to his belt and grasped his knife, but that was all. It was not the time for taking to headlong flight, an act which would have brought the whole band whooping and yelling at his heels.

Fortunately for the spy in the Indian camp, the night was darker now, a thin veil of cloud having swept over the stars, otherwise the fate of Dr Lascelles' expedition would have been sealed. As it was, the Indian kicked the form beside him heavily with his moccasined foot, and then walked slowly away in the direction of the horses.

Some men would have continued their retreat at once, perhaps hurriedly, but Joses was too old a campaigner for such an act. As he lay there, with his face buried deeply in the short herbage, he thought to himself that most probably the waking up of the Indian who had just gone, the kick, and the striding away, would have aroused some of the others, and in this belief he lay perfectly still for quite ten minutes.

Then feeling satisfied that he might continue his retreat, he was drawing himself together for a fresh start, when a man on his right leaped to his feet; another did the same, and after talking together for a few moments they too went off in the direction of the horses.

This decided Joses upon a fresh wait, which he kept up, till feeling that, safe or unsafe, he must make the venture, he once more started, crawling slowly along without making a sound, till he felt it safe to rise to his hands and knees, when he got over the ground far more swiftly, ending by springing to his feet, and listening intently for a few moments, when there was the faint neigh of a horse from the Indian camp.

"If one of ours hears that," muttered Joses, "he'll answer, and the Indians will be down upon us before we know where we are."

Chapter Four.: The Night Alarm.

Bart Woodlaw had not been keeping his renewed watch long before he heard a step behind him, and, turning sharply, found himself face to face with Dr Lascelles.

"Well, my boy," he said, "is all right?"

"I think so, sir. Did you hear anything?"

"No, my boy, I woke up and just came to see how matters were going. Any alarm?"

"Yes, sir, and no, sir," replied Bart.

"What do you mean?" exclaimed the Doctor sharply.

"Only that Joses woke up, sir, and I found him watching that mass of rock which you can see out yonder. That one sir—or—no!—I can't see it now."

"Why?" said the Doctor, in a quick low decisive tone; "is it darker now?"

"Very little, sir; but perhaps Joses was right: he said he thought there must be a fire out there to make it stand out so clearly, and—"

"Well? speak, my boy! Be quick!"

"Perhaps he was right, sir, for I cannot see the rock there at all."

"Where is Joses? Why did he not go and see?" exclaimed the Doctor sharply.

"He has been gone nearly an hour, sir, and I was expecting him back when you came."

"That's right! But which way? Joses must feel that there is danger, or he would not have left the camp like this."

Bart pointed in the direction taken by their follower, and the Doctor took a few hasty strides forward, as if to follow, but he came back directly.

"No. It would be folly," he said; "I should not find him out in this wild. Depend upon it, Bart, that was an Indian fire and camp out beyond the ridge yonder, and he suspected it. These old plainsmen read every sign of earth and sky, and we must learn to do the same, boy, for it may mean the saving of our lives."

"I'll try," said Bart earnestly. "I can follow trail a little now."

"Yes, and your eyes are wonderfully keen," replied the Doctor. "You have all the acute sense of one of these hunters, but you want the power of applying what you see, and learning its meaning."

Bart was about to reply, but the Doctor began walking up and down impatiently, for being more used than his ward in the ways of the plains, he could not help feeling sure that there was danger, and this idea grew upon him to such an extent that at last he roused the men from their sleep, bidding them silently get the horses ready for an immediate start, should it be necessary; and while this was going on, he went into the tent.

"Maude—my child—quick!" he said quietly. "Don't be alarmed, but wake up, and be ready for a long ride before dawn."

Maude was well accustomed to obey promptly all her father's orders, and so used to the emergencies and perils of frontier life that she said nothing, but rapidly prepared for their start, and in a few minutes she was ready, with all her little travelling possessions in the saddle-bags and valise that were strapped to her horse.

Just as the Doctor had seen that all was nearly ready, and that scarcely anything more remained to be done than to strike the little tent, Joses came running up.

"Well! what news?" said the Doctor, hurriedly.

"Injun—hundreds—mile away," said the plainsman in quick, sharp tones. "Hah! good!" he added, as he saw the preparations that had been made.

"Bart, see to Maude's horse. Down with the tent, Joses; Harry, help him. You, Juan and Sam, see to the horses."

Every order was obeyed with the promptitude displayed in men accustomed to a life on the plains, and in a very few minutes the tent was down, rolled up, and on the side of the waggon, the steeds were ready, and all mounting save Juan, who took his place in front of the waggon to drive its two horses, Dr Lascelles gave the word. Joses went to the front to act as pioneer, and pick a way unencumbered with stones, so that the waggon might go on in safety, and the camp was left behind.

Everything depended now upon silence. A shrill neigh from a mare would have betrayed them; even the louder rattle of the waggon wheels might have had that result, and brought upon them the marauding party, with a result that the Doctor shuddered to contemplate. There were moments when, in the face of such a danger, he felt disposed to make his way back to civilisation, dreading now to take his child out with him into the wilderness. But there was something so tempting in the freedom of the life; he felt so sanguine of turning his knowledge of metallurgy to some account; and what was more, it seemed so cowardly to turn back now, that he decided to go forward and risk all.

"We always have our rifles," he said softly to himself, "and if we can use them well, we may force the Indians to respect us if they will not treat us as friends."

And all this while the waggon jolted on over the rough ground or rolled smoothly over the flat plain, crushing down the thick buffalo-grass, or smashing some succulent, thorny cactus with a peculiar whishing sound that seemed to penetrate far through the silence of the night. They were journeying nearly due north, and so far they had got on quite a couple of miles without a horse uttering its shrill neigh, and it was possible that by now, silent as was the night, their cry might not reach the keen ears of their enemies, but all the same, the party proceeded as cautiously as possible, and beyond an order now and then given in a low voice, there was not a word uttered.

It was hard work, too, for, proceeding as they were in comparative darkness, every now and then a horse would place its hoof in the burrow of some animal, and nearly fall headlong. Then, too, in spite of all care and pioneering, awheel of the waggon would sink into some hollow or be brought heavily against the side of a rock.

Sometimes they had to alter their direction to avoid heavily-rising ground, and these obstacles became so many, that towards morning they came to a halt, regularly puzzled, and not knowing whether they were journeying away from or towards their enemies.

"I have completely lost count, Bart," said the Doctor.

"And if you had not," replied Bart, "we could not have gone on with the waggon, for we are right amongst the rocks, quite a mountain-side."

"Let's wait for daylight then," said the Doctor peevishly. "I begin to think we have done very wrong in bringing a waggon. Better have trusted to horses."

He sighed, though, directly afterwards, and was ready to alter his words, but he refrained, though he knew that it would have been impossible to have brought Maude if they had trusted to horses alone.

A couple of dreary hours ensued, during which they could do nothing but wait for daybreak, which, when it came at last, seemed cold and blank and dreary, giving a strange aspect to that part of the country where they were, though their vision was narrowed by the hills on all sides save one, that by which they had entered as it were into what was quite a horse-shoe.

Joses and Bart started as soon as it was sufficiently light, rifle in hand, to try and make out their whereabouts, for they were now beyond the region familiar to both in their long rides from ranche to ranche in quest of cattle.

They paused, though, for a minute or two to gain a sort of idea as to the best course to pursue, and then satisfied that there was no immediate danger, unless the Indians should have happened to strike upon their trail, they began to climb the steep rocky hill before them.

"Which way do you think the Indians were going, Joses?" said Bart, as they toiled on, with the east beginning to blush of a vivid red.

"Way they could find people to rob and plunder and carry off," said Joses gruffly, for he was weary and wanted his breakfast.

"Do you think they will strike our trail?"

"If they come across it, my lad—if they come across it."

"And if they do?"

"If they do, they'll follow it right to the end, and then that'll be the end of us."

"If we don't beat them off," said Bart merrily.

"Beat them off! Hark at him!" said Joses. "Why, what a boy it is. He talks of beating off a whole tribe of Indians as if they were so many Jack rabbits."

"Well, we are Englishmen," said Bart proudly.

"Yes, we are Englishmen," said Joses, winking to himself and laying just a little emphasis upon the men; "but we can't do impossibilities if we bes English."

"Joses, you're a regular old croaker, and always make the worst of things instead of the best."

"So would you if you was hungry as I am, my lad. I felt just now as if I could set to and eat one o' them alligators that paddles about in the lagoons, whacking the fishes in the shallows with their tails till they're silly, and then shovelling of them up with their great jaws."

"Well, for my part, Joses, I'd rather do as the alligators do to the fish."

"What, whack 'em with their tails? Why, you ain't got no tail, Master Bart."

"No, no! Eat the fish."

"Oh, ah! yes. I could eat a mess o' fish myself, nicely grilled on some bits o' wood, and yah! mind! look out!"

Joses uttered these words with quite a yell as, dropping his rifle, he stooped, picked up a lump of rock from among the many that lay about on the loose stony hill slope they were climbing, and hurled it with such unerring aim, and with so much force, that the hideous grey reptile they had disturbed, seeking to warm itself in the first sunbeams, and which had raised its ugly head threateningly, and begun to creep away with a low, strange rattling noise, was struck about the middle of its back, and now lay writhing miserably amidst the stones.

"I don't like killing things without they're good to eat," said Joses, picking up another stone, and seeking for an opportunity to crush the serpent's head— "Ah, don't go too near, boy; he could sting as bad as ever if he got a chance!"

"I don't think he'd bite now," said Bart.

"Ah, wouldn't he! Don't you try him, my boy. They're the viciousest things as ever was made. And, as I was saying, I don't—there, that's about done for him," he muttered, as he dropped the piece of rock he held right upon the rattlesnake's head, crushing it, and then taking hold of the tail, and drawing the reptile out to its full length—"as I was a-saying, Master Bart, I don't like killing things as arn't good to eat; but if you'll put all the rattlesnakes' heads together ready for me, I'll drop stones on 'em till they're quite dead."

"What a fine one, Joses!" said Bart, gazing curiously at the venomous beast.

"Six foot six and a half," said Joses, scanning the serpent. "That's his length to an 'alf inch."

"Is it? Well, come along; we are wasting time, but do you think rattlesnakes are as dangerous as people say?"

"Dangerous! I should think they are," replied Joses, as he shouldered his rifle; and they tramped rapidly on to make up for the minutes lost in killing the reptile. "You'd say so, too, if you was ever bit by one. I was once."

"You were?"

"I just was, my lad, through a hole in my leggings; and I never could understand how it was that that long, thin, twining, scaly beggar should have enough brains in her little flat head to know that it was the surest place to touch me right through that hole."

"It was strange," said Bart. "How was it?"

"Well, that's what I never could quite tell, Master Bart, for that bite, and what came after, seemed to make me quite silly like, and as if it took all the memory out of me. All I can recollect about it is that I was with—let me see! who was it? Ah! I remember now: our Sam; and we'd sat down one hot day on the side of a bit of a hill, just to rest and have one smoke. Then we got up to go, and, though we ought to have been aware of it, we warn't, there was plenty of snakes about I was just saying to Sam, as we saw one gliding away, that I didn't believe as they could sting as people said they could, when I suppose I kicked again' one as was lying asleep, and before I knew it a'most there was a sharp grab, and a pinch at my leg, with a kind of pricking feeling; and as I gave a sort of a jump, I see a long bit of snake just going into a hole under some stones, and he gave a rattle as he went.

"'Did he bite you?' says Sam.

"'Oh, just a bit of a pinch,' I says. 'Not much. It won't hurt me.'

"'You're such a tough un,' says Sam, by way of pleasing me, and being a bit pleased, I very stupidly said,—'yes, I am, old fellow, regular tough un,' and we tramped on, for I'd made up my mind that I wouldn't take no more notice of it than I would of the sting of a fly."

"Keep a good look-out all round, Joses," said Bart, interrupting him.

"That's what I am doing, Master Bart, with both eyes at once. I won't let nothing slip."

In fact, as they walked on, Joses' eyes were eagerly watching on either side, nothing escaping his keen sight; for frontier life had made him, like the savages, always expecting danger at every turn.

"Well, as I was a saying," he continued, "the bite bothered me, but I wasn't going to let Sam see that I minded the least bit in the world, but all at once it seemed to me as if I was full of little strings that ran from all over my body down into one leg, and that something had hold of one end of 'em, and kept giving 'em little pulls and jerks. Then I looked at Sam to see if he'd touched me, and his head seemed to have swelled 'bout twice as big as it ought to be, and his eyes looked wild and strange.

"'What's matter, mate?' I says to him, and there was such a ding in my ears that when I spoke to him, Master Bart, my voice seemed to come from somewhere else very far off, and to sound just like a whisper.

"'What's the matter with you?' he says, and taking hold of me, he gave me a shake. 'Here, come on,' he says. 'You must run.'

"And then he tried to make me run, and I s'pose I did part of the time, but everything kept getting thick and cloudy, and I didn't know a bit where I was going nor what was the matter till, all at once like, I was lying down somewhere, and the master was pouring something down my throat. Then I felt him seeming to scratch my leg as if he was trying to make it bleed, and then I didn't know any more about it till I found I was being walked up and down, and every now and then some one give me a drink of water as I thought, till the master told me afterwards that it was whisky. Then I went to sleep and dropped down, and they picked me up and made me walk again, and then I was asleep once more, and that's all. Ah, they bite fine and sharp, Master Bart, and I don't want any more of it, and so I tell you."

By this time they had pretty well reached the summit of the rocky hill they had been climbing, and obeying a sign from his companion, Bart followed his example, dropping down and crawling forward.

"I 'spect we shall find we look right over the flat from here," whispered Joses, sinking his voice for no apparent reason, save the caution engendered by years of risky life with neighbours at hand always ready to shed blood.

"And we should be easily seen from a distance, I suppose?" responded Bart.

"That's so, Master Bart. The Injun can see four times as far as we can, they say, though I don't quite believe it."

"It must be a clever Indian who could see farther than you can, Joses," said Bart quietly.

"Oh, I don't know," said the other, with a quiet chuckle; "I can see pretty far when it's clear. Look out."

Bart started aside, for he had disturbed another rattlesnake, which glided slowly away as if resenting the intrusion, and hesitating as to whether it should attack.

"You mustn't creep about here with your eyes shut," said Joses quietly. "It isn't safe, my lad,—not safe at all. Now you rest there behind that stone. We're close up to the top. Let me go the rest of the way, and see how things are down below."

Bart obeyed on the instant, and lay resting his chin upon his arms, watching Joses as he crept up the rest of the slope to where a few rough stones lay about on the summit of the hill, amongst which he glided and then disappeared.

Bart then turned his gaze backward, to look down into the Horse-shoe Valley he had quitted, thinking of his breakfast, and how glad he should be to return with the news that all was well, so that a fire might be lighted and a pleasant, refreshing meal be prepared. But the curve of the hill shut the waggon and those with it from view, so that he glanced round him to see what there was worthy of notice.

This was soon done. Masses of stone, with a few grey-looking plants growing amidst the arid cracks, a little scattered dry grass in patches, and a few bushy-looking shrubs of a dull sagey green; that was all. There were plenty of stones near, one of which looked like a safe shelter for serpent or lizard; and some horny-looking beetles were busily crawling about. Above all the blue sky, with the sun now well over the horizon, but not visible from where Bart lay, and having exhausted all the things worthy of notice, he was beginning to wonder how long Joses would be, when there was a sharp sound close at hand, as if a stone had fallen among some more. Then there was another, and this was followed by a low chirping noise like that of a grasshopper.

Bart responded to this with a very bad imitation of the sound, and, crawling from his shelter, he followed the course taken by his companion as exactly as he could, trying to track him by the dislodged stones and marks made on the few patches of grass where he had passed through. But, with a shrug of the shoulders, Bart was obliged to own that his powers of following a trail were very small. Not that they were wanted here, for at the end of five minutes he could make out the long bony body of Joses lying beside one of the smaller masses of stone that jagged the summit of the hill.

Joses was looking in his direction, and just raising one hand slightly, signed to him to come near.

There seemed to be no reason why Bart should not jump up and run to his side, but he was learning caution in a very arduous school, and carefully trailing his rifle, he crept the rest of the way to where the great stones lay; and as soon as he was beside his companion, he found, as he expected, that from this point the eye could range for miles and miles over widespreading plains; and so clear and bright was the morning air that objects of quite a small nature were visible miles away.

"Well!" said Joses gruffly, for he had volunteered no information, "see anything?"

"No," said Bart, gazing watchfully round; "no, I can see nothing. Can you?"

"I can see you; that's enough for me," was the reply. "I'm not going to tell when you ought to be able to see for yourself."

"But I can see nothing," said Bart, gazing eagerly in every direction. "Tell me what you have made out."

"Why should I tell you, when there's a chance of giving you a lesson in craft, my lad,—in craft."

"But really there seems to be nothing, Joses."

"And he calls his—eyes," growled the frontier man. "Why, I could polish up a couple o' pebbles out of the nearest river and make 'em see as well as you do, Master Bart."

"Nonsense!" cried the latter. "I'm straining hard over the plain. Which way am I to look?"

"Ah, I'm not going to tell you."

"But we are losing time," cried Bart. "Is there any danger?"

"Yes, lots."

"Where?"

"Everywhere."

"But can you see immediate danger?" cried Bart impatiently.

"Yes; see it as plain as plain."

"But where? No; don't tell me. I see it," cried Bart excitedly.

"Not you, young master! where?"

"Right away off from your right shoulder, like a little train of ants crawling over a brown path. I can see: there are men and horses. Is it a waggon-train? No, I am sure now. Miles away. They are Indians."

"Ha, ha, ha!" laughed Joses. "That's better. That's a good lesson before breakfast, and without a spy-glass. I shall make a man of you yet, Master Bart."

"Which way are they going?"

"Nay, I shan't tell you, my lad. That's for you to find out."

"Well, I will directly," said Bart, shading his eyes. "Where are we now? Oh, I see. Now I know. No; I don't, they move so slowly. Yes, I can see. They are going towards the north, Joses."

"Nor'-west, my lad," said the frontier man; "but that was a pretty good hit you made. Now what was the good of my telling you all that, and letting you be a baby when I want to see you a man."

"We've lost ever so much time, Joses."

"Nay, we have not, my lad; we've gained time, and your eyes have had such a eddication this morning as can't be beat."

"Well, let's get back now. I suppose we may get up and walk."

"Walk! what, do you want to have the Injuns back on us?"

"They could not see us here."

"Not see us! Do you suppose they're not sharper than that. Nay, my lad, when the Injuns come down upon us let's have it by accident. Don't let's bring 'em down upon us because we have been foolish."

Bart could not help thinking that there was an excess of care upon his companion's side, and said so.

"When you know the Injuns as well as I do, my lad, you won't think it possible to be too particular. But look here—you can see the Injuns out there, can't you?"

"Yes, but they look like ants or flies."

"I don't care what they look like. I only say you can see them, can't you?"

"Yes."

"And you know Injuns' eyes and ears are sharper than ours?"

"Not than yours."

"Well, I know that they are sharper than yours, Master Bart," said Joses, with a chuckle; "and now look here—if you can see them out there against the dry brown plain miles away, don't you think they could see us stuck up against the sky here in the bright morning sunshine, all this height above the ground?"

"Well, perhaps they could, if they were looking," said Bart rather sulkily.

"And they are looking this way. They always are looking this way and every way, so don't you think they are not. Now let's go down."

He set the example of how they should go down, by crawling back for some distance till he was below the ridge and beyond sight from the plain, Bart carefully following his example till he rose, when they started down the hill at as quick a trot as the rugged nature of the ground would permit, and soon after reached the waggon, which the Doctor had drawn into a position which hid it from the view of any one coming up from the entrance of the valley, and also placed it where, in time of peril, they might hold their own by means of their rifles, and keep an enemy at bay even if they did not beat him off.

Chapter Five.: "Surrounded by Indians."

A good breakfast and a few hours' rest seemed to put a different aspect upon the face of affairs; the day was glorious, and though the region they were in was arid and wanting in water, there was plenty to interest any one travelling on an expedition of research. A good look-out was kept for Indians, but the party seemed to have gone right away, and to give them ample time to get to a greater distance, Dr Lascelles determined, if he could find a spring anywhere at hand, to stay where they were for a couple of days.

"You see, Bart," he said, as they hunted about amongst the craggiest part of the amphitheatre where fortune or misfortune had led them, "it does not much matter where we go, so long as it is into a region where Europeans have not penetrated before. Many of these hills are teeming with mineral treasures, and we must come upon some of Nature's wasting store if we persevere."

"Then we might find metals here, sir?" said Bart eagerly.

"As likely here as anywhere else. These rocks are partly quartz, and at any time we may come upon some of the stone veined with gold, or stumble upon a place where silver lies in blocks."

"I hope," laughed Bart, "when we do, I may stumble right over one of the blocks and so be sure of examining it. I think I should know silver if I found it."

"I am not so sure," said the Doctor. "You've led a life of a kind that has not made you very likely to understand minerals, but I daresay we shall both know a little more about them before we have done—that is," he added with a sigh, "if the Indians will leave us alone."

"We must give them the slip, sir," said Bart, laughing.

"Perhaps we may, my boy; but we have another difficulty to contend with."

"What's that, sir; the distance?"

"No, Bart; I'm uneasy about the men. I'm afraid they will strike sooner or later, and insist upon going back."

"I'm not, sir," replied Bart. "I will answer for Joses, and he has only to say he means to go forward, and the others then will keep by his side. Mind that snake, sir."

The Doctor raised his rifle to fire, but refrained, lest the report should be heard, and drawing back, the rattlesnake did the same; then they continued their journey, the Doctor examining the rocks attentively as he went on, but seeing nothing worthy of notice.

"We must be well on our guard against these reptiles, Bart; that is the first I have seen, and they may prove numerous."

"They are numerous," said Bart; and he told of the number he had seen upon the slope above them.

"That settles me upon going forward this evening," said the Doctor, "for water seems to be very scarce. We must try and strike the river higher up, and follow its course. We shall then have plenty of water always within reach, and find wood and trees and hiding-places."

"But I thought you wanted to get into a mountainous part, sir, where precious minerals would be found," said Bart.

"Exactly, my dear boy, and that is just the place we shall reach if we persevere, for it is up in these rocky fastnesses, where the rivers have their sources, and sometimes their beds are sprinkled with the specks and also with pieces of gold that have been washed out of the sides of the mighty hills."

They went on thoughtfully for a time, the Doctor giving a chip here and a chip there as he passed masses of rock, but nothing rewarded him, and their walk was so uneventful that they saw nothing more than another rattlesnake, the valley being so solitary and deserted that, with the exception of a large hawk, they did not even see a bird.

They, however, found a tiny spring of water which trickled down among the rocks, and finally formed a little pool, ample for supplying their horses with water, and this discovery made the Doctor propose a return.

"I don't like leaving Maude for long," he said.

"Joses will watch over her, sir, as safely as you would yourself. You saved his life once he told me."

"He told you that!" exclaimed the Doctor.

"Yes, sir, when the rattlesnake bit him, and I don't think he would ever be ungrateful, though I think he feels hurt that you do not place more trust in him."

"Well, let him prove himself well worthy of my trust," said the Doctor, bluntly. "I have not found him so ready as he should be in helping me with my plans."

Here the Doctor became very silent and reserved, and though Bart asked him several questions, and tried to get him into conversation, he hardly spoke, but seemed moody and thoughtful till they were close upon the little camp.

This was hidden from them till they were almost there, for the upper end of the Horse-shoe Valley was extremely rugged, and their way lay in and out among heavy blocks of stone that seemed as if they had been hurled down from the mountain-side.

When they were just about to turn into the narrow opening where the waggon lay and the horses were tethered, the Doctor stooped down to examine some fragments that lay loose about their feet, and the consequence was that Bart went on alone. He was just about to give a peculiar whistle, one used commonly by himself and the men when they wished to signal their whereabouts, when he stopped short, half hidden by the rocks, raised his rifle to his shoulder, and stood ready to fire, while his face, tanned as it was by the sun, turned of a sickly hue.

For a moment he was about to fire. Then he felt that he must rush forward and save Maude. The next moment calmer reflection told him that such help and strength as he could command would be needed, and, slipping back out of sight, he ran to where he had left the Doctor.

He found him sitting down examining by means of a little magnifying-glass one of the fragments of rock that he had chipped off, while his rifle lay across his knee.

He seemed so calm and content that in those moments of emergency Bart almost shrank from speaking, knowing, as he did, how terrible would be the effect of his words.

Just then the Doctor looked up, saw his strange gaze, and dropping the fragments, he leaped to his feet.

"What is it?" he cried; "what is wrong?" and as he spoke the lock of his double rifle gave forth two ominous clicks twice over.

"They have come round while we have been away," whispered Bart hoarsely.

"They? Who? Our men?"

"No," panted Bart; "the camp is surrounded by Indians."

Chapter Six.: A Surgical Operation.

Dr Lascelles' first movement was to run forward to the help of his child, Bart being close behind.

Then with the knowledge that where there is terrible odds against which to fight, guile and skill are necessary, he paused for a moment, with the intention of trying to find cover from whence he could make deadly use of his rifle. But with the knowledge that Maude must be in the hands of the Indians, whose savage nature he too well knew, his fatherly instinct admitted of no pause for strategy, and dashing forward, he ran swiftly towards the waggon, with Bart close upon his heels.

The full extent of their peril was at once apparent, no less than twelve mounted Indians being at the head of the little valley in a group, every man in full war-paint, and with his rifle across his knees as he sat upon his sturdy Indian pony.

Facing them were Maude, Joses, Juan, and the other two men, who had apparently been taken by surprise, and who, rifle in hand, seemed to be parleying with the enemy.

The sight of the reinforcement in the shape of Bart, and Dr Lascelles made the Indians utter a loud "Ugh!" and for a moment they seemed disposed to assume the offensive, but to Bart's surprise they only urged their ponies forward a few yards, and then stopped.

"Get behind the waggon, quick, my child," panted the Doctor, as Bart rushed up to his old companion's side.

"They came down upon us all at once, master," said Joses. "They didn't come along the trail."

"Show a bold front," exclaimed the Doctor; "we may beat them off."

To his surprise, however, the Indians did not seem to mean fighting, one of them, who appeared to be the chief, riding forward a few yards, and saying something in his own language.

"What does he say?" said the Doctor, impatiently.

"I can't make him out," replied Joses. "His is a strange tongue to me."

"He is hurt," exclaimed Bart. "He is wounded in the arm. I think he is asking for something."

It certainly had that appearance, for the Indian was holding rifle and reins in his left hand, while the right arm hung helplessly by his side.

It was like weakening his own little force to do such a thing, knowing as he did how treacherous the Indian could be, but this was no time for hesitating, and as it seemed to be as Bart had intimated, the Doctor risked this being a manoeuvre on the part of the Indian chief, and holding his rifle ready, he stepped boldly forward to where the dusky warrior sat calm and motionless upon his horse.

Upon going close up there was no longer any room for doubt. The chief's arm was roughly bandaged, and the coarse cloth seemed to be eating into the terribly swollen flesh.

That was enough. All the Doctor's old instincts came at once to the front, and he took the injured limb in his hand.

He must have caused the Indian intense pain, but the fine bronzed-looking fellow, who had features of a keen aquiline type, did not move a muscle, while, as the Doctor laid his rifle up against a rock, the little mounted band uttered in chorus a sort of grunt of approval.

"It is peace, Bart," said the Doctor. "Maude, my child, get a bowl of clean water, towels, and some bandages. Bart, get out my surgical case."

As he spoke, he motioned to the chief to dismount, which he did, throwing himself lightly from his pony, not, as a European would, on the left side of the horse, but on the right, the well-trained animal standing motionless, and bending down its head to crop the nearest herbage.

"Throw a blanket down upon that sage-brush, Joses," continued the Doctor; and this being done, the latter pointed to it, making signs that the chief should sit down.

He did not stir for a few moments, but gazed searchingly round at the group, till he saw Maude come forward with a tin bowl of clean water and the bandages, followed by Bart, who had in his hand a little surgical case. Then he took a few steps forward, and seated himself, laying his rifle down amongst the short shrubby growth, while Juan, Sam, and Harry on the one side, the mounted Indians upon the other, looked curiously on.

Once there was a low murmur among the latter, as the Doctor drew a keen, long knife from its sheath at his belt; but the chief did not wince, and all were once more still.

"He has been badly hurt in a fight," said the Doctor, "and the rough surgery of his tribe or his medicine-man does not act."

"That's it, master," said Joses, who was standing close by with rifle ready in case of treachery. "His medicine-man couldn't tackle that, and they think all white men are good doctors. It means peace, master."

He pointed behind the Doctor as he spoke, and it was plain enough that at all events for the present the Indians meant no harm, for two trotted back, one to turn up a narrow rift that the little exploring party had passed unnoticed in the night, the other to go right on towards the entrance of the rough Horse-shoe.

"That means scouting, does it not?" said Bart.

"I think so," replied the Doctor. "Yes; these Indians are friendly, but we must be on our guard. Don't show that we are suspicious though. Help me as I dress this arm. Maude, my child, you had better go into the waggon."

"I am not afraid, father," she said, quietly.

"Stay, then," he said. "You can be of use, perhaps."

He spoke like this, for, in their rough frontier life, the girl had had more than one experience of surgery. Men had been wounded in fights with the Indians; others had suffered from falls and tramplings from horses, while on more than one occasion the Doctor had had to deal with terrible injuries, the results of gorings from fierce bulls. For it is a strange but well-known fact in those parts, that the domestic cattle that run wild from the various corrals or enclosures, and take to the plains, are ten times more dangerous than the fiercest bison or buffalo, as they are commonly called, that roam the wilds.

Meanwhile the rest of the band leaped lightly down from their ponies, and paying not the slightest heed to the white party, proceeded to gather wood and brush to make themselves a fire, some unpacking buffalo meat, and one bringing forward a portion of a prong-horn antelope.

The Doctor was now busily examining his patient's arm, cutting away the rough bandages, and laying bare a terrible injury.

He was not long in seeing its extent, and he knew that if some necessary steps were not taken at once, mortification of the limb would set in, and the result would be death.

The Indian's eyes glittered as he keenly watched the Doctor's face. He evidently knew the worst, and it was this which had made him seek white help, though of course he was not aware how fortunate he had been in his haphazard choice. He must have been suffering intense pain, but not a nerve quivered, not a muscle moved, while, deeply interested, Joses came closer, rested his arms upon the top of his rifle, and looked down.

"Why, he's got an arrow run right up his arm all along by the bone, master," exclaimed the frontier man; "and he has been trying to pull it out, and it's broken in."

"Right, Joses," said the Doctor, quietly; "and worse than that, the head of the arrow is fixed in the bone."

"Ah, I couldn't tell that," said Joses, coolly.

"I wish I could speak his dialect," continued the Doctor. "I shall have to operate severely if his arm is to be saved, and I don't want him or his men to pay me my fee with a crack from a tomahawk."

"Don't you be afraid of that, master. He won't wince, nor say a word. You may do what you like with him. Injuns is a bad lot, but they've got wonderful pluck over pain."

"This fellow has, at all events," said the Doctor. "Maude, my child, I think you had better go."

"If you wish it, father, I will," she replied simply; "but I could help you, and I should not be in the least afraid."

"Good," said the Doctor, laconically, as he lowered the injured arm after bathing it free from the macerated leaves and bark with which it had been bound up. Then with the Indian's glittering eyes following every movement, he took from his leather case of surgical instruments, all still wonderfully bright and kept in a most perfect state, a curious-looking pair of forceps with rough handles, and a couple of short-bladed, very keen knives.

"Hah!" said Joses, with a loud expiration of his breath, "them's like the pinchers a doctor chap once used to pull out a big aching tooth of mine, and he nearly pulled my head off as well."

"No; they were different to these, Joses," said the Doctor, quietly, as he took up a knife. "Feel faint, Bart?"

The lad blushed now. He had been turning pale.

"Well, I did feel a little sick, sir. It was the sight of that knife. It has all gone now."

"That's right, my boy. Always try and master such feelings as these. Now I must try and make him understand what I want to do. Give me that piece of stick, Bart, it will do to imitate the arrow."

Bart handed the piece of wood, which the Doctor shortened, and then, suiting the action to his words, he spoke to the chief:

"The arrow entered here," he said, pointing to a wound a little above the Indian's wrist, "and pierced right up through the muscles, to bury itself in the bone just here."

As he spoke, he pushed the stick up outside the arm along the course that the arrow had taken, and holding the end about where he considered the head of the arrow to be.

For answer the Indian gave two sharp nods, and said something in his own tongue which no one understood.

"Then," continued the Doctor, "you, or somebody else, in trying to extract the arrow, have broken it off, and it is here in the arm, at least six inches and the head."

As he spoke, he now broke the stick in two, throwing away part, and holding the remainder up against the Indian's wounded arm.

Again the chief nodded, and this time he smiled.

"Well, we understand one another so far," said the Doctor, "and he sees that I know what's the matter. Now then, am I to try and cure it? What would you like me to do?"

He pointed to the arm as he spoke, and then to himself, and the Indian took the Doctor's hand, directed it to the knife, and then, pointing to his arm, drew a line from the mouth of the wound right up to his elbow, making signs that the Doctor should make one great gash, and take the arrow out.

"All right, my friend, but that is not quite the right way," said the Doctor. "You trust me then to do my best for you?"

He took up one of the short-bladed knives as he spoke, and pointed to the arm.

The Indian smiled and nodded, his face the next moment becoming stern and fixed as if he were in terrible pain, and needed all his fortitude to bear it.

"Going to cut it out, master?" said Joses, roughly.

"Yes."

"Let's give the poor beggar a comforter then," continued Joses. "If he scalps us afterwards along with his copper crew, why, he does, but let's show him white men are gentlemen."

"What are you going to do?" said the Doctor, wonderingly.

"Show you directly," growled Joses, who leisurely filled a short, home-made wooden pipe with tobacco, lit it at the Indian's fire, which was now crackling merrily, and returned to offer it to the chief, who took it with a short nod and a grunt, and began to smoke rapidly.

"That'll take a bit o' the edge off it," growled Joses. "Shall I hold his arm?"

"No; Bart, will do that," said the Doctor, rolling up his sleeves and placing water, bandages, and forceps ready. "Humph! he cannot bend his arm. Hold it like that, Bart—firmly, my lad, and don't flinch. I won't cut you."

"I'll be quite firm, sir," said Bart, quietly; and the Doctor raised his knife.

As he did so, he glanced at where nine Indians were seated round the fire, expecting to see that they would be interested in what was taking place; but, on the contrary, they were to a man fully occupied in roasting their dried meat and the portions of the antelope that they had cut up. The operation on the chief did not interest them in the least, or if it did, they were too stoical to show it.

The Doctor then glanced at his savage patient, and laying one hand upon the dreadfully swollen limb, he received a nod of encouragement, for there was no sign of quailing in the chief's eyes; but as the Doctor approached the point of the knife to a spot terribly discoloured, just below the elbow, the Indian made a sound full of remonstrance, and pointing to the wound above the wrist, signed to his attendant that he should slit the arm right up.

"No, no," said the Doctor, smiling. "I'm not going to make a terrible wound like that. Leave it to me."

He patted the chief on the shoulder as he spoke, and once more the Indian subsided into a state of stolidity, as if there were nothing the matter and he was not in the slightest pain.

Here I pause for a few moments as I say— Shall I describe what the Doctor did to save the Indian's life, or shall I hold my hand?

I think I will go on, for there should be nothing objectionable in a few words describing the work of a man connected with one of the noblest professions under the sun.

There was no hesitation. With one quick, firm cut, the Doctor divided the flesh, piercing deep down, and as he cut his knife gave a sharp grate.

"Right on the arrowhead, Bart," he said quietly; and, withdrawing his knife, he thrust a pair of sharp forceps into the wound, and seemed as if he were going to drag out the arrow, but it was only to divide the shaft. This he seized with the other forceps, and drew out of the bleeding opening—a piece nearly five inches long, which came away easily enough.

Then, without a moment's hesitation, he sponged the cut for a while, and directly after, guiding them with the index finger of his left hand, he thrust the forceps once more into the wound.

There was a slight grating noise once again, a noise that Bart, as he manfully held the arm, seemed to feel go right through every nerve with a peculiar thrill. Then it was evident that the Doctor had fast hold of the arrowhead and he drew hard to take it out.

"I thought so," he said, "it is driven firmly into the bone."

As he spoke, he worked his forceps slightly to and fro, to loosen the arrowhead, and then, bearing firmly upon it, drew it out—an ugly, keen piece of nastily barbed iron, with a scrap of the shaft and some deer sinew attached.

The Doctor examined it attentively to see that everything had come away, and uttered a sigh of satisfaction, while the only sign the Indian gave was to draw a long, deep breath.

"There, Mr Tomahawk," said the Doctor, smiling, as he held the arm over the bowl, and bathed the injury tenderly with fresh relays of water, till it nearly ceased bleeding; "that's better than making a cut all along your arm, and I'll be bound to say it feels easier already."

The Indian did not move or speak, but sat there smoking patiently till the deep cut was sewn up, padded with lint, and bound, and the wound above the wrist, where the arrow had entered, was also dressed and bound up carefully.

"There: now your arm will heal," said the Doctor, as he contrived a sling, and placed the injured limb at rest. "A man with such a fine healthy physique will not suffer much, I'll be bound. Hah, it's quite a treat to do some of the old work again."

The chief waited patiently until the Doctor had finished. Then rising, he stood for a few moments with knitted brows, perfectly motionless; and the frontier man, seeing what was the matter, seemed to be about to proffer his arm, but the Indian paid no heed to him, merely gazing straight before him till the feeling of faintness had passed away, when he stooped and picked up the piece of arrow shaft and the head, walked with them to where his followers were sitting, and held them out for them to see. Then they were passed round with a series of grunts, duly examined, and finally found a resting-place in a little beaver-skin bag at the chiefs girdle, along with his paints and one or two pieces of so-called "medicine" or charms.

Meanwhile the Doctor was busy putting away his instruments, feeling greatly relieved that the encounter with the Indians had been of so friendly a nature.

At the end of a few minutes the chief came back with the large buffalo robe that had been strapped to the back of his pony, spread it before the Doctor, placed on it his rifle, tomahawk, knife, and pouch, and signed to him that they were his as a present.

"He means that it is all he has to give you, sir," said Bart, who seemed to understand the chief's ways quicker than his guardian, and who eagerly set himself to interpret.

"Yes, that seems to be his meaning," replied the Doctor. "Well, let's see if we can't make him our friend."

Saying which the Doctor stooped down, picked up the knife and hatchet and placed them in the chiefs belt, his rifle in the hollow of his arm, and finally his buffalo robe over his shoulders, ending by giving him his hand smilingly, and saying the one word friend, friend, two or three times over.

The chief made no reply, but gravely stalked back to his followers, as if affronted at the refusal of his gift, and the day passed with him lying down quietly smoking in the sage-brush, while the occupants of the Doctor's little camp went uneasily about their various tasks, ending by dividing the night into watches, lest their savage neighbours should take it into their heads to depart suddenly with the white man's horses—a favourite practice with Indians, and one that in this case would have been destructive of the expedition.

Chapter Seven.: Another Alarm.

To the surprise and satisfaction of Bart, all was well in the camp at daybreak when he looked round; the horses were grazing contentedly at the end of their tether ropes, and the Indians were just stirring, and raking together the fire that had been smouldering all the night.

Breakfast was prepared, and they were about to partake thereof, when the Doctor took counsel with Joses as to what was best to be done.

"Do you think they will molest us now?" he asked.

"No, master, I don't think so, but there's no knowing how to take an Indian. I should be very careful about the horses though, for a good horse is more than an Indian can resist."

"I have thought the same; and it seems to me that we had better stay here until this party has gone, for I don't want them to be following us from place to place."

"There's a band of 'em somewhere not far away," said Joses, "depend upon it, so p'r'aps it will be best to wait till we see which way they go, and then go totherwise."

Soon after breakfast the chief came up to the waggon and held out his arm to be examined, smiling gravely, and looking his satisfaction, as it was very plain that a great deal of the swelling had subsided.

This went on for some days, during which the Indians seemed perfectly content with their quarters, they having found a better supply of water; and to show their friendliness, they made foraging expeditions, and brought in game which they shared in a very liberal way.

This was all very well, but still it was not pleasant to have them as neighbours, and several times over the Doctor made up his mind to start and continue his expedition, and this he would have done but for the fact of his being sure that their savage friends, for this they now seemed to be, would follow them.

At the end of ten days the chief's arm had wonderfully altered, and with it his whole demeanour, the healthy, active life he led conducing largely towards the cure. But he was always quiet and reserved, making no advances, and always keeping aloof with his watchful little band.

"We are wasting time horribly," said the Doctor, one morning. "We'll start at once."

"Why not wait till night and steal off?" said Maude.

"Because we could not hide our trail," said Bart. "The Indians could follow us. I think it will be best to let them see we don't mind them, and go away boldly."

"That's what I mean to do," said the Doctor, and directly they had ended their meal, the few arrangements necessary were made, and after going and shaking hands all round with the stolid Indians, the horses were mounted, the waggon set in motion, and they rode back along the valley. Passing the Indian camp, they arrived at the opening through which, bearing off to the west, the Indians reached the plains, and for hours kept on winding in and out amongst the hills.

It was after sundown that the Doctor called a halt in the wild rocky part that they had reached, a short rest in the very heat of the day being the only break which they had had in their journey. In fact, as darkness would soon be upon them, it would have been madness to proceed farther, the country having become so broken and wild that it would have been next to impossible to proceed without wrecking the waggon.

Their usual precautions were taken as soon as a satisfactory nook was found with a fair supply of water, and soon after sunrise next morning, all having been well during the night, the Doctor and Bart started for a look round while breakfast was being prepared, Bart taking his rifle, as there was always the necessity for supplying the wants of the camp.

"I wonder whether we shall see any more of the Indians," said Bart, as they climbed up amongst the rocks to what looked almost like a gateway formed by a couple of boldly scarped masses, in whose strata lines various plants and shrubs maintained a precarious existence.

"I wonder they have not followed us before now," replied the Doctor. "Mind how you come. Can you climb it?"

For answer, Bart leaped up to where the Doctor had clambered as easily as a mountain sheep, and after a little farther effort they reached the gate-like place, to find that it gave them a view right out on to the partly-wooded country beyond. For they had left the level, changeless plain on the other side of the rocks, and the sight of a fresh character of country was sufficient to make the Doctor eagerly take the little telescope he carried in a sling, and begin to sweep the horizon.

As he did so, he let fall words about the beauty of the country.

"Splendid grazing land," he said, "well-watered. We must have a stay here." Then lowering his glass, so as to take the landscape closer in, he uttered an ejaculation of astonishment.

"Why, Bart," he said, "I'm afraid here are the Indians Joses saw that night."

"Let me look, sir," cried Bart, stretching out his hand for the glass, but only to exclaim, "I can see them plainly enough without. Why, they cannot be much more than a mile away."

"And they seem to be journeying in our direction," replied the Doctor. "Let's get back quickly, and try if we cannot find another hiding-place for the waggon."

Hurrying back, Bart started the idea that these might be the main body of their friendly Indians.

"So much the better for us, Master Bart, but I'm afraid that we shall not be so lucky again."

"I half fancied I saw our chief amongst them," said Bart, giving vent to his sanguine feelings.

"More than half fancy, Bart," replied the Doctor, "for there he sits upon his horse."

He pointed with his glass, and, to Bart's astonishment, there in the little wilderness of rocks that they had made their halting-place for the night, was the chief with his eleven followers who were already tethering their horses, and making arrangements to take up their quarters close by them as of old.

"Do you think they mean to continue friendly?" asked Bart uneasily, for he could not help thinking how thoroughly they were at the mercy of the Indians if they proved hostile.

"I cannot say," replied the Doctor. "But look here, Bart, take the chief with you up to the gap, and show him the party beyond. His men may not have seen them, and we shall learn perhaps whether they are friends or foes."

On reaching the waggon, as no attempt was made by the Indians to join them or resume intercourse, Bart went straight up to the chief, and made signs to him to follow, which he proceeded to do upon his horse, but upon Bart, pointing upwards to the rocky ascent, he leaped off lightly, and the youth noticed that he was beginning to make use of his injured arm.

In a very short time they had climbed to the opening between the rocks, where, upon seeing that there was open country beyond, the Indian at once crouched and approached cautiously, dropping flat upon the earth next moment, and crawling over the ground with a rapidity that astonished his companion, who was watching his face directly after, to try and read therefrom whether he belonged to the band of Indians in the open park in the land beyond.

To Bart's surprise, the chief drew back quickly, his face changed, and his whole figure seemed to be full of excitement.

He said a few words rapidly, and then, seeing that he was not understood, he began to make signs, pointing first to the opening out into the plain, and then taking out his knife, and striking with it fiercely. Then he pointed once more to the opening, and to his wounded arm, going through the motions of one drawing a bow.

"Friends, friends, friends," he then said in a hoarse whisper, repeating the Doctor's word, and then shaking his head and spitting angrily upon the ground, and striking with his knife.

He then signed to Bart, to follow, and ran down the steep slope just as one of his followers cantered hastily up.

Both had the same news to tell in the little camp, and though the Doctor could not comprehend the Indian chief's dialect, his motions were significant enough, as he rapidly touched the barrels of his followers' rifles, and then those of the white party, repeating the word, "Friends."

The next moment he had given orders which sent a couple of his men up the rocks, to play the part of scouts, while he hurriedly scanned their position, and chose a sheltered place, a couple of hundred yards back, where there was ample room for the horses and waggon, which were quietly taken there, the rocks and masses of stone around affording shelter and cover in case of attack.

"There's no doubt about their being friends now, Bart," said the Doctor; "we must trust them for the future, but I pray Heaven that we may not be about to engage in shedding blood."

"We won't hurt nobody, master," said Joses, carefully examining his rifle, "so long as they leave us alone; but if they don't, I'm afraid I shall make holes through some of them that you wouldn't be able to cure."

Just then the Indian held up his hand to command silence, and directly after he pointed here and there to places that would command good views of approaching foes, while he angrily pointed to Maude, signing that she should crouch down closely behind some sheltering rocks.

The Doctor yielded to his wishes, and then, in perfect silence, they waited for the coming of the Indian band, which if the trail were noted, they knew could not be long delayed.

If Bart had felt any doubt before of these Indians with them being friendly, it was swept away now by the thorough earnestness with which they joined in the defence of their little stronghold. On either side of him were the stern-looking warriors, rifle in hand, watchful of eye and quick of ear, each listening attentively for danger while waiting for warnings from the scouts who had been sent out.

As Bart thought over their position and its dangers, he grew troubled at heart about Maude, the sister and companion as she had always seemed to him, and somehow, much as he looked up to Dr Lascelles, who seemed to him the very height of knowledge, strength, and skill, it filled his mind with forebodings of the future as he wondered how they were to continue their expedition to the end without happening upon some terrible calamity.

"Maude ought to have been left with friends, or sent to the city. It seems to me like madness to have brought her here."

Just then Dr Lascelles crept up cautiously behind him, making him start and turn scarlet as a hand was laid upon his shoulder; for it seemed to him as if the Doctor had been able to read his thoughts.

"Why, Bart," he said, smiling, "you look as red as fire; you ought to look as pale as milk. Do you want to begin the fight?"

"No," said Bart, sturdily; "I hope we shan't have to fight at all, for it seems very horrid to have to shoot at a man."

"Ever so much more horrid for a man to shoot at you," said Joses in a hoarse whisper as he crawled up behind them. "I'd sooner shoot twelve, than twelve should shoot me."

"Why have you left your post?" said the Doctor, looking at him sternly.

"Came to say, master, that I think young miss aren't safe. She will keep showing herself, and watching to see if you are all right, and that'll make the Indians, if they come, all aim at her."

"You are right, Joses," said the Doctor, hastily; and he went softly back to the waggon, while Joses went on in a grumbling whisper:

"I don't know what he wanted to bring her for. Course we all like her, Master Bart, but it scares me when I think of what it might lead to if we get hard pressed some of these days."

"Don't croak, Joses," whispered Bart; and then they were both silent and remained watching, for the chief held up his hand, pointing towards the rocks beyond, which they knew that their enemies were passing, and whose tops they scanned lest at any moment some of the painted warriors might appear searching the valley with their keen dark eyes.

The hours passed, and the rocks around them grew painfully heated by the ardent rays that beat down upon them. Not a breath of air reached the corner where such anxious guard was kept; and to add to the discomfort of the watchers, a terrible thirst attacked them.

Bart's lips seemed cracking and his throat parched and burning, but this was all borne in fortitude; and as he saw the Indians on either side of him, bearing the inconveniences without a murmur, he forebore to complain.

Towards mid-day, when the heat was tremendous, and Bart was wondering why the chief or Dr Lascelles did not make some movement to see whether the strange Indians had gone, and at the same time was ready to declare to himself that the men sent out as scouts must have gone to sleep, he felt a couple of hands placed upon his shoulders from behind, pressing him down, and then a long brown sinewy arm was thrust forward, with the hand pointing to the edge of the ridge a quarter of a mile away.

Dr Lascelles had not returned, and Joses had some time before crept back to his own post, so that Bart was alone amongst their Indian friends.

He knew at once whose was the pointing arm, and following the indicated direction, he saw plainly enough first the head and shoulders of an Indian come into sight, then there was apparently a scramble and a leap, and he could see that the man was mounted. And then followed another and another, till there was a group of half a dozen mounted men, who had ridden up some ravine to the top from the plain beyond, and who were now searching and scanning the valley where the Doctor's encampment lay.

Now was the crucial time. The neigh of a horse, the sight of an uncautiously exposed head or hand, would have been sufficient to betray their whereabouts, and sooner or later the attack would have come.

But now it was that the clever strategy of the chief was seen, for he had chosen their retreat not merely for its strength, but for its concealment.

Bart glanced back towards the waggon, and wondered how it was that this prominent object had not been seen. Fortunately, however, its tilt was of the colour of the surrounding rocks, and it was pretty well hidden behind some projecting masses.

For quite a quarter of an hour this group of mounted Indians remained full in view, and all the time Bart's sensations were that he must be seen as plainly as he could see his foes; but at last he saw them slowly disappear one by one over the other side of the ridge; and as soon as the last had gone the chief uttered a deep "Ugh!"

There was danger though yet, and he would not let a man stir till quite half an hour later, when his two scouts came in quickly, and said a few words in a low guttural tone.

"I should be for learning the language of these men if we were to stay with them, Bart," said the Doctor; "but they may leave us at any time, and the next party we meet may talk a different dialect."

The chief's acts were sufficient now to satisfy them that the present danger had passed, and soon after he and his men mounted and rode off without a word.

Chapter Eight.: Rough Customers.

There was nothing to tempt a stay where they were, so taking advantage of their being once more alone, a fresh start was made along the most open course that presented itself, and some miles were placed between them and the last camp before a halt was made for the night.

"We shan't do no good, Master Bart," said Joses, as they two kept watch for the first part of the night. "The master thinks we shall, but I don't, and Juan don't, and Sam and Harry don't."

"But why not?"

"Why not, Master Bart? How can you 'spect it, when you've got a young woman and a waggon and a tent along with you. Them's all three things as stop you from getting over the ground. I don't call this an exploring party; I call it just a-going out a-pleasuring when it's all pain."

"You always would grumble, Joses; no matter where we were, or what we were doing, you would have your grumble. I suppose it does you good."

"Why, of course it does," said Joses, with a low chuckling laugh. "If I wasn't to grumble, that would all be in my mind making me sour, so I gets rid of it as soon as I can."

That night passed without adventure, and, starting at daybreak the next morning, they found a fine open stretch of plain before them, beyond which, blue and purple in the distance, rose the mountains, and these were looked upon as their temporary destination, for Dr Lascelles was of opinion that here he might discover something to reward his toils.

The day was so hot and the journey so arduous, that upon getting to the farther side of the plain, with the ground growing terribly broken and rugged as they approached the mountain slopes, a suitable spot was selected, and the country being apparently quite free from danger, the tent was set up, and the quarters made snug for two or three days' rest, so that the Doctor might make a good search about the mountain chasms and ravines, and see if there were any prospect of success.

The place reached was very rugged, but it had an indescribable charm from the varied tints of the rocks and the clumps of bushes, with here and there a low scrubby tree, some of which proved to be laden with wild plums.

"Why, those are wild grapes too, are they not?" said Bart, pointing to some clustering vines which hung over the rocks laden with purpling berries.

"That they be," said Joses; "and as sour as sour, I'll bet. But I say, Master Bart, hear that?"

"What! that piping noise?" replied Bart. "I was wondering what it could be."

"I'll tell you, lad," said Joses, chuckling. "That's young wild turkeys calling to one another, and if we don't have a few to roast it shan't be our fault."

The Doctor was told of the find, and after all had been made snug, it was resolved to take guns and rifles, and search for something likely to prove an agreeable change.

"For we may as well enjoy ourselves, Bart, and supply Madam Maude here with a few good things for our pic-nic pot."

The heat of the evening and the exertion of the long day's journey made the party rather reluctant to stir after their meal, but at last guns were taken, and in the hope of securing a few of the wild turkeys, a start was made; but after a stroll in different directions, Joses began to shake his head, and to say that it would be no use till daybreak, for the turkeys had gone to roost.

Walking, too, was difficult, and there were so many thorns, that, out of kindness to his child, the Doctor proposed that they should return to the tent; signals were made to the men at a distance, and thoroughly enjoying the cool, delicious air of approaching eve, they had nearly reached the tent, when about a hundred yards of the roughest ground had to be traversed—a part that seemed as if giants had been hurling down huge masses of the mountain to form a new chaos, among whose mighty boulders, awkward thorns, huge prickly cacti, and wild plums, grew in profusion.

"What a place to turn into a wild garden, Bart!" said the Doctor, suddenly.

"I had been thinking so," cried Maude, eagerly. "What a place to build a house!"

"And feed cattle, eh?" said the Doctor. "Very pretty to look at, my child, but I'm afraid that unless we could live by our guns, we should starve."

"Hough—hough—hough!" came from beyond a rugged piece of rock.

"O father!" cried Maude, clinging to his arm.

"Don't hold me, child," he said fiercely, "leave my arm free;" and starting forward, gun in hand, he made for the place from whence the hideous half-roaring, half-grunting noise had come.

Before he had gone a dozen steps the sound was repeated, but away to their right. Then came the sharp reports of two guns, and, evidently seeing something hidden from her father and Bart, Maude sprang forward while they followed.

"Don't go, Missy, don't go," shouted Juan, and his cry was echoed by Harry; but she did not seem to hear them, and was the first to arrive at where a huge bear lay upon its flank, feebly clawing at the rock with fore and hind paw, it having received a couple of shots in vital parts.

"Pray keep back, Maude," cried Bart, running to her side.

"I wanted to see it," she said with an eager glance around at her father, who came up rapidly. "What is it?"

"It's the cub half grown of a grizzly bear," said Dr Lascelles, speaking excitedly now. "Back, girl, to the tent; the mother must be close at hand."

"On, forward; she's gone round to the right," shouted the men behind, who had been trying to get on by another way, but were stopped by the rocks.

"Back, girl!" said the Doctor again. "Forward all of you, steadily, and make every shot tell. Where is Joses?"

Just then the deep hoarse grunting roar came again from a hollow down beyond them, and directly after, as they all hurried forward, each man ready to fire at the first chance, they heard a shot, and directly after came in sight of Joses, with his double rifle to his shoulder taking aim at a monstrous bear that, apparently half disabled by his last shot, was drawing itself up on a great shelving block of stone, and open mouthed and with blood and slaver running from its glistening ivory fangs, was just turning upon him to make a dash and strike him down.

Just then a second shot rang out, and the bear rolled over, but sprang to its feet again with a terrific roar, and dashed at her assailant.

It was impossible to fire now, lest Joses should be hit; and though he turned and fled, he was too late, for the bear, in spite of its huge, ox-like size, sprang upon him, striking him down, and stood over him.

But now was the time, and the Doctor's and Bart's rifles both rang out, the latter going down on one knee to take careful aim; and as the smoke cleared away the bear was gone.

"She's made for those rocks yonder," cried Juan, excitedly. "We'll have her now, master. She didn't seem hurt a bit."

"Be careful," cried the Doctor. "Maude, help poor Joses. Go forward, Bart, but mind. She may be fatally wounded now."

Bart was for staying to help the man who had so often been his companion, but his orders were to go on; he knew that Joses could not be in better hands; and there was the inducement to slay his slayer to urge him forward as he ran with his rifle at the trail over the rocks, and was guided by the savage growling he could hear amidst some bushes to where the monster was at bay.

It was fast approaching the moment when all would be in gloom, and Bart knew that it would be impossible for them to camp where they were with a wounded grizzly anywhere near at hand. Slain the monster must be, and at once; but though the growling was plain enough, the bear was not visible, and ammunition is too costly out in the desert for a single charge to be wasted by a foolish shot.

Juan, Harry, and Sam were all in position, ready to fire, but still the animal did not show itself, so they went closer to the thicket, and threw in heavy stones, but without the least effect, till Juan suddenly exclaimed that he would go right in and drive the brute out.

Bart forbade this, however, and the man contented himself with going a little closer, and throwing a heavy block in a part where they had not thrown before.

A savage grunt was the result, and judging where the grizzly lay, Juan, without waiting for counsel, raised his rifle and fired, dropping his weapon and running for his life the next moment, for the shot was succeeded by a savage yell, and the monster came crashing out in a headlong charge, giving Juan no cause for flight, since his butt made straight for Bart, open mouthed, fiery-eyed, and panting for revenge.

Bart's first instinct was to turn and run, his second to stand his ground and fire right at the monster, taking deadly aim.

But in moments of peril like his there is little time for the exercise of judgment, and ere he could raise his rifle to his shoulder and take careful aim the bear was upon him, rising up on its hind legs, not to hug him, as is generally supposed to be the habits of these beasts, but to strike at him right and left with its hideously armed paws.

Bart did not know how it happened, but as the beast towered up in its huge proportions, he fired rapidly both barrels of his piece, one loaded with heavy shot for the turkeys, the other with ball, right into the monster's chest.

As he fired Bart leaped back, and it was well that he did so, for the grizzly fell forward with a heavy thud, almost where he had been standing, clawed at the rocks and stones for a few moments, and then lay perfectly still—dead.

Chapter Nine.: First Searches for Gold.

The three men uttered a loud cheer, and ran and leaped upon their fallen enemy, but Bart ran back, loading his piece as he went, to where he had left the Doctor with poor Joses.

Bart felt his heart beat heavily, and there was a strange, choking feeling of pain at his throat as he thought of rough, surly-spoken Joses, the man who had been his guide and companion in many a hunt and search for the straying cattle; and now it seemed to him that he was to lose one who he felt had been a friend.

"Is he—"

Bart panted out this much, and then stopped in amazement, for, as he turned the corner of some rocks that lay between him and the tent, instead of addressing the Doctor, he found himself face to face with Joses, who, according to Bart's ideas, should have been lying upon the stones, hideously clawed from shoulder to heel by the monster's terrible hooks. On the contrary, the rough fellow was sitting up, with his back close to a great block of stone, his rifle across his knees, and both hands busy rolling up a little cigarette.

"Why, Joses," panted Bart, "I thought—"

"As I was killed? Well, I ain't," said Joses, roughly.

"But the bear—she struck you down—I saw her claw you."

"You see her strike me down," growled Joses; "but she didn't claw me, my lad. She didn't hit out far enough, but she's tore every rag off my back right into ribbons, and I'm waiting here till the Doctor brings me something else and my blanket to wear."

"O Joses, I am glad," cried Bart, hoarsely; and his voice was full of emotion as he spoke, while he caught the rough fellow's hands in his.

"Don't spoil a fellow's cigarette," growled Joses roughly, but his eyes showed the pleasure he felt. "I say are you glad, though?"

"Glad?" cried Bart, "indeed, indeed I am."

"That's right, Master Bart. That's right. It would have been awkward if I'd been killed."

"Oh, don't talk about it," cried Bart, shuddering.

"Why not, my lad? It would though. They'd have had no end of a job to dig down in this stony ground. But you've killed the bear among you?"

"Yes; she's dead enough."

"That's well. Who fired the shot as finished her? Don't say you let Juan or Sam, or I won't forgive you."

"I fired the last, and brought her down," said Bart quietly enough.

"That's right," said Joses, "that's right; you ought to be a good shot now."

"But are you not hurt at all?" asked Bart.

"Well, I can't say as I arn't hurt," replied Joses, "because she knocked all the wind out of me as she sent me down so quickly, and she scratched a few bits of skin off as well as my clothes, but that don't matter: skin grows again, clothes don't. Humph, here comes the Doctor with the things."

"A narrow escape for him, Bart. But how about the grizzly?"

"Dead, sir, quite dead," replied Bart. "Are we likely to see Mr Grizzly as well?"

"No, I think not, my boy. Mother and cubs generally go together."

"Now, Joses, let me dress your back."

"No, thank ye, master, I can dress myself, bless you."

"No, no, I mean apply some of this dressing to those terrible scratches."

"Oh, if that's what you mean, master, go on. Wouldn't they be just as well without?"

"No, no; turn round, man."

Joses obeyed, and Bart shuddered as he saw the scores made by the monster's hideous claws, though Joses took it all quietly enough, and after the dressing threw his blanket over his shoulders, to walk with his master and Bart, to have a look at the grizzly lying there in the gathering shades of night.

It was a monster indeed, being quite nine feet long, and massive in proportion, while its great sharp curved claws were some of them nearly six inches from point to insertion in the shaggy toes.

Such a skin was too precious as a trophy to be left, and before daylight next morning, Juan, Harry, and Sam were at work stripping it off, Bart, when he came soon after, finding them well on with their task, Joses being seated upon a fragment of rock contentedly smoking his cigarette and giving instructions, he being an adept at such matters, having stripped off hundreds if not thousands of hides in his day, from bison cattle and bear down to panther and skunk.

"I ain't helping, Master Bart," he said apologetically, "being a bit stiff this morning."

"Which is a blessing as it ain't worse," said Harry; "for you might have been much worse, you know."

"You mind your own business," growled Joses. "You're whipping off great bits o' flesh there and leaving 'em on the skin."

"Well, see how hard it is when it's cold," grumbled Harry; and then to Juan, "I shan't take no notice of him. You see he's a bit sore."

Harry was quite right, poor Joses being so sore that for some days he could not mount his horse, and spent his time in drying the two bear-skins in the sun, and dressing them on the fleshy side, till they were quite soft and made capital mats for the waggon.

One morning, however, he expressed himself as being all right, and whatever pains he felt, he would not show the slightest sign, but mounted his horse, and would have gone forward, only the Doctor decided to spend another day where they were, so as to more fully examine the rocks, for he fancied that he had discovered a metallic deposit in one spot on the previous night.

It was settled, then, that the horses should go on grazing in the little meadow-like spot beside a tiny stream close by the waggon, and that the Doctor, Juan, Joses, and Bart should explore the ravine where the Doctor thought he had found traces of gold, while Sam and Harry kept watch by the camp.

For days past the neighbourhood had been well hunted over, and with the exception of a snake or two, no noxious or dangerous creature had been seen; the Indians seemed to have gone right away, and under the circumstances, all was considered safe.

Explorations had shown them that the place they were in rose like, as it were, a peninsula of rocks from amidst a sea of verdure. This peninsula formed quite a clump some miles round, and doubtless it had been chosen as a convenient place by the bear, being only connected with the mountain slope by a narrow neck of débris from the higher ground.

As the party went on, the Doctor told Bart, that his intention was to journey along by the side of the mountain till he found some valley or canyon, up which they could take the waggon, and then search the rocks as they went on whenever the land looked promising.

Upon this occasion, after a few hours' walk, the Doctor halted by the bed of a tiny stream, and after searching about in the sands for a time he hit upon a likely place, took a small portion of the sand in a shallow tin bowl, and began to wash it, changing the water over and over again, and throwing away the lighter sand, till nothing was left but a small portion of coarser fragments, and upon these being turned out in the bright sunshine and examined, there were certainly a few specks of gold to be seen, but so minute that the Doctor threw them away with a sigh.

"We must have something more promising than that," he said. "Now I think, Bart, you had better go along that ridge of broken rock close up to the hills, and walk eastward for a few miles to explore. I will go with Juan to the west. Perhaps we shall find a likely place for going right up into the mountains. We'll meet here again at say two hours before sundown. Keep a sharp look-out."

They parted, and for the next two hours Bart and Joses journeyed along under what was for the most part a wall of rock fringed at the top with verdure, and broken up into chasms and crevices which were filled with plants of familiar or strange growths.

Sometimes they started a serpent, and once they came upon a little herd of antelopes, but they were not in search of game, and they let the agile creatures go unmolested.

The heat was growing terrific beneath the sheltered rock-wall, and at last, weakened by his encounter with the bear Joses began to show signs of distress.

"I'd give something for a good drink of water," he said. "I've been longing this hour past, and I can't understand how it is that we haven't come upon a stream running out into the plain. There arn't been no chance of the waggon going up into the mountains this way."

"Shall we turn back?"

"Turn back? No! not if we have to go right round the whole world," growled Joses. "Come along, my lad, we'll find a spring somewheres."

For another hour they tramped on almost in silence, and then all at once came a musical, plashing sound that made Joses draw himself up erect and say with a smile:

"There's always water if you go on long enough, my lad. That there's a fall."

And so it proved to be, and one of extreme beauty, for a couple of hundred yards farther they came upon a nook in the rough wall, where the water of a small stream poured swiftly down, all foam and flash and sparkle, and yet in so close and compact a body that, pulling a cow-horn from his pocket, Joses could walk closely up and catch the pure cold fluid as it fell.

"There, Master Bart," he said, filling and rinsing out the horn two or three times, "there you are. Drink, my lad, for you want it bad, as I can see."

"No, you drink first, Joses," said the lad; but the rough frontier man refused, and it was not until Bart had emptied the horn of what seemed to be the most delicious water he had ever tasted, that Joses would fill and drink.

When he did begin, however, it seemed as if he would never leave off, for he kept on pouring down horn after horn, and smacking his lips with satisfaction.

"Ah, my lad!" he exclaimed at last, "I've drunk everything in my time, whiskey, and aguardiente, and grape wine, and molasses rum, but there isn't one of 'em as comes up anywhere like a horn of sparkling water like that when you are parched and burnt up with thirst."

"It is delicious, Joses," said Bart; "but now had we not better go back?"

"Yes, if we mean to be to our time; but suppose we go a little lower down there into the plain, and try if there's anything like what the master's hunting for in the sands."

They went down for about a quarter of a mile to where there was a smooth sandy reach, and a cup being produced, they set to and washed several lots of sand, in each case finding a few specks but nothing more, and at last they gave it up, when Joses pointed to some footprints in the soil, where there was evidently a drinking-place made by deer.

"What are those?" said Bart, "panthers?"

"Painters they are, my lad, and I daresay we could shoot one if we had time. Make a splendid skin for little Miss. I dessay we could find a skunk or two hereabouts. Eh! nasty? Well, they are, but their fur's lovely."

They saw neither panther nor skunk, though footprints, evidently made the previous night, were plentiful about the stream; and now, as time was getting on, they sturdily set themselves to their backward journey, Joses praising the water nearly all the way, when he was not telling of some encounter he had had with Indian or savage beast in his earlier days.

"Do you think we shall see any more of the Indians, Joses?" said Bart at last.

"What, Old Arrow—in—the—arm!"

"Yes."

"Sure to," said Joses. "He's a good fellow that is. 'Taint an Indian's natur to show he's fond of you, but that chap would fight for the master to the last."

"It seemed like it the other day, but it was very strange that he should go off as he did."

"Not it, my lad. He's gone to watch them Injuns, safe."

"Then he will think us ungrateful for going away."

"Not he. Depend upon it, he'll turn up one of these days just when we don't expect it, and sit down just as if nothing had happened."

"But will he find our trail over such stony ground?"

"Find it? Ah! of course he will, and before you know where you are."

They trudged on in silence now, for both were growing tired, but just about the time appointed they came within sight of their starting-place, the Doctor meeting them a few minutes later.

"What luck?" he asked.

"Nothing but a glorious spring of water, and a stream with some specks of gold in the washing."

"I have done little better, Bart, but there is a valley yonder that leads up into the mountains, and with care I think we can get the waggon along without much difficulty."

Chapter Ten.: A sure-footed Beast.

An early start was made next morning, and following the course mapped out by the Doctor, they soon reached an opening in the hills, up which they turned, to find in the hollow a thread-like stream and that, as they proceeded, the mountains began to open out before them higher and higher, till they seemed to close in the horizon like clouds of delicate amethystine blue.

Every now and then the travelling was so bad that it seemed as if they must return, but somehow the waggon and horses were got over the obstacles, and a short level cheered them on to fresh exertions, while, as they slowly climbed higher and higher, there was the satisfaction of knowing that there was less likelihood of molestation from Indians, the dangerous tribes of the plains, Comanches and Apachés, rarely taking their horses up amongst the rugged portions of the hills.

Maude, in her girlish freshness of heart, was delighted with the variety of scenery, while to Bart all was excitement. Even the labour to extricate the waggon from some rift, or to help to drag it up some tremendous slope, was enjoyable.

Then there were little excursions to make down moist ravines, where an antelope might be bagged for the larder; or up to some dry-looking flat, shut in by the hills, where grouse might be put up amongst the sage-brush and other thin growth, for six hard-working men out in these brisk latitudes consume a great deal of food, and the stores in the waggon had to be saved as much a possible.

One way and the other the larder was kept well supplied, and while Dr Lascelles on the one hand talked eagerly of the precious metal he hoped to discover, Joses was always ready with promises of endless sport.

"Why, by an' by, Master Bart," he said one day as they journeyed slowly on, "we shall come to rivers so full of salmon that all you've got to do is to pull 'em out."

"If you can catch them," said Bart, laughing.

"Catch 'em, my boy? Why, they don't want no catching. I've known 'em come up some rivers so quick and fast that when they got up to the shallows they shoved one another out on to the sides high and dry, and all you'd got to do was to catch 'em and eat 'em."

"Let's see, that's what the Doctor calls a traveller's tale, Joses."

"Yes; this traveller's tale," said Bart's companion gruffly. "You needn't believe it without you like, but it's true all the same."

"Well, I'll try and believe it," said Bart, laughing, "but I didn't know salmon were so stupid as that."

"Stupid! they aren't stupid, my lad," replied Joses sharply. "Suppose you and millions of people behind you were walking along a narrow bit o' land with a river on each side of you, and everybody was pushing on from behind to get up to the end of the bit of land, where there wasn't room for you all, and suppose you and hundreds more got pushed into the water on one side or on the other, that wouldn't be because you were so very stupid, would it?"

"No," said Bart, "that would be because I couldn't help it."

"Well, it's just the same with the salmon, my lad. Millions of 'em come up from out of the sea at spawning time, and they swim up and up till the rivers get narrower and shallower, and all those behind keep pushing the first ones on till thousands die on the banks, and get eaten by the wolves and coyótes that come down then to the banks along with eagles and hawks and birds like them."

"I beg your pardon, Joses, for not believing you," said Bart, earnestly. "I see now."

"Oh, it's all right enough," said the rough fellow bluntly. "I shouldn't have believed it if I hadn't seen it, and of course it's only up the little shallow streams that shoot off from the others."

This conversation took place some days after they had been in the mountains, gradually climbing higher, and getting glorious views at times, of hill and distant plain. Bart and Joses were out "after the pot," as the latter called it, and on this occasion they had been very unfortunate.

"I tell you what it is," said Joses at last, "we shall have to go lower down. The master won't never find no gold and silver up here, and food'll get scarcer and scarcer, unless we can come upon a flock of sheep."

"A flock of sheep up here!" said Bart incredulously.

"I didn't say salmon, I said sheep," grunted Joses. "Now, say you don't believe there is sheep up here."

"You tell me there are sheep up here," said Bart, "and I will believe you."

"I don't say there are; I only hope there are," said Joses; "for if we could get one or two o' them in good condition, they're the best eating of anything as goes on four legs."

"But not our sort of sheep?"

"No, of course not. Mountain sheep, my lad, with great horns twisted round so long and thick you get wondering how the sheep can carry 'em, and—there, look!"

He caught Bart by the shoulder, and pointed to a tremendous slope, a quarter of a mile away, where, in the clear pure air, the lad could see a flock of about twenty sheep evidently watching them.

"They're the shyest, artfullest things as ever was," whispered Joses. "Down softly, and let's back away; we must circumvent them, and get behind 'em for a shot."

"Too late," said Bart; and he was right, for suddenly the whole herd went off at a tremendous pace along a slope that seemed to be quite a precipice, and the next moment they were gone.

"That's up for to-day," said Joses, shouldering his rifle. "We may go back and try and pick up a bird or two. To-morrow we'll come strong, and p'r'aps get a shot at the sheep, as we know they are here."

They were fortunate enough to shoot a few grouse on their way back, and next morning at daybreak, Bart and the four men started after the sheep, the Doctor preferring to stay by the waggon and examine some of the rocks.

As the party climbed upwards towards the slope where the sheep had been seen on the previous day, Joses was full of stories about the shy nature of these animals.

"They'll lead you right away into the wildest places," he said, "and then, when you think you've got them, they go over some steep cut, and you never see 'em again. Some people say they jump head first down on to the rocks, and lets themselves fall on their horns, which is made big on purpose, and then bounces up again, but I don't believe it, for if they did, they'd break their necks. All the same, though, they do jump down some wonderful steep places and run up others that look like walls. Here, what's Sam making signals for! Go softly."

They crept up to their companion, and found that he had sighted a flock of eleven sheep on a slope quite a couple of miles away, and but for the assurance of Joses that it was all right, and that they were sheep, Bart would have said it was a patch of a light colour on the mountain.

As they approached cautiously, however, trying to stalk the timid creatures, Bart found that his men were right, and they spent the next two hours in cautious approach, till they saw that the sheep took alarm and rushed up to the top of the slope, disappeared for a moment, and then came back, to stand staring down at their advancing enemies.

"It's all right," exclaimed Joses, "we can get the lot if we like, for they can't get away. Yonder's a regular dip down where they can't jump. Keep your rifles ready, my boys, and we'll shoot two. That'll be enough."

As they spread out and slowly advanced, the sheep ran back out of sight, but came back again, proving Joses' words, that there was a precipice beyond them and their enemies in front.

Four times over, as the hunting party advanced, did the sheep perform this evolution, but the last time they did not come back into sight.

"They're away hiding down among the bushes," said Joses. "Be ready. Now then close in. You keep in the middle here, Master Bart, and have the first shot. Pick a good fat one."

"Yes," panted Bart, who was out of breath with the climbing, and to rest him Joses called a halt, keeping a sharp look-out the while to left and right, so that the sheep might not elude them.

At the end of a few minutes they toiled up the slope once more, Joses uttering a few words of warning to his young companion.

"Don't rush when you get to the top, for it slopes down there with a big wall going right down beyond, and you mightn't be able to stop yourself. Keep cool, we shall see them together directly."

But they did not see the sheep cowering together as they expected, for though the top of the mountain was just as Joses had described, sloping down after they had passed the summit and then going down abruptly in an awful precipice, no sheep were to be seen, and after making sure that none were hidden, the men passed on cautiously to the edge, Bart being a little way behind, forcing his way through some thick bushes.

Just then a cry from Joses made him hurry to the edge, but he was too late to see what three of them witnessed, and that was the leap of a magnificent ram, which had been standing upon a ledge ten feet below them, and which, as soon as it heard the bushes above its head parted, made a tremendous spring as if into space, but landed on another ledge, fifty feet below, to take off once more for another leap right out of sight.

"We must go back and round into the valley," said Juan. "We shall find them all with their necks broken."

"You'll be clever if you do," said Joses, in a savage growl. "They've gone on jumping down like that right to the bottom, Master Bart, and—"

"Is that the flock?" said Bart, pointing to where a similar wall of rock rose up from what seemed to be part of a great canyon.

"That's them," said Joses, counting, "eight, nine, ten, eleven, and all as fresh as if they'd never made a jump. There, I'll believe anything of 'em after that."

"Why, it makes one shudder to look down," said Bart, shrinking back.

"Shudder!" said Joses, "why, I'd have starved a hundred times before I'd have made a jump like that. No mutton for dinner to-day, boys. Let's get some birds."

And very disconsolately and birdless, they made their way back to the camp.

Chapter Eleven.: Bears and for Bears.

Bart was sufficiently observing to notice, even amidst the many calls he had upon his attention, that Dr Lascelles grew more and more absorbed and dreamy every day. When they first started he was always on the alert about the management of the expedition, the proportioning of the supplies and matters of that kind; but as he found in a short time that Bart devoted himself eagerly to everything connected with the successful carrying out of their progress, that Joses was sternly exacting over the other men, and that Maude took ample care of the stores, he very soon ceased troubling himself about anything but the main object which he had in view.

Hence it was then that he used to sling a sort of game-bag over his shoulder directly after the early morning meal, place a sharp, wedge-like hammer in his belt, shoulder his double rifle, and go off "rock-chipping," as Joses called it.

"I don't see what's the good of his loading one barrel with shot, Master Bart, for he never brings in no game; and as for the stones—well, I haven't seen a single likely bit yet."

"Do you think he ever will hit upon a good mine of gold or silver, Joses?" said Bart, as they were out hunting one day.

"Well, Master Bart, you know what sort of a fellow I am. If I'd got five hundred cows, I should never reckon as they'd have five hundred calves next year, but just calculate as they wouldn't have one. Then all that come would be so many to the good. Looking at it fairly, I don't want to dishearten you, my lad, but speaking from sperience, I should say he wouldn't."

"And this will all be labour in vain, Joses?"

"Nay, I don't say that, Master Bart. He might find a big vein of gold or silver; but I never knew a man yet who went out in the mountains looking for one as did."

"But up northward there, men have discovered mines and made themselves enormously rich."

"To be sure they have, my lad, but not by going and looking for the gold or silver. It was always found by accident like, and you and me is much more like to come upon a big lead where we're trying after sheep or deer than he is with all his regular trying."

"You think there are mineral riches up in the mountains then?"

"Think, Master Bart! Oh, I'm sure of it. But where is it to be found? P'r'aps we're walking over it now, but there's no means of telling."

"No," said Bart thoughtfully, "for everything about is so vast."

"That's about it, my lad, and all the harm I wish master is that he may find as much as he wants."

"I wish he may, Joses," said Bart, "or that I could find a mine for him and Miss Maude."

"Well, my lad, we'll keep our eyes open while we are out, only we have so many other things to push, and want to push on farther so as to get among better pasture for the horses. They don't look in such good condition as they did."

There was good reason for this remark, their halting-places during the past few days having been in very sterile spots, where the tall forbidding rocks were relieved by very little that was green, and patches of grass were few.

But these were the regions most affected by the Doctor, who believed that they were the most likely ones for discovering treasure belonging to nature's great storehouse, untouched as yet by man. In these barren wilds he would tramp about, now climbing to the top of some chine, now letting himself down into some gloomy forbidding ravine, but always without success, there being nothing to tempt him to say, "Here is the beginning of a very wealthy mine."

Every time they journeyed on the toil became greater, for they were in most inaccessible parts of the mountain range, and they knew by the coolness of the air that they must now be far above the plains.

Bart and Joses worked hard to supply the larder, the principal food they obtained being the sage grouse and dusky grouse, which birds they found to be pretty plentiful high up in the mountains wherever there was a flat or a slope with plenty of cover; but just as they were getting terribly tired of the sameness of this diet, Bart made one morning a lucky find.

They had reached a fresh halting-place after sundown on the previous night—one that was extremely attractive from the variety of the high ground, the depths of the chasms around, and the beauty of the cedars that spread their flat, frond-like branches over the mountain-sides, which were diversified by the presence of endless dense thickets.

"It looks like a deer country," Joses had said as they were tethering the horses amongst some magnificent grass.

These words had haunted Bart the night through, and hence, at the first sight of morning on the peaks up far above where they were, he had taken his rifle and gone off to see what he could find.

Three hours' tramp produced nothing but a glimpse of some mountain sheep far away and at a very great height.

He was too weary and hungry to think of following them, and was reluctantly making for the camp, when all at once a magnificent deer sprang up from amongst a thicket of young pines, and bounded off at an astounding rate.

It seemed madness to fire, but, aiming well in front, Bart drew trigger, and then leaped aside to get free of the smoke. As he did so, he just caught a glimpse of the deer as it bounded up a steep slope and the next moment it was gone.

Bart felt that he had not hit it, but curiosity prompted him to follow in the animal's track, in the hope of getting a second shot, and as he proceeded, he could not help wishing for the muscular strength of these deer, for the ground, full of rifts and chasms, over which he toiled painfully in a regular climb, the deer had bounded over at full speed.

It took him some time to get to the spot where he had last seen the deer, when, to his intense surprise and delight, he found traces of blood upon the stones, and upon climbing higher, he found his way blocked by a chasm.

Feeling sure that the animal would have cleared this at a bound, he lowered himself down by holding on by a young pine which bent beneath his weight. Then he slipped for a few feet, made a leap, and came down amongst some bushes, where, lying perfectly dead, was the most beautiful deer he had ever seen.

Unfortunately hunger and the knowledge that others are hungry interfere with romantic admiration, and after feasting his eyes, Bart began to feast his imagination on the delight of those in the camp with the prospect of venison steaks. So, in regular hunter's fashion, he proceeded to partially skin and dress the deer, cutting off sufficient for their meal, and leaving the other parts to be fetched by the men.

There were rejoicings in camp that morning, and soon after breakfast Bart started off once more, taking with him Joses, Juan, and Sam, all of whom were exceedingly willing to become the bearers of the meat in which they stood in such great need.

The Doctor had gone off in another direction, taking with him Maude as his companion, and after the little party had returned to the camp, Bart was standing thoughtfully gazing at a magnificent eminence, clothed almost to the top with cedars, while in its rifts and ravines were dark-foliaged pines.

"I wonder whether we should find anything up there, Joses," said Bart.

"Not much," said the frontier man. "There'd be deer, I daresay, if the sound of your rifle and the coming of the sheep hadn't sent them away."

"Why should the sheep send them away?" asked Bart.

"I don't know why they should," said Joses; "all I know is that they do. You never find black-tailed deer like you shot and mountain sheep living together as neighbours. It arn't their nature."

"Well, what do you say to taking our rifles and exploring?"

"Don't mind," said Joses, looking round. "Horses are all right, and there's no fear of being overhauled by Injuns up here, so let's go and take Sam with us, but you won't get no more deer."

"Well, we don't want any for a day or two. But why shouldn't I get another?"

"Because they lie close in the thickest part of the cover in the middle of the day, and you might pretty well tread upon them before they'd move."

They started directly after, and for about two hours did nothing but climb up amidst cedar and pine forest. Sometimes amongst the trunks of big trees, sometimes down in gashes or gullies in the mountain-side, which were full of younger growths, as if the rich soil and pine seeds had been swept there by the storms and then taken root.

"I tell you what it is, Master Bart," said Joses, suddenly coming to a halt, to roll up and light his cigarito, a practice he never gave up, "it strikes me that we've nearly got to the end of it."

"End of what?" asked Bart.

"This clump of hills. You see if when we get to the top here, it don't all go down full swoop like a house wall right bang to the plain."

"What, like the place where the mountain sheep went down?"

"That's it, my lad, only without any go up on the other side. It strikes me that we shall find it all plain on this side, and that if we can't find a break in the wall with a regular gulch, we shall have to go back with our horses and waggon and try some other way."

"Well, come along and let's see," said Bart; and once more they climbed on for quite half-an-hour, when they emerged from the trees on to a rugged piece of open rocky plain, with scattered pines gnarled and twisted and swept bare by the mighty winds, and as far as eye could reach nothing but one vast, well-watered plain.

"Told you so," said Joses; "now we shall either have to keep up here in the mountain or go down among the Injuns again, just as the master likes."

"Let's come and sit down near the edge here and rest," said Bart, who was fascinated by the beauty of the scene, and, going right out upon a jutting promontory of stone, they could look to right and left at the great wall of rock that spread as far as they could see. In places it seemed to go sheer down to the plain, in others it was broken into ledges by slips and falls of rock; but everywhere it seemed to shut the great plain in from the west, and Bart fully realised that they would have to find some great rift or gulch by which to descend, if their journey was to be continued in this direction.

"How far is it down to the plain?" said Bart, after he had been feasting his eyes for some time.

"Four to five thousand feet," said Joses. "Can't tell for certain. Chap would fall a long way before he found bottom, and then he'd bounce off, and go on again and again. I don't think the mountain sheep would jump here."

As they sat resting and inhaling the fresh breeze that blew over the widespreading plain, Bart could not help noticing the remains of a grand old pine that had once grown right at the edge of the stupendous precipice, but had gradually been storm-beaten and split in its old age till the trunk and a few jagged branches only remained.

One of these projected from its stunted trunk close down by the roots, and seemed thrust out at right angles over the precipice in a way that somehow seemed to tempt Bart.

He turned his eyes from it again and again, but that branch fascinated him, and he found himself considering how dangerous it would be, and yet how delightful, to climb right out on that branch till it bent and bent, and would bear him no further, and then sitting astride, dance up and down in mid air, right over the awful depths below.

So strange was the attraction that Bart found his hands wet with perspiration, and a peculiar feeling of horror attacked him; but what was more strange, the desire to risk his life kept growing upon him, and as he afterwards told himself, he would no doubt have made the mad venture if something had not happened to take his attention.

Joses was leaning back with half-closed eyes, enjoying his cigárito, and Bart was half rising to his knees to go back and round to where the branch projected, just to try it, he told himself, when they heard a shout away to the left, and that shout acted like magic upon Bart.

"Why, that's Sam," he said, drawing a breath full of relief, just as if he had awakened from some terrible nightmare.

"I'd 'bout forgotten him," said Joses lazily. "Ahoy! Oho!—eh!" he shouted back. Then there was another shout and a rustling of bushes, a grunting noise, and Bart seized his rifle.

"He has found game," he said.

Then he nearly let fall his piece, and knelt there as if turned to stone, for, to his horror, he suddenly saw Sam down upon his hands and knees crawling straight out on the great gnarled branch that overhung the precipice, keeping to this mode of progression for a time, and then letting his legs go down one on each side of the branch, and hitching himself along, yelling lustily the while for help.

"He has gone mad," cried Bart, and as he spoke he thought of his own sensations a few minutes before, and how he had felt tempted to do this very thing.

"No, he arn't," said Joses, throwing the remains of his cigárito over the precipice, and lifting his rifle; "he's got bears after him."

Almost as he spoke the great rough furry body of an enormous black bear came into sight, and without a moment's hesitation walked right out along the branch after the man.

"There's another," cried Bart, "shoot, Joses, shoot. I dare not."

It seemed that Joses dare not either, or else the excitement paralysed him, for he only remained like Bart, staring stupidly at the unwonted scene before them as a second bear followed the first, which, in spite of Sam's efforts to get into safety, had overtaken him, crept right upon him, and throwing its forepaws round him and the branches as well, hugged him fast, while the second came close up and stood there growling and grunting and patting at its companion, who, fortunately for Sam, was driving the claws at the ends of its paws deeply into the gnarled branch.

"If I don't fire they'll kill him," muttered Joses, as the huge branch visibly bent with the weight of the three bodies now upon it. "If I kill him instead it would be a mercy, so here goes."

He raised his rifle, took careful aim, and was about to draw the trigger, but forbore, as just then the report of Bart's piece rang out, and the second bear raised itself up on its hind legs, while the foremost backed a couple of feet, and stood growling savagely with its head turned towards where it could see the smoke.

That was Bart's opportunity, and throwing himself upon his breast, and steadying his rifle upon a piece of rock, he fired again, making the foremost bear utter a savage growl and begin tearing furiously at its flank.

Then Joses' rifle spoke, and the first bear reared up and fell over backwards, a second shot striking the hindmost full in the head, and one after the other the two monsters fell headlong, the first seeming to dive down, making a swimming motion with its massive paws, the second turning over back downwards.

They both struck the rock about fifty feet below the branch, and this seemed to make them glance off and fly through the air at a fearful rate, spinning over and over till they struck again at an enormous distance below, and then plunged out of sight, leaving Bart sick with horror to gaze upon the unfortunate Sam.

Chapter Twelve.: Sam gets a Fright.

Bart was brought to his senses by Joses, who exclaimed sharply:

"Load, my lad, load; you never know when you may want your piece."

Bart obeyed mechanically as Joses shouted:

"Now then, how long are you going to sit there?"

Sam, who was seated astride the gnarled old limb, holding on tightly with both hands, turned his head slightly and then turned it back, staring straight down into the awful depths, as if fascinated by the scene below.

"Here, hi! Don't sit staring there," cried Joses. "Get back, man."

Sam shook his head and seemed to cling the more tightly.

"Are you hurt, Sam?" cried Bart.

Sam shook his head.

"Why don't you speak?" roared Joses, angrily. "Did the beasts claw you?"

Sam shook his head, but otherwise he remained motionless, and Bart and Joses went round to where the tree clung to the rocky soil, and stood gazing out at their companion and within some fifteen feet of where he clung.

"What's the matter, Sam; why don't you come back?" asked Bart.

The man responded with a low groan.

"He must be badly hurt, Joses," exclaimed Bart. "What are we to do?"

"Wait a moment till I think," said Joses. "He's hurt in his head, that's what's the matter with him."

"By the bears' claws?"

"No, my lad, they didn't hurt him. He's frit."

"Frightened?" said Bart.

"Yes! He's lost his nerve, and daren't move."

"Let's say a few encouraging words to him."

"You may say thousands, and they won't do no good," said Joses. "He's got the fright and badly too."

"But the bears are gone?"

"Ay, that they are, my lad; but the fall's there, and that's what he's afraid of. I've seen men look like that before now, when climbing up mountains."

"But it would be so easy to get back, Joses. I could do it directly."

"So could he if he hadn't lost his nerve. Now what's to be done?"

"Shall I creep out to him?" said Bart eagerly.

"What, you? what good would it do? You don't think you could carry him back like a baby?"

"No," said Bart, "but I might help him."

"You couldn't help him a bit," growled Joses, "nor more could I. All the good you could do would be to make him clutch you and then down both would go at once, and what's the use of that."

"If we had brought a lasso with us."

"Well, if we had," said Joses, "and could fasten it round him, I don't believe we could haul him off, for he'd only cling all the tighter, and perhaps drag us over the side."

"What is to be done then?" said Bart. "Here, Sam, make an effort, my lad. Creep back; it's as easy as can be. Don't be afraid. Here, I will come to you."

He threw down his gun, and before Joses could stop him, he climbed out to the projecting limb, and letting his legs go down on either side, worked himself along till he was close behind Sam, whom he slapped on the back.

"There," cried Bart. "It's easy enough. Don't think of how deep down it is. Now I'm going back. You do the same. Come along."

As he spoke and said encouraging things to Sam, Bart felt himself impelled to gaze down into the depths beneath him, and as he did so, the dashing bravery that had impelled him to risk his life that he might encourage his follower to creep back, all seemed to forsake him, a cold perspiration broke out on face and limbs, accompanied by a horrible paralysing sense of fear, and in an instant he was suffering from the same loss of nerve as the man whom he wished to help.

Bart's hands clutched at the rough branch, and he strove to drive his finger nails into the bark in a spasmodic effort to save himself from death. He was going to fall. He knew that he was. Nothing could save him—nothing, and in imagination he saw himself lose his hold of the branch, slip sidewise, and go down headlong as the bears had fallen, to strike against the rocks, glance off, and then plunge down, down, swifter and swifter into space.

The sensation was fearful, and for the time being he could make no effort to master it. One overwhelming sense of terror had seized upon him, and this regularly froze all action till he now crouched as helpless and unnerved as the poor fellow before him who never even turned his head, but clung to the branch as if insensible to everything but the horrors of his position.

Joses shouted to him, and said something again and again, but Bart only heard an indistinct murmur as he stared straight down at the tops of the pines and other trees half a mile below him; and then came a dreamy, wondering feeling, as to how much pain he should feel when he fell; how long he would be going down all that distance; whether he should have to fall on the tops of the pine-trees, or amongst the rough ravines of rock.

And so on, thought after thought of this kind, till all at once, as if out of a dream, a voice seemed to say to him:

"Well, I shouldn't have thought, Master Bart, as I'd taught all these years, was such a coward!"

The words stung him, and seemed to bring him back to himself.

Coward! what would Maude think of him for being such a coward? Not that it would much matter if he fell down there and were smashed to death. What would the Doctor, who had given him so many lessons on presence of mind, coolness in danger, and the like? And here was he completely given up to the horror of his position, making no effort when it was perhaps no harder to get back than it had been to get forward.

"I won't think of the depth," said Bart, setting his teeth, and, raising himself upright, he hitched himself a few inches back.

Then the feeling of danger came upon him once more, and was mastering him again rapidly, when the great rough voice of old Joses rang out loudly in a half-mocking, half-angry tone:

"And I thought him such a brave un too."

"And so I will be," muttered Bart, as he made a fresh effort to recover from his feeling of panic; and as he did so, he hitched himself along the branch towards the main trunk with his back half turned, threw one leg over so that he was in a sitting position, and the next minute he was standing beside Joses, with his heart beating furiously, and a feeling of wonderment coming over him as to why it was that he had been so frightened over such a trifling matter.

"That's better, my lad," said Joses quietly; and as Bart gazed on the rough fellow's face, expecting revilings and reproaches at his cowardice, he saw that the man's bronzed and swarthy features looked dirty and mottled, his eyes staring, and that he was dripping with perspiration.

Just then Joses gripped him by the shoulder in a way that would have made him wince, only he did not want to show the white feather again, and he stood firm as his companion said:

"'Taint no use to talk like that to him. It won't touch him, Master Bart. It's very horrid when that lays hold of you, and you can't help it."

"No," said Bart, feeling relieved, "I could not help it."

"Course you couldn't, my lad. But now we must get old Sam back, or he'll hang there till he faints, and then drop."

"O Joses!" cried Bart.

"I only wish we could get a bear on the bough beyond him there. That would make him scuffle back."

"Frighten him back?" said Bart.

"Yes; one fright would be bigger than the other, and make him come," said Joses.

"Do you think that if we frightened him, he would try to get back then?" whispered Bart.

"I'm sure of it," said Joses.

"Do as I do then," said Bart, as he picked up his rifle. Then speaking loudly he exclaimed:

"Joses; we must not leave the poor fellow there to die of hunger. He can't get back, so let's put him out of his misery at once. Where shall I aim at? His heart?"

"No, no, Master Bart; his head. Send a bullet right through his skull, and it'll be all over at once. You fire first."

Without a moment's hesitation, Bart rested the barrel of his rifle against the trunk, took careful aim, and fired so that the bullet whistled pretty closely by Sam's ear.

The man started and shuddered, seeming as if he were going to sit up, but he relapsed into the former position. "I think I can do it, Master Bart, this time," said Joses; and laying his piece in a notch formed by the bark, he took careful aim, and fired, his bullet going through Sam's hat, and carrying it off to go fluttering down into the abyss.

This time Sam did not move, and Bart gazed at Joses in despair.

"He's too artful, Master Bart," whispered the latter: "he knows we are only doing it to frighten him. I don't know how to appeal to his feelings, unless I was to say, 'here's your old wife a-coming, Sam,' for he run away from her ten years ago. But it wouldn't be no good. He wouldn't believe it."

Bart hesitated for a few moments as he reloaded his rifle, and then he shouted to Sam:

"Now, no nonsense, Sam. You must get back."

The man paid no heed to him, and Bart turned to Joses to say loudly:

"We can't leave him here like this. He must climb back or fall, so if he won't climb back the sooner he is out of his misery the better."

"That's a true word," said Joses.

"Give me your axe then," said Bart, and Joses drew it from his belt, when Bart took it, and after moistening his hands, drove it into the branch just where it touched the tree, making a deep incision, and then drove it in again, when a white, wedge-shaped chip flew out, for the boy had been early in life taught the use of the axe.

Then cutting rapidly and well, he sent the chips flying, while every stroke sent a quiver along the great branch.

Still Sam clung to the spot where he had been from the first, and made no effort to move; and at last, when he was half-way through the branch, Bart stopped short in despair, for the pretence of cutting it off had not the slightest effect upon Sam.

"Tired, Master Bart?" cried Joses just then; and snatching away the axe, he began to apply it with tremendous effect, the chips flying over the precipice, and a great yawning opening appearing in the upper part of the branch.

"Don't cut any farther, Joses," whispered Bart; "it will give way."

"I shall cut till it begins to, Master Bart," replied the man; and as he spoke he went on making the chips fly, but still without effect, for Sam did not move.

"I shall have to give up directly, my lad," whispered Joses, with a peculiar look; "but I'll have one more chop."

He raised the axe, and delivered another sharp blow, when there was a loud crack as if half a dozen rifles had gone off at once, and almost before the fact could be realised the branch went down, to remain hanging only by a few tough portions of its under part.

Bart and Joses looked over the precipice aghast at what they had done, and gazed down at Sam's wild face, as, with his legs dislodged from their position, he seemed to have been turned right over, and to be clinging solely in a death grip with his arms.

Then, with cat-like alacrity, he seemed to wrench himself round, holding on to the lower part of the bough with his legs; and the next moment he was climbing steadily up, with the bough swinging to and fro beneath his weight.

It was a question now of the toughness of the fibres by which the bough hung; and the stress upon the minds of the watchers was terrible, as they crouched there, gazing over the edge of the awful precipice, momentarily expecting to see branch and man go headlong down as the bears had fallen before them.

But Sam climbed steadily up during what seemed to be a long time, but which was only a few moments, reaching at last the jagged points where the branch was broken, when there came an ominous crack, and Sam paused, as if irresolute.

"Keep it up," panted Bart, and his words seemed to electrify the man, who made one or two more clutches at the branch, and then he was in safety beside his companions, staring stupidly from one to the other.

"I didn't think I was going to get back," he said at last. "It was you cutting the branch did it. I shouldn't have moved else."

There was no show of resentment—no annoyance at having been treated in this terrible manner. Sam only seemed very thankful for his escape, and trotting off to where he had dropped his rifle when pursued by the bears, he rejoined his companions, and proceeded with them back towards the camp; for they had not the least idea where to find a way down into the plain, even if they had entertained any desire to try and get the skins and some steaks off the bears.

As they journeyed on, Sam related how he had suddenly come upon one of the bears feeding upon the fruit of a clump of bushes, and as the animal seemed tame and little disposed to fly from him he had refrained from firing, but had picked up a lump of rock and thrown it at the beast.

The stone hit its mark, and uttering a loud grunting yell, the bear charged its assailant, Sam to his horror finding that the cry had brought a second enemy into the field, when he dropped his rifle, fled for his life, and took refuge from the following danger in the way and with the result that we have seen.

Chapter Thirteen.: Black Boy amuses himself.

Upon learning the fact that they had so nearly crossed the ridge of mountains, the Doctor resolved next day to proceed as far as the point where the adventure with the bears had taken place, and there endeavour, by the aid of his glass, to determine which direction to take: whether to find a ravine by which they might descend into the plain, or whether it would be better to remain amongst these mountains, and here continue his search.

The place was reached in due time, and for the time being there seemed to be no chance of getting down into the plain, either to search for the bears or to pursue their course in that direction.

The Doctor examined the slopes and ravines, plunged down into the most sheltered chasms, and chipped at the fragments of rock, but no sign of silver rewarded the search, and their journey would have been useless but for the fact that, as they were making a circuit, Joses suddenly arrested them, for he had caught a glimpse of a little flock of mountain sheep, and these he and Bart immediately set themselves to try and stalk.

It was no easy task, for the little group were upon a broad shelf high above them, and in a position that gave them an excellent opportunity for seeing approaching danger. But this time, after taking a long circuit, the hunters were rewarded by finding themselves well within shot, and only separated from the timid beasts by some rugged masses of rock.

These they cautiously approached, crawling upon hands and knees, when, after glancing from one to the other by way of signal, Bart and Joses fired exactly together, with the result that a splendid young ram made a bound into the air and rolled over the edge of the shelf, falling crashing down amongst the bushes and loose stones, to land at last but a very short distance from where the Doctor was awaiting his companions' return.

The most remarkable part of the little hunt, though, was the action of the rest of the flock, which went off with headlong speed to the end of the shelf of the mountain, where they seemed to charge the perpendicular face of the rock and run up it like so many enlarged beetles, to disappear directly after over the edge of the cliff upon which they had climbed.

"At last!" panted Bart eagerly. "We shall have something good in the larder to-day instead of running short."

"Just you wait till you've tasted it," said Joses, as he came up, drew his knife, and he and Sam rapidly dressed the sheep, getting rid of the useless parts, and dividing it so that each might have a share of the load back to camp, where Joses' words proved true, the various joints being declared to be more delicious than any meat the eaters had tasted yet.

In these thorough solitudes amongst the hills the practice of keeping watch had not been so strictly attended to as during the journeying in the plains, for the horse—Indians seldom visited these rugged places,—in fact, none but the searchers after mineral treasures were likely to come into these toilsome regions. Hence it was then that the next night the party were so wanting in vigilance.

Harry had been appointed to the latter half of the night, and after diligently keeping guard through the earlier hours, Joses awakened his successor, and fully trusting in his carrying out his duties, went and lay down in his blanket, and in a few seconds was fast asleep.

That morning at sunrise, after a delicious night's rest, Bart rose to have a look round before breakfast, when to his horror he saw that the camp was apparently in the hands of the Indians, who had been allowed by the negligent sentinel to approach while those who would have defended it slept.

Bart's first movement was to seize his gun, his next to arouse the Doctor.

Then he stopped short, sorry for what he had done, for just then, free from all sling and stiffness in his wounded arm, their old friend the chief came striding across the open space before the waggon, and upon seeing Bart held out his hands in token of friendship.

Bart shook hands with him, and as he glanced round he could see that the faces of those around were all familiar except one, whom the chief had beckoned to approach, which the strange Indian did with a stately air, when a short conversation between them and the chief took place, after which the new-comer turned to Bart, and said in very fair English:

"The great chief Beaver-with-the-Sharp-Teeth bids me tell you that he has been back to his people to fetch one of his warriors who can speak the tongue of the pale-faced people, and I am that warrior. The great chief Beaver-with-the-Sharp-Teeth says it is peace, and he comes to see his friends and the great medicine-man, who brought him back to life when wounded by the poisonous arrows of the Indian dogs of the plains."

"We are very glad to see Beaver-with-the-Sharp-Teeth again," cried Bart heartily, "and delighted to find he has brought a great warrior who can speak our language."

"So that it flows soft and sweet," said a hoarse voice, and Joses stood up. "How are you, chief?"

The hearty, friendly look and extended hand needed no interpretation, and the greeting between them was warm enough to bring smiles into the faces of all the Indians, who had no scruple soon afterwards about finishing the mountain mutton.

After the breakfast Bart and the Doctor learned that the chief Beaver, as it was settled to call him, had been off really on purpose to get an interpreter, knowing that he could find the trail of his friends again; and this he had done, following them right into the mountains, and coming upon them as we have seen.

Conversation was easy now, and Bart learned that their friends had had a severe fight in the plains a short time before the first meeting, and that the Beaver had felt sure that he would die of his wound, and be left in the wilderness the same as they had left fifteen of their number, the odds against them having been terribly great.

Later on came questions, the Beaver being anxious to know why the Doctor's party were there.

"You have not come upon the war-path," the Beaver said, "for you are weak in number, and you have brought a woman. Why are you here?"

Then the Doctor explained his object—to find a vein of either gold or silver somewhere in the mountains; and as soon as it was all interpreted, the chief laughed outright.

"He does not set much store by the precious metals, Bart," said the Doctor, "and when I see the simplicity of their ways, it almost makes me ashamed of our own."

Just then the Beaver talked earnestly for a few moments with the warrior who interpreted, and returned to the Doctor.

"The Beaver-with-the-Sharp-Teeth says you gave him life when all was growing black, and he thought to see his people never more; and now he says that he rejoices that he can take his brother across the plains to where a great river runs deep down by the side of a mighty mountain, where there is silver in greater quantities than can be carried away."

"Does the chief know of such a place?" cried the Doctor, excitedly.

"Yes; he and I have seen it often," said the Indian.

"And will he take me there?"

"Yes; the Beaver will take his brother there, and give it all into his hands."

"At last!" cried the Doctor excitedly. Then in a low voice, "Suppose it should not prove to be silver after all?"

"I know it is silver," said the Indian, quietly. "Look," he cried, taking a clumsily-made ring from his medicine-bag. "That came from there, so did the ring upon the lariat of the chief."

"Ask him when he will take me there!" cried the Doctor.

"He says now," replied the Indian, smiling at the Doctor's eagerness and excitement. "It is a long way, and the plains are hot, and there is little water; but we can hunt as we go, and all will be well."

"You know the way from here down into the plain?" said the Doctor. "It is a long way, is it not?"

The Indian smiled. "It is a very short journey," he said. "I know the way."

In effect they started as soon as the camp was struck, and the Beaver, leading the way, took them down a deep gulch, of whose existence they were unaware, by which they made an easy descent into the plain, and into which they passed with such good effect that at sunset the bold bluff where the adventure with the bears had taken place stood up in the distance, with the steep wall falling away on either side, looking diminutive in the distance, and very different to what it really was.

They had had a rapid progress over a long range of perfectly level plain, the horses, after the toils in the mountains, seeming quite excited at having grass beneath their feet; and hence it was that when they were camping for the night, and Bart's beautiful cob with long mane and tail had been divested of saddle and bridle, and after being watered was about to be secured by its lariat to the tether-peg, the excitable little creature, that had been till now all docility and tractableness, suddenly uttered a shrill neigh, pranced, reared up, and before Bart could seize it by the mane, went off across the plain like the wind.

The loss of such a beast would have been irreparable, and the Doctor and Joses ran to untether their horses to join pursuit, but before they could reach them, the Beaver and half a dozen of his men were after the cob at full speed, loosing their lariats as they rode and holding them over their heads ready to use as lassoes as soon as they could get within reach of the fugitive.

No easy task this, for as, dolefully enough, Bart looked on from the waggon, he could see his little horse keeping a long distance ahead, while now the Indians seemed to be making to the left to try and cut the restive little creature off, as he made for a wild-looking part of the plain about a couple of miles away.

Bart was helpless, for there was no horse of their own left that was of the slightest use for pursuit of his swift little cob, and all he could do was to stare after those engaged in the pursuit in a hopeless way as the truant galloped on at full speed, swishing its tail, tossing its head, and apparently revelling in its newly-found liberty.

All at once Bart became aware of the fact that one of the Indians had been for some minutes watching him attentively, and the man had uttered a low guttural laugh as if he were enjoying the youth's misfortune.

"I wonder how he would like it," thought Bart, as he darted an indignant look at the Indian, who sat upon his swift pony like a group cut in bronze. "He might just as well have gone after Black Boy, for his pony looks as if it could go."

Just then the Indian threw himself lightly from his nag and drew near to Bart, with the horse-hair rein in his hand. Then he made signs to the young fellow to mount.

"Do you mean that you will lend me the pony to go after my own?" said Bart eagerly.

The Indian did not understand his words, but evidently realised their meaning, for he smiled and nodded, and placed the rein in Bart's hand, when he leaped into the saddle, or rather into the apology for a saddle, for it was only a piece of bison hide held on by a bandage, while a sort of knob or peg was in the place of the pommel, a contrivance invented by the Indians to hold on by when attacking a dangerous enemy, so as to lie as it were alongside of their horse, and fire or shoot arrows beneath its neck, their bodies being in this way thoroughly protected by their horses.

The Indian smiled and drew back when Bart touched the pony with his heel, the result being that, instead of going off at a gallop, the little restive beast reared up, pawing at the air with its hoofs, and nearly falling backwards upon its rider.

The Indian looked on intently as if ready to leap forward and seize the bridle should Bart be dismounted. But the lad kept his seat, and the pony went on all fours again, but only to begin kicking furiously, to dislodge the strange white-faced being upon its back. It was like an insult to an animal that had been accustomed to carry true-blooded Indians all its life, dressed in skins ornamented with feathers and neatly painted up for special occasions, to have a pale-faced, undersized human animal in strange clothes mounted upon it; and the proper thing seemed to be to kick him off as soon as it could.

These seemed to be the ideas of the Indian pony as exemplified by its acts; but the wildest of animals of the horse family cannot always do as they please, and it was evidently with something like astonishment that the little steed found Bart, still fixed firmly upon its back instead of flying over its head or slipping off backwards over the tail.

This being so, the pony began to what is called "buck," that is to say, instead of letting its back remain in an agreeable hollow curve, one which seems to have been made by nature on purpose to hold a human being, it curved its spine in the opposite direction, arching it as a cat would, but of course in a modified way, and then began leaping up from the earth in a series of buck jumps, all four hoofs from the ground at once.

Still, in spite of this being the most difficult form of horse trouble to master, Bart kept his seat. He was jerked about a great deal, but he had been long used to riding restive horses, and he sat there as coolly as if in a chair.

Then the Indian pony uttered a few shrill snorts and squeaks, throwing up its head, and finally turning round, first on one side then upon the other, it tried to bite its rider's legs—attacks which Bart met by a series of sharp blows, given with the lariat that was coiled by the horse's neck.

These pranks went on for a few minutes, the Indian looking smilingly on the while, till, seeing that Bart was not to be dislodged, the pony began to back and finally lay down.

This of course dismounted the rider, and with a snort of triumph the pony sprang to its feet again, evidently meaning to bound off after Black Boy and enjoy a turn of freedom.

The pony had reckoned without its rider, for Bart was too old at such matters to leave his grasp of the rein, and the Indian cob's first knowledge of its mistake was given by a sharp check to its under jaw, round which the horse-hair rope was twitched, the next by finding its rider back in his old place where he had leaped as lightly as could be.

The Indian gave an approving grunt, and uttering what was quite a sigh, the pony resigned itself to its fate, and obeying the touch of Bart's heel, went off at a fine springing gallop.

It was a long chase and an arduous one, for Black Boy seemed to laugh to scorn all attempts at capture—of course these were horse-laughs—and led his pursuers a tremendous run; and had it not been for his master, late as he was in the field, the cob would not have been captured that night. As it was, Bart went off at speed, setting at defiance prairie-dogs' burrows, and other holes that might be in his way, and at last he contrived to cut off a corner so as to get nearer to his nag, when, taking the rein beneath his leg, he placed both hands to his mouth and uttered a long shrill cry.

It acted like magic upon Black Boy, who recognised it directly as his master's call, and having had his frolic, he trotted slowly towards where Bart cantered on, suffered himself to be caught, and the party returned in triumph, none the worse, save the tiring, for the adventure.

Chapter Fourteen.: The Silver Canyon.

A week's arduous journey over a sterile stretch of country, where water was very scarce and where game was hard to approach, brought them at last in reach of what looked to be a curiously formed mountain far away in the middle of an apparently boundless plain. Then it struck Bart that it could not be a mountain, for its sides were perpendicular, and its top at a distance seemed to be perfectly flat, and long discussions arose between him and the Doctor as to the peculiarity of the strange eminence standing up so prominently right in the middle of the plain.

While they were discussing the subject, the Beaver and his English-speaking follower came to their side, and pointing to the mountain, gave them to understand that this was their destination.

"But is there silver there?" said the Doctor eagerly, when the Indian smiled and said quietly, "Wait and see."

The mountain on being first seen appeared to be at quite a short distance, but at the end of their first day's journey they seemed to have got no nearer, while after another day, though it had assumed more prominent proportions, they were still at some distance, and it was not until the third morning that the little party stood on the reedy shores of a long narrow winding lake, one end of which they had to skirt before they could ride up to the foot of the flat-topped mountain which looked as if it had been suddenly thrust by some wondrous volcanic action right from the plain to form what appeared to be a huge castle, some seven or eight hundred feet high, and with no ravine or rift in the wall by which it could be approached.

All Bart's questions were met by the one sole answer from the Indian, "Wait and see;" and in this spirit the savages guided them along beneath the towering ramparts of the mountain, whose scarped sides even a mountain sheep could not have climbed, till towards evening rein was drawn close under the mighty rocks, fragments of which had fallen here and there, loosened by time or cut loose by the shafts of storms to lie crumbling about its feet.

There seemed to be no reason for halting there, save that there was a little spring of water trickling down from the rocks, while a short distance in front what seemed to be a wide crack appeared in the plain, zigzagging here and there, one end going off into the distance, the other appearing to pass round close by the mountain; and as soon as they were dismounted and the horses tethered, the Beaver signed to Bart and the Doctor to accompany him, while the interpreter followed close behind.

It was a glorious evening, and after the heat of the day, the soft, cool breeze that swept over the plain was refreshing in the extreme; but all the same Bart felt very hungry, and his thoughts were more upon some carefully picked sage grouse that Joses and Maude were roasting than upon the search for silver; but the Doctor was excited, for he felt that most likely this would prove to be the goal of their long journey. His great fear was that the Indians in their ignorance might have taken some white shining stone or mica for the precious metal.

The crack in the plain seemed to grow wider as they approached, but the Indians suddenly led them off to the right, close under the towering flank of the mountain, and between it and a mass of rock that might have been split from it at some early stage in the world's life.

This mass was some forty or fifty feet high, and between it and the parent mountain there was a narrow rift, so narrow in fact that they had to proceed in single file for about a hundred yards, winding in and out till, reaching the end, the Indians stood upon a broad kind of shelf of rock in silence as the Doctor and Bart involuntarily uttered a cry of surprise.

For there was the crack in the plain below their feet, and they were standing upon its very verge where it came in close to the mountain, whose top was some seven hundred feet above their heads, while here its perpendicular side went down for fully another thousand to where, in the solemn dark depths of the vast canyon or crack in the rocky crust of the earth, a great rushing river ran, its roar rising to where they stood in a strangely weird monotone, like low echoing thunder.

The reflections in the evening sky lighted up the vast rift for a while, and Bart forgot his hunger in the contemplation of this strange freak of nature, of a river running below in a channel whose walls were perfectly perpendicular and against which in places the rapid stream seemed to beat and eddy and swirl, while in other parts there were long stretches of pebbly and rocky shore. For as far as Bart could judge, the walls seemed to be about four hundred feet apart, though in the fading evening light it was hard to tell anything for certain.

A more stupendous work of nature had never met Bart's eye, and his first thoughts were natural enough— How should he manage to get to the top of that flat mountain?—How should he be able to lower himself down into the mysterious shades of that vast canyon, and wander amongst the wonders that must for certain be hidden there?

Just then the Beaver spoke. He had evidently been taking lessons from the interpreter, as, smiling loftily and half in pity at the eagerness of men who could care for such a trifle as white ore when they had horses and rifles, he pointed up at the perpendicular face of the mountain and then downward at the wall of the canyon, and said:—

"Silver—silver. Beaver give his brother. Medicine-man."

"He means there is silver here, sir, and he gives it to you," said Bart eagerly.

"Yes. Give. Silver," said the chief, nodding his head, and holding out his hand, which the Doctor grasped, Bart doing the same by the other.

"I am very grateful," said the Doctor at last, while his eyes kept wandering about, "but I see none."

"Silver—silver," said the chief again, as he looked up and then down, ending by addressing some words in the Indian dialect to the interpreter, who pointed in the direction of the camp.

"The Beaver-with-Sharp-Teeth says, let us eat," he said.

This brought back Bart's hunger so vividly to his recollection that he laughed merrily and turned to go.

"Yes," he said, "let us eat by all means. Shall we come in the morning and examine this place, sir?"

"Yes, Bart, we will," said the Doctor, as they turned back; "but I'm afraid we shall be disappointed. What was that?"

"An Indian," said Bart. "I saw him glide amongst the rocks. Was it an enemy?"

"No; impossible, I should say," replied the Doctor. "One of our own party. Our friends here would have seen him if he had been an enemy, long before we should."

"And so you think there is no silver here, sir?" said Bart.

"I can't tell yet, my boy. There may be, but these men know so little about such things that I cannot help feeling doubtful. However, we shall see, and if I am disappointed I shall know what to do."

"Try again, sir?" said Bart.

"Try again, my boy, for there is ample store in the mountains if we can find it."

"Yes," he said, as they walked back, "this is going to be a disappointment." He picked up a piece of rock as he went along between the rocks; "this stone does not look like silver-bearing stratum. But we'll wait till the morning, Bart, and see."

Chapter Fifteen.: Dangerous Neighbours.

Upon reaching the waggon it was to find Joses smiling and sniffing as he stood on the leeward side of the fire, so as to get the full benefit of the odour of the well-done sage grouse which looked juicy brown, and delicious enough to tempt the most ascetic of individuals, while Maude laughed merrily to see the eager glances Bart kept directing at the iron rod upon which the birds had been spitted and hung before the fire.

"Don't you wish we had a nice new loaf or two, Bart?" she said, looking very serious, and as if disappointed that this was not the case.

"Oh, don't talk about it," cried Bart.

"I won't," said Maude, trying to appear serious. "It makes you look like a wolf, Bart."

"And that's just how I feel," he cried—"horribly like one."

Half an hour later he owned that he felt more like a reasonable being, for not only had he had a fair portion of the delicate sage grouse, but found to his delight that there was an ample supply of cakes freshly made and baked in the ashes while he had been with the Doctor exploring.

Bart took one turn round their little camp before lying down to sleep, and by the wonderfully dark, star-encrusted sky, the great flat-topped mountain looked curiously black, and as if it leaned over towards where they were encamped, and might at any moment topple down and crush them.

So strange was this appearance, and so thoroughly real, that it was a long time before Bart could satisfy himself that it was only the shadow that impressed him in so peculiar a way. Once he had been about to call the attention of the Doctor to the fact, but fortunately, as he thought, he refrained.

"He lay down directly," said Bart to himself as he walked on, and then he stopped short, startled, for just before him in the solemn stillness of the great plain, and just outside the shadow cast by the mountain, he saw what appeared to be an enormously tall, dark figure coming towards him in perfect silence, and seeming as if it glided over the sandy earth.

Bart's heart seemed to stand still. His mouth felt dry. His breath came thick and short. He could not run, for his feet appeared to be fixed to the ground, and all he felt able to do was to wait while the figure came nearer and nearer, through the transparent darkness, till it was close upon him, and said in a low voice that made the youth start from his lethargy, unchaining as it did his faculties, and giving him the power to move:

"Hallo, Bart! I thought you were asleep."

"I thought you were, sir," said Bart.

"Well, I'm going to lie down now, my boy, but I've been walking in a silver dream. Better get back."

He said no more, but walked straight to the little camp, while, pondering upon the intent manner in which his guardian seemed to give himself up to this dream of discovering silver, Bart began to make a circuit of the camp, finding to his satisfaction that the Beaver had posted four men as sentinels, Joses telling his young leader afterwards when he lay down that the chief had refused to allow either of the white men to go on duty that night.

"You think he is to be trusted, don't you, Joses?" asked Bart sleepily.

"Trusted? Oh yes, he's to be trusted, my lad. Injuns are as bad as can be, but some of 'em's got good pyntes, and this one, though he might have scalped the lot of us once upon a time, became our friend as soon as the Doctor cured his arm. And it was a cure too, for now it's as strong and well as ever. I tell you what, Master Bart."

No answer.

"I tell you what, Master Bart."

No answer.

"I say, young one, are you asleep?"

No reply.

"Well, he has dropped off sudden," growled Joses. "I suppose I must tell him what another time."

Having made up his mind to this, the sturdy fellow gave himself a bit of a twist in his blanket, laid his head upon his arm, and in a few seconds was as fast asleep as Bart.

The latter slept soundly all but once in the night, when it seemed to him that he had heard a strange, wild cry, and, starting up on his elbow, he listened attentively for some moments, but the cry was not repeated, and feeling that it must have been in his dreams that he had heard the sound, he lay down again and slept till dawn, when he sprang up, left every one asleep, and stole off, rifle in hand, to see if he could get a shot at a deer anywhere about the mountain, and also to have a look down into the tremendous canyon about whose depths and whose rushing stream he seemed to have been dreaming all the night.

He recollected well enough the way they had gone on the previous evening, and as he stepped swiftly forward, there, at the bottom of the narrow rift between the mass of fallen rock and the mountain, was the pale lemon-tinted horizon, with a few streaks above it flecking the early morning sky and telling of the coming day.

"The canyon will look glorious when the sun is up," said Bart to himself; "but I don't see any game about, and—oh!—"

Click—click—click—click went the locks of his double rifle as he came suddenly upon a sight which seemed to freeze his blood, forcing him to stand still and gaze wildly upon what was before him.

Then the thought of self-preservation stepped in, and as if from the lessons taught of the Indians, he sprang to shelter, sheltering himself behind a block of stone, his rifle ready, and covering every spot in turn that seemed likely to contain the cruel enemy that had done this deed.

For there before him—but flat upon his back, his arms outstretched, his long lance beneath him—lay one of the friendly Indians, while his companion lay half raised upon his side, as if he had dragged himself a short distance so as to recline with his head upon a piece of rock. His spear was across his legs, and it was very evident that he had been like this for some time after receiving his death wound.

For both were dead, the morning light plainly showing that in their hideous glassy eyes, without the terrible witness of the pool of blood that had trickled from their gaping wounds.

Bart shuddered and felt as if a hand of ice were grasping his heart. Then a fierce feeling of rage came over him, and his eyes flashed as he looked round for the treacherous enemies who had done this deed.

He looked in vain, and at last he stole cautiously out of his lurking-place; then forgot his caution, and ran to where the Indians lay, forgetting, in his eagerness to help them, the horrors of the scene.

But he could do nothing, for as he laid his hand upon the breast of each in turn, it was to find that their hearts had ceased to beat, and they were already cold.

Racing back to the camp, he spread his news, and the Beaver and his little following ran off to see for themselves the truth of his story, after which they mounted, and started to find the trail of the treacherous murderers of their companions, while during their absence the Doctor examined the two slaughtered Indians, and gave it as his opinion that they had both been treacherously stabbed from behind.

It was past mid-day before the Beaver returned to announce that there had only been two Indians lurking about their camp.

"And did you overtake them?" said Bart.

The chief smiled in a curious, grim way, and pointed to a couple of scalps that hung at the belts of two of his warriors.

"They were on foot. We were mounted," he said quietly. "They deserved to die. We had not injured them, or stolen their wives or horses. They deserved to die."

This was unanswerable, and no one spoke, the Indians going off to bury their dead companions, which they did simply by finding a suitable crevice in the depths of the ravine near which they had been slain, laying them in side by side, with their medicine-bags hung from their necks, their weapons ready to their hands, and their buffalo robes about them, all ready for their use in the happy hunting-grounds.

This done they were covered first with bushes, and then with stones, and the Indians returned to camp.

Chapter Sixteen.: In Nature's Storehouse.

All this seemed to add terribly to the sense of insecurity felt by the Doctor, and Joses was not slow to speak out.

"We may have a mob of horse-Injun down upon us at any moment," he growled. "I don't think we're very safe."

"Joses is right," said the Doctor; "we must see if there is a rich deposit of silver here, and then, if all seems well, we must return, and get together a force of recruits so as to be strong enough to resist the Indians, should they be so ill advised as to attack us, and ready to work the mines."

"'Aven't seen no mines yet," growled Joses.

The Doctor coughed with a look of vexation upon his countenance, and, beckoning to the chief, he took his rifle. Bart rose, and leaving Joses in charge of the camp, they started for the edge of the canyon.

There was no likelihood of enemies being about the place after the event of the morning; but to the little party every shrub and bush, every stone, seemed to suggest a lurking-place for a treacherous enemy. Still they pressed on, the chief taking them, for some unknown reason, in the opposite route along beneath the perpendicular walls of the mountain, which here ran straight up from the plain.

They went by a rugged patch of broken rock, and by what seemed to be a great post stuck up there by human hands, but which proved, on a nearer approach, to be the remains of a moderate-sized tree that had been struck by lightning, the whole of the upper portion having been charred away, leaving only some ten feet standing up out of the ground.

A short distance farther on, as they were close in by the steep wall of rock, they came to a slight projection, as if a huge piece had slipped down from above, and turning sharply round this, the Beaver pointed to a narrow rift just wide enough to allow of the passage of one man at a time.

He signed to the Doctor to enter, and climbing over a few rough stones, the latter passed in and out of sight.

"Bart! quick, my boy! quick!" he said directly after, and the lad sprang in to help him, as he thought, in some perilous adventure, but only to stop short and stare at the long sloping narrow passage fringed with prickly cactus plants, which slope ran evidently up the side of the mountain.

"Why, it's the way up to the top," cried Bart. "I wonder who made it."

"Dame Nature, I should say, my boy," said the Doctor. "We must explore this. Why, what a natural fortification! One man could hold this passage against hundreds."

Just then the chief appeared below them, for they had climbed up a few yards, and signed to them to come down.

The Doctor hesitated, and then descended.

"Let's see what he has to show, Bart. I have seen no silver yet."

They followed the Beaver down, and he led them straight back, past the camp, through the narrow ravine, once more to the shelf of rock overlooking the canyon, and now, in the full glow of the sunny afternoon, they were able to realise the grandeur of the scene where the river ran swiftly down below, fully a thousand feet, in a bed of its own, shut out from the upper world by the perpendicular walls of rock.

At the first glance it seemed that it would be impossible to descend, but on farther examination there seemed in places to be rifts and crevices and shelves, dotted with trees and plants of the richest growth, where it might be likely that skilful climbers could make a way down.

From where they stood the river looked enchanting, for while all up in the plain was arid and grey, and the trees and shrubs that grew there seemed parched and dry, and of a sickly green, all below was of the richest verdant hues, and lovely groves of woodland were interspersed with soft patches of waving grass that flourished where stormy winds never reached, and moisture and heat were abundant.

Still this paradise-like river was not without signs of trouble visiting it at times, and these remained in huge up-torn trees, dead branches, and jagged rocks, splintered and riven, that dotted the patches of plain from the shores of the river to the perpendicular walls of the canyon.

Bart needed no telling that these were the traces of floods, when, instead of the bright silver rushing river, the waters came down from the mountains hundreds of miles to the north, and the great canyon was filled to its walls with a huge seething yellow flow, and in imagination he thought of what the smiling emerald valley would be after such a visitation.

But he had little time for thought, the chief making signs to the Doctor to follow him, first laying down his rifle and signing to the Doctor to do the same.

Dr Lascelles hesitated for a moment, and then did as the chief wished, when the Beaver went on for a few yards to where the shelf of rock seemed to end, and there was nothing but a sheer fall of a thousand feet down to the stones and herbage at the bottom of the canyon, while above towered up the mountain which seemed like a Titanic bastion round which the river curved.

Without a moment's hesitation the chief turned his face to them, lowered himself over the edge of the shelf down and down till only his hands remained visible. Then he drew himself up till his face was above the rock, and made a sign to the Doctor to come on.

"I dare not go, Bart," said the Doctor, whose face was covered with dew. "Would you be afraid to follow him, my boy?"

"I should be afraid, sir," replied Bart laying down his rifle, "but I'll go."

"No, no, I will not be such a coward," cried the Doctor; and going boldly to the edge, he refrained from looking over, but turned and lowered himself down, passing out of Bart's sight; and when the latter crept to the edge and looked down, he could see a narrow ledge below with climbing plants and luxuriant shrubs, but no sight of the Doctor or his guide.

Bart remained motionless—horror-stricken as the thought came upon him that they might have slipped and gone headlong into the chasm below; but on glancing back he saw one of the Indians who was of the party smiling, and evidently quite satisfied that nothing was wrong.

This being so, Bart remained gazing down into the canyon, listening intently, and wondering whither the pair could have gone.

It was a most wonderful sight to look down at that lovely silver river that flashed and sparkled and danced in the sunshine. In places where there were deep, calm pools it looked intensely blue, as it reflected the pure sky, while other portions seemed one gorgeous, dazzling damascene of molten metal, upon which Bart could hardly gaze.

Then there was the wonderful variety of the tints that adorned the shrubs and creepers that were growing luxuriantly wherever they could obtain a hold.

There were moments when Bart fancied that he could see the salmon plash in the river, but he could make out the birds in the depths below as they floated and skimmed about from shore to shore, and over the tops of the trees that looked like shrubs from where he crouched.

Just then, as he was forgetting the absence of the Doctor in an intense desire to explore the wonders of the canyon, to shoot in the patches of forest, to fish in the river, and find he knew not what in those wondrous solitudes where man had probably never yet trod, he heard a call, and, brought back to himself from his visionary expedition, he shouted a reply.

"The Beaver's coming to you, Bart. Lower yourself down, my boy, and come."

These—the Doctor's words—sounded close at hand, but the speaker was invisible.

"All right; I'll come," cried Bart; and as he spoke a feeling of shrinking came over him, and he felt ready to draw back. But calling upon himself, he went closer to the edge, trying to look under, and the next moment there was the head of the Beaver just below, gazing up at him with a half-mocking smile upon his face.

"You think I'm afraid," said Bart, looking down at him, "but I can't help that. I'll come all the same;" and swiftly turning, he lowered himself down till his body was hanging as it were in space, and only his chest and elbows were on the shelf.

Then for a moment he seemed to hesitate, but he mastered the shrinking directly after, and lowered himself more and more till he hung at the extremity of his hands, vainly seeking for a foothold.

"Are you there, Beaver?" he shouted, and he felt his waist seized and his sides pinioned by two strong hands, his own parted company from the shelf, and he seemed to fall a terrible distance, but it was only a couple of feet, and he found himself standing upon the solid rock, with the shelf jutting out above his head, and plenty of room to peer about amongst the clustering bushes that had here made themselves a home.

The chief smiled at his startled look, and pointing to the left, Bart glanced sidewise at where the precipice went down, and then walked onward cautiously along a rugged shelf not much unlike the one from which he had descended, save that it was densely covered with shrubby growth.

This shelf suddenly ended in a rift like a huge crevice in the face of the mountain, but there was a broad crack before it, and this it was necessary to leap before entering the rift.

Bart stopped short, gazing down into what seemed an awful abyss, but the Beaver passed him lightly, as if there were no danger whatever, and lightly leaped across to some rough pieces of rock.

The distance was nothing, but the depths below made it seem an awful leap, till Bart felt that the Doctor must have gone over it before him, and without further hesitation he bounded across and stood beside the chief, who led the way farther into the rift to where, some fifty feet from the entrance, the Doctor was standing, hammer in hand, gazing intently at the newly chipped rock and the fragments that lay around.

"At last, Bart!" he cried joyously.

"What! Is it a vein?" said Bart, eagerly.

"A vein, boy? It is a mountain of silver—a valley of silver. Here are great threads of the precious metal, and masses of ore as well. It seems as if it ran right down the sides of the canyon, and from what the Indian appears to know, it does, Bart, I never expected to make such a find as this."

As he spoke, he handed pieces of the rock to Bart, who found that in some there were angular pieces of what seemed to be native silver, while others were full of threads and veins, or appeared as pieces of dull metalliferous stone.

"It is a huge fortune—wealth untold, Bart," said the Doctor.

"Is it, sir?" said Bart coolly, for he could not feel the same rapture as the Doctor.

"Is it, boy? Yes! enormous wealth."

"But how are we to carry it away, sir?" asked Bart dryly.

"Carry it away! Why, do you not understand that this mine will want working, and that we must have a large number of men here? But no; you cannot conceive the greatness of this find."

As he spoke, the Doctor hurried to the mouth of the rift, and then cautiously lowered himself into the chasm, over which Bart had leaped, clinging to the stout stems of the various shrubs.

For a few moments Bart hesitated. Then he followed till they were both quite a hundred feet below the shelf, and the part of the rift they had first entered, and were able to creep right out till they were level with the side of the canyon, and able to look down to the river.

But the Doctor did not care to look down upon the river, for tearing away some of the thick growth from the rock, he cast it behind him, so that it fell far out into the canyon. Then two or three pieces of rock followed, and somehow Bart felt more interested in their fall than in the search for silver, listening in the hope of hearing them crash down deep in the great stream.

"Yes; as I thought," cried the Doctor, excitedly, "the vein or mass runs right down the side of this vast canyon, Bart—the Silver Canyon, we must call it. But come, let's get back. I must tell my child. Such a discovery was never made before. Discovery, do I say! Why, these poor ignorant Indians must have known of it for years, perhaps for generations, and beyond working up a few pieces to make themselves rings for their horses' lariats, or to secure their saddles, they have left is as it is."

As he spoke, he was already climbing up towards the shelf, his excitement in his tremendous find making him forget the risks he kept running, for to one in cool blood, the face of the rock, the insecurity of the shrubs to which he clung, and the many times that silver-veined stones gave way beneath his feet, were very terrible, and Bart drew his breath hard, climbing slowly after his companion till at last they stood once more upon the shelf.

And all this time the Beaver was looking calmly on, following each movement, helping his white friends to climb where it was necessary, and seeming half amused at the Doctor's intense eagerness. In fact, Bart fancied that at times he looked rather contemptuously on at the Doctor's delight with what he found, for it was so much whitey-grey metallic stone to him, and as nothing beside the possession of a fine swift pony, or an ample supply of powder and lead.

Chapter Seventeen.: Untrustworthy Sentinels.

They soon reached the little camp, where the Doctor eagerly communicated his news to his child, and then taking Joses aside he repeated it to him.

"Well, that's right, master. I'm glad, of course; and I hope it'll make you rich, for you want it bad enough after so many years of loss with your cattle."

"It has made me rich—I am rich, Joses!" cried the Doctor, excitedly.

"That's good, master," said the man, coolly. "And now what's going to be done? Are we to carry the mountain back to the old ranche?"

The Doctor frowned.

"We shall have to return at once, Joses, to organise a regular mining party. We must have plenty of well-armed men, and tools, and machinery to work this great find. We must go back at once."

"Now, master?"

"No, no, perhaps not for a week, my man," said the Doctor, whose nervous excitement seemed to increase. "I must thoroughly investigate the extent of the silver deposit, descend into the canyon, and ascend the mountain. Then we must settle where our new town is to be."

"Ah, we're going to have a new town, are we, master?"

"To be sure! Of course! How could the mining adventure be carried on without?"

Joses shook his head.

"P'r'aps we shall stay here a week then, master?" he said at last.

"Yes; perhaps a fortnight."

"Then if you don't mind, master, I think we'll move camp to that little patch of rocks close by that old blasted tree that stands up like a post. I've been thinking it will be a better place; and if you'll give the word, I'll put the little keg of powder in a hole somewhere. I don't think it's quite right to have it so near our fire every day."

"Do what you think best, Joses," said the Doctor, eagerly. "Yes; I should bury the powder under the rocks somewhere, so that we can easily get it again. But why do you want to move the camp?"

"Because that's a better place, with plenty of rocks for cover if the Injuns should come and look us up."

"Let us change, then," said the Doctor, abstractedly; and that afternoon they shifted to the cluster of rocks near the blasted tree, close under the shelter of the tall wall-like mountain-side. Rocks were cleared from a centre and piled round; the waggon was well secured; a good place found for the horses; and lastly, Joses lit his cigarette, and then took the keg of gunpowder, carried it to a convenient spot near the withered tree, and buried it beneath some loose stones.

The Beaver smiled at the preparations, and displayed his knowledge of English after a short conversation with the interpreter by exclaiming:

"Good—good—good—very good!"

A hasty meal was snatched, and then the Doctor went off again alone, while the Beaver signed to Bart to follow him, and then took him past the narrow opening that led to the way up the mountain, and showed him a second opening, through which they passed, to find within a good open cavernous hollow at the foot of the mountain wall, shut in by huge masses of rock.

"Why, our horses would be safe here, even if we were attacked," exclaimed Bart.

"Horses," said the Beaver, nodding. "Yes; horses."

There was no mistaking the value of such a place, for there was secure shelter for at least a hundred horses, and the entrance properly secured—an entrance so narrow that there was only room for one animal to pass through—storm or attack from the hostile Indians could have been set at defiance.

"Supposing a town to be built here somewhere up the mountain, this great enclosure would be invaluable," said Bart, and, hurrying back, he fetched Joses to inspect the place.

"Ah, that's not bad," said the rough frontier man. "Why, Master Bart, what a cattle corral that would make! Block the mouth up well, they'd be clever Injuns who got anything away. Let's put the horses in here at once."

"Do you think it is necessary, Joses?" said Bart.

"It's always necessary to be safe out in the plain, my lad," replied Joses. "How do we know that the Injuns won't come to-night to look after the men they've lost? Same time, how do we know they will? All the same, though, you can never be too safe. Let's get the horses inside, my lad, as we have such a place, and I half wish now we'd gone up the mountain somewhere to make our camp. You never know when danger may come."

"Horses in there," said Bart to the Beaver, and he pointed to the entrance.

The chief nodded, and seemed to have understood them all along by their looks and ways, so that when the horses belonging to the English party were driven in that evening he had those of his own followers driven in as well, and it was settled that Joses was to be the watchman that night.

It was quite sundown when the Doctor returned, this time with Maude, whom he had taken to be an eye-witness of his good fortune. Bart went to meet them, and that glorious, glowing evening they sat in their little camp, revelling in the soft pure air, which seemed full of exhilaration, and the lad could not help recalling afterwards what a thoroughly satisfied, happy look there was in his guardian's countenance as he sat there reckoning up the value of his grand discovery, and making his plans for the future.

Then came a very unpleasant episode, one which Bart hid from the Doctor, for he would not trouble him with bad news upon a night like that; but all the same it caused the lad intense annoyance, and he went off to where Joses was smoking his cigárito and staring at the stars.

"Tipsy! drunk!" he exclaimed. "What! Sam and Juan? Where could they get the stuff?"

"They must have crept under the waggon, and broken a hole through, for the brandy lay there treasured up in case of illness."

"I'll thrash 'em both till they can't crawl!" cried Joses, wrathfully. "I didn't think it of them. It's no good though to do it to-night when they can't understand. Let them sleep it off to-night, my boy, and to-morrow morning we'll show the Beaver and his men what we do to thieves who steal liquor to get drunk. I wouldn't have thought it of them."

"What shall you do to them, Joses?" said Bart.

"Tie them up to that old post of a tree, my boy, and give them a taste of horse-hair lariat on the bare back. That's what I'll do to them. They're under me, they are, and I'm answerable to the master. But there, don't say no more; it makes me mad, Master Bart. Go back now, and let them sleep it out. I'm glad I moved that powder."

"So am I, Joses," said Bart; and after a few more, words he returned to the little camp, to find the two offenders fast asleep.

Bart was very weary when he lay down, after glancing round to see that all proper precautions had been taken; and it seemed to him that he could not have been asleep five minutes when he felt a hand laid upon his mouth, and another grasp his shoulder, while on looking up, there, between him and the star-encrusted sky, was a dark Indian face.

For a moment he thought of resistance. The next he had seen whose was the face, and obeying a sign to be silent, he listened while the Beaver bent lower, and said in good English, "Enemy. Indians coming."

Bart rose on the instant, and roused the Doctor, who immediately awakened Maude, and obeying the signs of the Indian, they followed him into the shadow of the mountain, for the Beaver shook his head fiercely at the idea of attempting to defend the little camp.

It all took place in a few hurried moments, and almost before they were half-way to their goal there was a fierce yell, the rush of trampling horses, and a dark shadowy body was seen to swoop down upon the camp. While before, in his excitement, Bart could realise his position, he found himself with the Doctor and Maude beyond the narrow entrance, and on the slope that seemed to lead up into the mountains.

As soon as Maude was in safety, Bart and the Doctor returned to the entrance, to find it well guarded by the Indians; and if the place were discovered or known to the enemy, it was very plain that they could be easily kept at bay if anything like a determined defence were made, and there was no fear of that.

Then came a sort of muster or examination of their little force, which, to Bart's agony, resulted in the discovery that while all the Indians were present, and Harry was by their side, Joses, Sam, and Juan were away.

In his excitement, Bart did not realise why this was. Now he recalled that when he lay down to sleep the two offenders had been snoring stertorously, and it was evident that they were helplessly stupefied when the Indians came, and were taken.

But Joses?

Of course he was at his post, and the question now was, would he remain undiscovered, or would the Indians find the hiding-place of the horses, and after killing Joses sweep them all away?

It was a terrible thought, for to be left alone in that vast plain without horses seemed too hard to be borne. At the first blush it made Bart shudder, and it was quite in despair that with cocked rifle he waited for morning light, which seemed as if it would never come.

Bart's thoughts were many, and frequent were the whispered conversations with the Doctor, as to whether the Indians would not find the cache of the horses as soon as it was daylight by their trail, though to this he had answered that the ground all around was so marked by horses' hoofs that it was not likely that any definite track would be made out.

Then moment by moment they expected their own hiding-place to be known, and that they would be engaged fighting for their lives with their relentless foes; but the hours wore on, and though they could hear the buzz of many voices, and sometimes dark shadowy forms could be made out away on the plain, the fugitives were in dense shadow, and remained unmolested till the break of day.

By this time Bart had given Maude such comforting intelligence as he could, bidding her be hopeful, for that these Indians must be strangers to the place, or they would have known of the way up the mountain, and searched it at once.

"But if they found it in the morning, Bart," she said, "what then?"

"What then?" said Bart, with a coolness he did not feel. "Why, then we shall have to kill all the poor wretches—that's all."

Maude shuddered, and Bart returned to where the Beaver was at the opening, watching the place where the enemy had been plundering the waggon, and had afterwards stirred up the camp fire and were seated round.

"Joses was glad that he had put away the powder," thought Bart, as he saw the glare of the fire. "I begin to wish it had been left."

Chapter Eighteen.: Two Horrors.

Morning at last, and from their hiding-place the fugitives could see that the Indians were in great numbers, and whilst some were with their horses, others were gathered together in a crowd about the post-like tree-trunk half-way between the gate of the mountains, as Bart called it, and the camp.

The greatest caution was needed to keep themselves from the keen sight of the Indians, who had apparently seen nothing of the horses' trail; and as far as Bart could tell, Joses was so far safe. Still it was like this:— If the Indians should begin to examine the face of the rock, they must find both entries, and then it was a question of brave defence, though it seemed impossible but that numbers must gain the mastery in the end.

"Poor Joses!" thought Bart, and the tears rose to his eyes. "I'd give anything to be by his side, to fight with him and defend the horses."

Then he began to wonder how many charges of powder he would have, and how long he could hold out.

"A good many will fall before they do master him," thought Bart, "if he's not captured already. I wonder whether they have hurt Juan and Sam."

Just then the crowd about the post fell back, and the Doctor put his glass to his eye, and then uttered a cry of horror.

He glanced round directly to see if Maude had heard him, but she, poor girl, had fallen fast asleep in the niche where they had placed her, to be out of reach of bullets should firing begin.

"What is it, sir?" cried Bart. "Ah, I see. How horrible! The wretches! May I begin to shoot?"

"You could do no good, and so would only bring the foe down upon my child," said the Doctor sternly.

"But it is Juan, is it not?" cried Bart, excitedly.

"Yes," said the Doctor, using the glass, "and Sam. They have stripped the poor fellows almost entirely, and painted Death's heads and cross-bones upon their hearts."

"Oh yes," cried Bart, in agony, "I can see;" and he looked with horror upon the scene, for there, evidently already half dead, their breasts scored with knives, and their ankles bound, Juan and Sam were suspended by means of a lariat, bound tightly to their wrists, and securely twisted round the upper part of the old blasted tree. The poor fellows' hats and a portion of their clothes lay close by them, and as they hung there, inert and helpless, Bart, and his companion saw the cruel, vindictive Indians draw off to a short distance, and joining up into a close body, they began to fire at their prisoners, treating them as marks on which to try their skill with the rifle.

The sensation of horror this scene caused was indescribable, and Bart turned to the Doctor with a look of agony in his eyes.

"Quick!" he said; "let us run out and save them. Oh, what monsters! They cannot be men."

The Indian who acted as interpreter spoke rapidly to the chief, who replied, and then the Indian turned to the Doctor and Bart.

"The Beaver-with-Sharp-Teeth says if we want to go out to fight, they are so many we should all be killed. We must not go."

"He is right, Bart," said the Doctor, hoarsely. "I am willing enough to fight, but the presence of Maude seems to unman me. I dare not attempt anything that would risk her life."

"But it is so horrible," cried Bart, peering out of his hiding-place excitedly, but only to feel the Beaver's hand upon his shoulder, forcing him down into his old niche.

"Indian dog see," whispered the Beaver, who was rapidly picking up English words and joining them together.

The sharp report of rifle after rifle was heard now, and after every shot there was a guttural yell of satisfaction.

"They will kill them, sir," panted Bart, who seemed as if he could hardly bear to listen to what was going on.

"They must have been dead, poor fellows, when they were hung up there, Bart. I would that we dared attack the monsters."

"Can you see any sign of Joses, sir?" asked Bart.

"No, my boy; no sign of him, poor fellow! Heaven grant that he be not seen."

All this time the Indians were rapidly loading and firing at the two unfortunate men, and, to Bart's horror, he could hear bullet after bullet strike them, the others hitting the rocky face of the mountain with a sharp pat, and in the interval of silence that followed those in hiding could hear some of the bullets afterwards fall.

Every time the savages thought they had hit their white prisoners they uttered a yell of triumph, and Dr Lascelles knew that this terrible scene was only the prologue to one of a far more hideous nature, when, with a fiendish cruelty peculiar to their nature, they would fall upon their victims with their knives, to flay off their scalps and beards, leaving the terribly mutilated bodies to the birds and beasts of the plains.

"I could hit several of them, I'm sure," panted Bart, eagerly. "Pray, sir, let's fire upon them, and kill some of the wretches. I never felt like this before, but now it seems as if I must do something to punish those horrible fiends."

"We could all fire and bring down some of them, Bart," whispered the Doctor; "but there are fully a hundred there, my boy, and we must be the losers in the end. They would never leave till they had killed us every one."

Bart hung his head, and stood there resting upon his rifle, wishing that his ears could be deaf to the hideous yelling and firing that kept going on, as the Indians went on with their puerile sport of wreaking their empty vengeance upon the bodies of the two men whom they had slain.

Twenty times over the Doctor raised his rifle, and as often let it fall, as he knew what the consequences of his firing would be, while, when encouraged by this act on the part of his elder, Bart did likewise, it was for the Beaver to press the barrel down with his brown hand, shaking his head and smiling gravely the while.

"The Beaver-with-Sharp-Teeth," said the interpreter, "says that the young chief must wait till the Indian dogs are not so many; then he shall kill all he will, and take all their scalps."

"Ugh!" shuddered Bart, "as if I wanted to take scalps! I could feel pleased though if they killed and took the scalps of all these wretches. No, I don't want that," he muttered, "but it is very horrible, and it nearly drives me mad to see the cruel monsters shooting at our two poor men. How they can—"

"Good heavens!" ejaculated the Doctor; "what's that?"

They were all gazing intently at the great post where the firing was going on, and beyond it at the group of Indians calmly loading and firing, with a soft film of smoke floating away above their heads, when all at once, just in their midst, there was a vivid flash of light, and the air seemed to be full of blocks of stone, which were driven up with a dense cloud of smoke. Then there was a deafening report, which echoed back from the side of the mountain; a trembling of the ground, as if there had been an earthquake; the great pieces of stone fell here and there; and then, as the smoke spread, a few Indians could be seen rushing hard towards where their companions were gathered with their horses, while about the spot where the earth had seemed to vomit forth flame, rocks and stones were piled-up in hideous confusion, mingled with quite a score of the bodies of Indians.

There was no hesitation on the part of the survivors. The Great Spirit had spoken to them in his displeasure, and those who had not been smitten seized their horses, those which had no riders now kept with them, and the whole band went off over the plain at full speed; while no sooner were they well away upon the plain, than the Beaver and his party laid their rifles aside, and dashed out, knife and hatchet in hand, killing two or three injured men before the Doctor could interfere, as he and Bart ran out, followed by Harry.

It was a hideous sight, and perhaps it was a merciful act the killing of the wretches by the Beaver and his men, for they were horribly injured by the explosion, while others had arms and legs blown off. Some were crushed by the falling stones, others had been killed outright at first; and as soon as he had seen but a portion of the horrors, the Doctor sent Bart back to bid Maude be in no wise alarmed, for the enemy were gone, but she must not leave the place where she was hiding for a while.

Bart found her looking white and trembling with dread, but a few words satisfied her, and the lad ran back, to pass the horrible mass of piled-up stones and human beings with a shudder, as he ran on and joined the Doctor and Joses, who was standing outside his hiding-place, perfectly unharmed, and leaning upon his rifle.

Bart was about to burst forth into a long string of congratulations, but somehow they all failed upon his lips. He tried to speak, but he choked and found it impossible. All he could do for a few moments was to catch the great rough hands of Joses in his, and stand shaking them with all his might.

Joses did not reply; he only looked a little less grim than usual as he returned Bart's grip with interest.

"Why, you thought the Injun had got me, did you, Master Bart? You thought the Injun had got me. Well, they hadn't this time, you see, but I 'spected they'd find me out every moment. I meant to fight it out though till all my powder was gone, and then I meant to back the horses at the Injun, and make them kick as long as I could, for of course you wouldn't have been able to come."

"I am glad you are safe, Joses," cried Bart, at last. "It is almost like a miracle that they didn't find you, and that the explosion took place. It must have been our keg of powder, Joses, that you hid under the stones."

"Think so, Master Bart?" said Joses, as if deeply astonished.

"Yes," cried Bart, "it must have been that."

"Yes," said the Doctor. "The wretches must have dropped a burning wad, or something of that kind."

"But it was very horrible," cried Bart.

"Yes, horrible," assented the Doctor.

"But it saved all us as was left, Master," said Joses, gruffly. "They'd have found us out else, and served us the same as they did poor old Sam and old Juan. What beasts Injun is."

"Yes, it saved our lives, Joses, and it was as it were a miracle. But there, don't let's talk about it. We must take steps to bury those poor creatures, and that before my child comes out. Do you think the enemy will come back?" he continued, turning to the interpreter.

"The Beaver-with-Sharp-Teeth says no: not for days," was the reply; and, willingly enough, the Indians helped their white friends to enlarge the hole ploughed out by the explosion of the powder keg, which was easily done by picking out a few pieces of rock, when there was ample room for the dead, who, after some hour or two's toil, were buried beneath the stones.

The remains of the two poor fellows, Juan and Sam, were buried more carefully, with a few simple rites, and then, saddened and weary, the Doctor turned to seek Maude.

Bart was about to follow him, when Joses took him by the sleeve.

"I wouldn't say anything to the master, but I must tell you."

"Tell me what?"

"About the explosion, Master Bart."

"Well, I saw it," said Bart.

"Yes, but you didn't see how it happened."

"I thought we had decided that."

"Well, you thought so, but you wasn't right, and I didn't care to brag about it; but I did it, Master Bart."

"You fired that powder, and blew all those poor wretches to eternity!" cried Bart, in horror.

"Now don't you get a looking like that, Master Bart. Why, of course I did it. Where's the harm? They killed my two poor fellows, and they'd have killed all of us, and set us up to shoot at if they'd had the chance."

"Well, Joses, I suppose you are right," said Bart, "but it seems very horrible."

"Deal more horrible if they'd killed Miss Maude."

"Oh, hush! Joses," cried Bart excitedly, "Tell me, though, how did you manage it."

"Well, you see, Master Bart, it was like this. I stood looking on at their devilry till I felt as if I couldn't bear it no longer, and then all at once I recollected the powder, and I thought that if I could put a bullet through the keg it would blow it up, and them too."

"And did you, Joses?"

"Well, I did, Master Bart, but it took me a long while for it. I knew exactly where it was, but I couldn't see it for the crowd of fellows round, and I daren't shoot unless I was sure, or else I should have brought them on to me like a shot."

"Of course, of course, Joses," cried Bart, who was deeply interested.

"Well, Master Bart, I had to wait till I thought I should never get a chance, and then they opened right out, and I could see the exact spot where to send my bullet, when I trembled so that I daren't pull trigger, and when I could they all crowded up again."

"But they gave you another chance, Joses?" cried Bart excitedly.

"To be sure they did, my lad, at last, and that time it was only after a deal of dodging about that there was any chance, and, laying my rifle on the rock, I drew trigger, saw the stones, flash as the bullet struck, just, too, when they were all cheering, the beasts, at what they'd done to those two poor fellows."

"And then there was the awful flash and roar, Joses?"

"Yes, Master Bart, and the Injuns never knew what was the matter, and that's all."

"All, Joses?"

"Yes, Master Bart, and wasn't it enough? But you'd better not tell the master; he might say he didn't object to an Injun or two killed in self-defence, but that this was wholesale."

Bart promised to keep the matter a secret, and he went about for the rest of the day pondering upon the skill of Joses with the rifle, and what confidence he must have had in his power to hit the keg hidden under the stones to run such a risk, for, as he said, a miss would have brought down the Indians upon him, and so Bart said once more.

"Yes, Master Bart; but then, you see, I didn't miss, and we've got rid of some of the enemy and scared the rest away."

Chapter Nineteen.: Beating up for Recruits.

The cause of the explosion remained a secret between Bart and Joses, and in the busy times that followed there was but little opportunity for dwelling upon the trouble. The Doctor was full of the discovery and the necessity for taking steps to utilise its value, for now they were almost helpless—the greater part of their ammunition was gone; their force was weakened by the loss of two men; and, worst of all, it was terribly insecure, for at any moment the Indians might get over their fright, and come back to bury their dead. If this were so, they would find that the task had already been done, and then they would search for and find the occupants of the camp.

This being so, the Doctor suddenly grew calm.

"I've made my plans," he said, quietly.

"Yes?" exclaimed Maude and Bart, in a breath.

"We must go straight back to our starting-place, and then on to Lerisco, and there I must get the proper authorisations from the government, and afterwards organise a large expedition of people, and bring them here at once."

He had hardly made this announcement when the Beaver came slowly up to stand with his follower the interpreter behind, and looking as if he wished to say something in particular.

The Doctor rose, and pointed to a place where his visitor could sit down, but the chief declined.

"Enemy," he said sharply. "Indian dogs."

Then he turned round quickly to the interpreter.

"The Beaver-with-Sharp-Teeth says the Apachés will be back to-night to see why the earth opened and killed their friends."

"Indeed! So soon?" said the Doctor.

"The chief says we must go from here till the Indian dogs have been. Then we can come back."

"That settles it, Bart," exclaimed the Doctor. "We'll start at once."

The preparations needed were few, and an hour later they were retreating quickly across the plain, the coming darkness being close at hand to veil their movements, so that when they halted to rest in the morning they were a long distance on their way, and sheltered by a patch of forest trees that looked like the remains of some tract of woodland that had once spread over the plain.

It was deemed wise to wait till evening, and taking it in turns, they watched and slept till nearly sundown.

The Beaver had had the last watch, and he announced that he had seen a large body of Apachés going in the direction of the canyon, but at so great a distance off across the plain that there was no need for alarm.

They started soon afterwards, and after a very uneventful but tedious journey, they reached the spot where they had first encountered the Beaver and his followers. Here the Indians came to a halt: they did not care to go farther towards the home of the white man, but readily entered into a compact to keep watch near the Silver Canyon, and return two moons hence to meet the Doctor and his expeditionary party, when they were once more on their way across the plains.

The journey seemed strange without the company of the chief and his men, and during many of their halts but little rest was had on account of the necessity for watchfulness. The rest of the distance was, however, got over in safety, and they rode at last into the town of Lerisco, where their expedition having got wind soon after they had started, their return was looked upon as of people from the dead.

For here the Doctor encountered several old friends and neighbours from their ranches, fifteen or even twenty miles from the town, and they were all ready with stories of their misfortunes, the raids they had had to endure from the unfriendly Indians; and the Doctor returned to his temporary lodgings that night satisfied that he had only to name his discovery to gain a following of as many enterprising spirits as he wished to command.

There was a good deal to do, for the Doctor felt that it would not be very satisfactory to get his discovery in full working order, and then have it claimed by the United States Government, or that of the Republic then in power in those parts.

He soon satisfied himself, however, of the right course to pursue, had two or three interviews with the governor, obtained a concession of the right to work the mine in consideration of a certain percentage of silver being paid to the government; and this being all duly signed and sealed, he came away light-hearted and eager to begin.

His first care was to make arrangements for the staying of Maude in some place of safety, and he smiled to himself as he realised how easy this would be now that he was the owner of a great silver mine. It was simplicity itself.

No sooner did Don Ramon the governor comprehend what was required than an invitation came from his lady, a pleasant-looking Spanish-Mexican dame, who took at once to the motherless girl, and thus the difficulty was got over, both the governor and his wife declaring that Maude should make that her home.

Then the Doctor rode out to three or four ranches in the neighbourhood, and laid his plan before their owners, offering them such terms of participation that they jumped at the proposals; and the result was that in a very short time no less than six ranches had been closed, the female occupants settled in the town, and their owners, with their waggons, cattle, mules, horses, and an ample supply of stores, were preparing for their journey across the forest to the Silver Canyon.

There was a wonderfully attractive sound in that title—The Silver Canyon, and it acted like magic on the men of English blood, who, though they had taken to the dress, and were burned by the sun almost to the complexion of the Spanish-Americans amongst whom they dwelt, had still all the enterprise and love of adventure of their people, and were ready enough to go.

Not so the Mexicans. There was a rich silver mine out in the plains? Well, let it be there; they could enjoy life without it, and they were not going to rob themselves of the comfort of basking in the sun and idling and sauntering in the evenings. Besides, there were the Indians, and they might have to fight, a duty they left to the little army kept up by the republic. The lancers had been raised on purpose to combat with the Indians. Let them do it. They, the Mexican gentlemen, preferred their cigáritos, and to see a bolero danced to a couple of twanging guitars.

The Englishmen laughed at the want of enterprise by the "greasers," as they contemptuously called the people, and hugged themselves as they thought of what wealth there was in store for them.

One evening, however, Bart, who was rather depressed at the idea of going without his old companion Maude, although at the same time he could not help feeling pleased at the prospect of her remaining in safety, was returning to his lodgings, which he shared with Joses, when he overtook a couple of the English cattle-breeders, old neighbours of the Doctor, who were loudly talking about the venture.

"I shouldn't be a bit surprised," said one, "if this all turns out to be a fraud."

"Oh no, I think it's all right."

"But there have been so many cheats of this kind."

"True, so there have," said the other.

"And if the Doctor has got us together to take us right out there for the sake of his own ends?"

"Well, I shouldn't care to be him," said the other, "if it proves to be like that."

They turned down a side lane, and Bart heard no more, but this was enough to prove to him that the Doctor's would be no bed of roses if everything did not turn out to be as good as was expected.

He reported this to the Doctor, who only smiled, and hurried on his preparations.

Money was easily forthcoming as soon as it was known that the government favoured the undertaking; and at last, with plenty of rough mining implements, blasting powder, and stores of all kinds, the Doctor's expedition started at daybreak one morning, in ample time to keep the appointment with the Beaver.

"I say, Master Bart," said Joses, as he sat upon his strong horse side by side with Bart, watching their train go slowly by, "I think we can laugh at the Apachés now, my lad; while, when the Sharp-Toothed Beaver joins us with his dark-skinned fighting men, we can give the rascals such a hunting as shall send 'em north amongst the Yankees with fleas in their ears."

"It's grand!" cried Bart, rousing himself up, for he had been feeling rather low-spirited at parting from Maude, and it had made him worse to see the poor girl's misery when she had clung to her father and said the last good-byes. Still there was the fact that the governor and his lady were excellent people, and the poor girl would soon brighten up.

And there sat Bart, on his eager little horse, Black Boy, which kept on champing its bit and snorting and pawing the ground, shaking its head, and longing, after weeks of abstinence, to be once more off and away on a long-stretching gallop across the plains.

There were men mounted on horses, men on mules, greasers driving cattle or the baggage mules, some in charge of the waggons, and all well-armed, eager and excited, as they filed by, a crowd of swarthy, poncho-wearing idlers watching them with an aspect of good-humoured contempt and pity on their faces, as if saying to themselves, "Poor fools! what a lot of labour and trouble they are going through to get silver and become rich, while we can be so much more happy and comfortable in our idleness and dirt and rags!"

A couple of miles outside the town the mob of idlers to the last man had dropped off, and, bright and excited, the Doctor rode up in the cheery morning sunshine.

"I'm going to ride forward, Bart," he cried, "so as to lead the van and show the line of march.

You keep about the middle, and mind there's no straggling off to right or left. You, Joses, take the rear, and stand no tricks from stragglers. Every man is to keep to his place and do his duty. Strict discipline is to be the order of the day, and unless we keep up our rigid training we shall be in no condition to encounter the Indians when they come."

"What are these coming after us?" cried Bart, looking back at a cloud of dust.

"Lancers," said Joses.

"Surely there is no trouble with the governor now," exclaimed the Doctor, excitedly, as a squadron of admirably mounted cavalry, with black-yellow pennons to their lances, came up at a canter, their leader riding straight up to the Doctor.

"Don Ramon sends me to see you well on the road, Don Lascelles," he cried. "We are to set you well upon your journey."

As he spoke, he turned and raised his hand, with the result that the next in command rode forward with a troop of the body of cavalry, to take the lead till they had reached the first halting-place, where the lancers said farewell, and parted from the adventurers, both parties cheering loudly when the soldiery rode slowly back towards Lerisco, while the waggon-train continued its long, slow journey towards the mountains.

Chapter Twenty.: The Thirsty Desert.

The journey was without adventure. Signs of Indians were seen, and this made those of the train more watchful, but there was no encounter with the red men of the desert, till an alarm was spread one morning of a party of about twenty well-mounted Indians being seen approaching the camp, just as it was being broken up for a farther advance towards the mountains.

The alarm spread; men seized their rifles, and they were preparing to fire upon the swiftly approaching troop, when Bart and Joses set spur to their horses, and went off at full gallop, apparently to encounter the enemy.

But they had not been deceived. Even at a distance Bart knew his friend the Beaver at a glance, and the would-be defenders of the camp saw the meeting, and the hearty handshaking that took place.

This was a relief, and the men of the expedition gazed curiously at the bronzed, well-armed horsemen of the plains, who sat their wiry, swift little steeds as if they were part and parcel of themselves, when they rode up to exchange greetings with the Doctor.

From that hour the Beaver's followers took the place of the lancers, leading the van and closing up the rear, as well as constantly hovering along the sides of the long waggon-train, which they guarded watchfully as if it were their own particular charge.

The Doctor placed implicit reliance in the chief, who guided them by a longer route, but which proved to be one which took them round the base of the two mountainous ridges they had to pass, and thus saved the adventurers a long and arduous amount of toil with the waggons in the rugged ground.

At last, when they were well in sight of the flat-topped mountain, and the Doctor was constantly reining in his horse to sweep the horizon with his glass in search of the Apachés, the chief rode up to say that he and his men were about to advance on a scouting expedition to sweep the country between them and the canyon, while the train was to press on, always keeping a watchful look-out until their Indian escort returned.

The Beaver and his men scoured off like the wind, and were soon lost to view, while that night and the next day the long train moved slowly over the plain to avoid the dense clumps of prickly cactus and agaves, suffering terribly from thirst, for what had been verdant when Bart was there last was now one vast expanse of dust, which rose thickly in clouds at the tramp of horse or mule.

The want of water was beginning to be severely felt; and as they went sluggishly on, towards the second evening horses and mules with drooping heads, and the cattle lowing piteously, Bart, as he kept cantering from place to place to say a few encouraging words, knew that he could hold out no hope of water being reached till well on in the next day, and he would have urged a halt for rest, only that the Doctor was eager for them to get as well on their way as possible.

Night at last, a wretched, weary night of intense heat, and man and beast suffering horribly from thirst. The clouds had gathered during the night, and the thunder rolled in the distance, while vivid flashes of lightning illumined the plains, but no rain fell, and when morning broke, after the most painful time Bart had ever passed, he found the Doctor looking ghastly, his eyes bloodshot, his lips cracked, and that even hardy Joses was suffering to as great an extent.

The people were almost in a state of mutiny, and ready to ask the Doctor if he had dragged them to this terrible blinding waste to perish from thirst; while it was evident that if water was not soon reached half the beasts must fall down by the way.

As it was, numbers of the poor animals were bleeding from the mouth and nostrils from the pricks received as they eagerly champed the various plants of the cactus family.

"Let us push on," said the Doctor; "everything depends upon our getting on to that shallow lake, for there is no water in the way;" but with every desire to push on, the task became more laborious every hour,—the cattle were constantly striving to stray off to right or left in search of something to quench their maddening thirst, while, go where he would, the Doctor was met by fierce, angry looks and muttered threats.

It would have been easy enough for the men to ride on to find water, but there was always the fear that if they did, the Indians would select just that moment for marching down and driving off their cattle and plundering the waggons. Such an attack would have been ruin, perhaps death to all, so there was nothing for it but to ride sullenly on in company with the now plodding cattle, hour after hour.

"Why don't the Beaver come back, Joses?" cried Bart, pettishly. "If he were here, his men could take care of the cattle and waggons, while we went on for water. The lake can't be many miles ahead."

"A good ways yet," said Joses. "That mountain looks close when it's miles away. Beaver's watching the Injuns somewhere, or he'd have been back before now. Say, Master Bart, I'm glad we haven't got much farther to go. If we had, we shouldn't do it."

"I'm afraid not," replied Bart, and then they both had to join in the task of driving back the suffering cattle into the main body, for they would keep straying away.

And so the journey went on all that day through the blinding, choking dust and scorching heat, which seemed to blister and sting till it was almost unbearable.

"Keep it up, my lads," Bart kept on saying. "There's water ahead. Not much farther now."

"That mountain gets farther away," said one of the newcomers. "I don't believe we shall ever get there."

This was a specimen of the incessant complaining of the people, whom the heat and thirst seemed to rob of every scrap of patience and endurance that they might have originally possessed.

But somehow, in spite of all their troubles, the day wore on, and Bart kept hopefully looking out for a glimpse of the water ahead.

They ought to have reached it long before, but the pace of the weary oxen had been most painfully slow. Then the wind, what little there was, had been behind them, seeming as out of the mouth of some furnace, and bringing back upon them the finely pulverised dust that the cattle raised.

At last, towards evening, the sky began again to cloud over, and the mountain that had appeared distant seemed, by the change in the atmosphere, to be brought nearer to them. Almost by magic, too, the wind fell. There was a perfect calm, and then it began to blow from the opposite quarter, at first in soft puffs, then as a steady, refreshing breeze, and instantly there was a commotion in the camp,—the cattle set off at a lumbering gallop; the mules, heedless of their burdens, followed suit; the horses snorted and strained at their bridles, and Joses galloped about, shouting to the teamsters in charge of the waggons, who were striving with all their might to restrain their horses.

"Let them go, my lads; unhitch and let them go, or they'll have the waggons over."

"Stampede! stampede!" some of the men kept shouting, and all at once it seemed that the whole of the quadrupeds were in motion; for, acting upon Joses' orders, the teams were unhitched, and away the whole body swept in a thundering gallop onward towards the mountain, leaving the waggons solitary in the dusty plain.

Every now and then a mule freed itself of its pack, and began kicking and squealing in delight at its freedom, while the cattle tossed their horns and went on in headlong gallop.

For once the wind had turned, the poor suffering beasts had sniffed the soft moist air that had passed over the shallow lake, and their unerring instinct set them off in search of relief.

There was no pause, and all the mounted men could do was to let their horses keep pace with the mules and cattle, only guiding them clear of the thickest part of the drove. And so they thundered on till the dusty plain was left behind, and green rank herbage and thickly growing water-plants reached, through which the cattle rushed to the shallow water at the edge of the lake.

But still they did not stop to drink, but rushed on and on, plashing as they went, till they were in right up to their flanks. Then, and then only, did they begin to drink, snorting and breathing hard, and drawing in the pure fresh water.

Some bellowed with pleasure as they seemed to satisfy their raging thirst; others began to swim or waded out till their nostrils only were above the surface; while the mules, as soon as they had drunk their fill, started to squeal and kick and splash to the endangerment of their loads. The horses behaved the most soberly, contenting themselves with wading in to a respectable distance, and then drinking when the water was undisturbed and pure, as did their masters; the Doctor, Joses, and Bart bending down and filling the little metal cups they carried again and again.

It was growing dark as they turned from the shallow water of the lake, the mules following the horses placidly enough, and the lumbering cattle contentedly obeying the call of their masters, and settling themselves down directly to crop the rich rank grasses upon the marshy shores.

A short consultation was held now, and the question arose whether they had been observed by Indians, who might come down and try to stampede the cattle.

The matter was settled by one-half the men staying to guard them, while the other half went back to fetch up the waggons, the mule-drivers having plenty to do in collecting the burdens that had been kicked off, but which the mules submitted patiently enough to have replaced.

Still it was long on towards midnight before the waggons had all been drawn up to the shores of the lake, whose soft moist grasses seemed like paradise to the weary travellers over the desolate, dusty plains; and no sooner had Bart tethered Black Boy, and seen him contentedly cropping the grass, than, forgetful of Indians, hunger, everything but the fact that he was wearied out, he threw himself down, and in less than a minute he was fast asleep.

Chapter Twenty One.: Taking full Possession.

Waking with the bright sun shining over the waters of the lake, the cattle quietly browsing, and the well-watered horses enjoying a thoroughly good feed, the troubles of the journey over the dreary plain were pretty well forgotten, and as fires were lit and meals prepared, there were bright faces around ready to give the Doctor a genial "good morning."

Soon after those on the look-out, while the rest made a hearty meal to prepare them for the toil of the day, announced Indians, and arms were seized, while men stood ready to run to their horses and to protect their cattle.

But there was no need for alarm, the new-comers being the Beaver and his followers, who stated that they had come upon signs of Indians, and found that they had been by the mountain within the past day or two. But they had followed the trail, and found that their enemies had gone due north, following the course of the Great Canyon, and it was probable that they had finished their raid into these southern parts, and would not return.

"If they do," said the Beaver, with contemptuous indifference, "our young men shall kill them all. Their horses will be useful. They are no good to live, for they are thieves and murderers without mercy."

The rest of the journey was soon achieved, and the waggons drawn up in regular order close beside the mountain, while, after due inspection of the cavernous place where Joses had remained concealed with the horses, it was decided as a first step to construct with rocks a semi-circular wall, whose two ends should rest against the perpendicular mountain-side, and this would serve as a corral for the cattle, and also act as a place of retreat for a certain number to protect them, the horses being kept in Joses' Hole, as Bart christened the place.

There was plenty of willing labour now that the goal had been reached, and a few of the principals had been with the Doctor to inspect the vein of silver, from which they came back enthusiastic to a degree.

Leaving the greater part busy over the task of forming the cattle corral or enclosure, the Doctor called upon Bart and Joses, with three or four of his leading followers, to make the ascent of the mountain, and to this end a mysterious-looking pole was brought from the Doctor's waggon, and given to one of the men to carry. A pick and some ropes and pegs were handed to Joses, Bart received a bag, and thus accoutred they started.

"Where are we going?" said one of the party, as he saw that they were walking straight for the perpendicular wall.

"Up to the top of the mountain," replied the Doctor.

"Have you ever been up?" the man asked, staring at him wonderingly.

"No; but I believe the ascent will be pretty easy, and I have a reason for going."

"Is he mad?" whispered the man to Bart. "Why, nothing but a fly could climb up there."

"Mad? No," replied Bart, smiling. "Wait a bit, and you'll see."

"Well, I wouldn't have believed there was a way through here!" said the man, slapping his leg, and laughing heartily, as they reached the narrow slit, crept through, and then stood with the long slope above them ready for the ascent. "It seems as if nature had done it all in the most cunning way, so as to make a hiding-place."

"And a stronghold and fort for us," said Bart. "I think when once we get this place in order, we may set at defiance all the Indians of the plains."

"If they don't starve us out, or stop our supply of water," said Joses, gruffly. "Man must eat and drink."

By this time the Doctor was leading the way up the long rugged slope, that seemed as if it had been carved by water constantly rushing down, though now it was perfectly dry. It was not above ten feet wide, and the walls were in places almost perpendicular.

It was a toilsome ascent, for at varying intervals great blocks of stone barred the path, with here and there corresponding rifts; but a little labour enabled the party to surmount these, and they climbed on till all at once the path took a new direction, going back as it were upon itself, but always upward at a sufficiently stiff angle, so as to form a zigzag right up the face of the mountain.

"It is one of the wonders of the world," exclaimed the Doctor, enthusiastically.

"It's a precious steep one, then," grumbled Joses.

"I can hardly understand it yet," continued the Doctor, "unless there has been a tremendous spring of water up on high here. It seems almost impossible for this path to be natural."

"Do you think it was made by men, sir?" said Bart.

"It may have been, but it seems hardly possible. Some great nation may have lived here once upon a time, but even then this does not look like the work of man. But let us go on."

It was quite a long journey to where the path turned again, and then they rested, and sat down to enjoy the sweet pure breeze, and gaze right out over the vast plain, which presented a wondrous panorama even from where they were, though a far grander view awaited them from the top, which they at last set off to reach.

There were the same difficulties in the way; huge blocks of stone, over which they had to climb; rifts that they had to leap, and various natural ruggednesses of this kind, to seem in opposition to the theory that the zigzag way was the work of hands, while at every halting-place the same thought was exchanged by Bart and the Doctor— "What a fortress! We might defend it against all attacks!"

But the Doctor had one other thought, and that was, how high did the silver lode come up into the mountain, and would they be able to commence the mining up there?

"At all events, Bart," he said, "up here will be our stores and treasure-houses. Nothing can be more safe than this."

At last, after a breathless ascent, Bart, who was in advance, sprang upon the top, and uttered a loud cheer, but only to stop short as he gazed round in wonder at the comparatively level surface of the mountain, and the marvellous extent of the view around. Whether there was silver, or whether there was none, did not seem to occur to him: all he wanted was to explore the many wide acres of surface, to creep down into the rifts, to cautiously walk along at the very edge of this tremendous precipice, which went sharply down without protection of any natural parapet of rock. Above all, he wanted to get over to the farther side, and, going to the edge, gaze right into the glorious canyon with the rugged sides, and try from this enormous height to trace its course to right and left as it meandered through the plain.

"What a place to live in!" thought Bart, for there were grass, flowers, bushes, stunted trees, and cactuses, similar to those below them on the plain. In fact, it seemed to Bart as if this was a piece—almost roughly rounded—of the plain that had been left when the rest sank down several hundred feet, or else that this portion had been thrust right up to stand there, bold and bluff, ready to defy the fury of any storms that might blow.

The Doctor led the way half round, till he found what he considered a suitable spot near the edge on the northern side of the mountain; and there being no need to fear the Indians any longer, he set Joses to work with the pick to clear out a narrow rift, into which the pole they had brought was lowered, and wedged up perpendicularly with fragments of rock, one of which Bart saw was almost a mass of pure silver; then staves were set against the bottom, and bound there for strength; then guy ropes added, and secured to well-driven-down pegs; and lastly, as a defiance to the Indians, and a declaration of the place being owned by the government, under whose consent they had formed the expedition, the national flag was run up, amidst hearty cheers, and its folds blew out strongly in the breeze.

"Now," said the Doctor, "we are under the protection of the flag, and can do as we please."

"Don't see as the flag will be much protection," growled Joses; "but it'll bring the Injun down on us before long."

The Doctor did not hear these words, for he was beginning to explore the top of the mountain, and making plans for converting the place into a stronghold. Bart heard them, however, and turned to the grumbler.

"Do you think the Indians will notice the flag, Joses?" he said.

"Do I think the Injuns will notice it, Master Bart? Why, they can't help noticing it. Isn't it flap, flap, flapping there, and asking them to come as hard as it can. Why, they'll see that bit o' rag miles and miles away, and be swooping down almost before we know where we are. Mark my words if they'll not. We shall have to sleep with one eye open and the other not shut, Master Bart, that's what we shall have to do."

"Well, we shall be strong enough now to meet any number," said Bart.

"Yes, if they don't catch us just as we are least expecting it. Dessay the Doctor knows best, but we shall never get much of that silver home on account of the Apachés."

"Oh yes, we shall, Joses," said Bart, merrily. "Wait a bit, and you will see that the Indians can be beaten off as easily as possible, and they'll soon be afraid to attack us when they find how strong we are. Perhaps they'll be glad to make friends. Now, come and have a look round."

Joses obeyed his young leader, shouldering his rifle, and following him in a surly, ill-used sort of way, resenting everything that was introduced to his notice as being poor and unsatisfactory.

"Glad to see trees up here, Master Bart," he said, as the lad made a remark, by a patch whose verdure was a pleasant relief to the eye after the glare from the bare rock. "I don't call them scrubs of things trees. Why, a good puff of wind would blow them off here and down into the plain."

"Then why hasn't a good puff of wind blown them off and down into the plain?" said Bart.

"Why haven't they been blown off—why haven't they been blown off, Master Bart? Well, I suppose because the wind hasn't blowed hard enough."

Bart laughed, and they went on along the edge of the tremendous cliff till they came above the canyon, down into which Bart, never seemed weary of gazing. For the place had quite a fascination for him, with its swift, sparkling river, beautiful wooded islands, and green and varied shores. The sides of the place, too, were so wondrously picturesque; here were weather-stained rocks of fifty different tints; there covered with lovely creepers, hanging in festoons or clinging close to the stony crevices that veined the rocky face in every direction. The shelves and ledges and mossy nooks were innumerable, and every one, even at that great height, wore a tempting look that drew the lad towards it, and made him itch to begin the exploration.

"What a lovely river, Joses!" he cried.

"Lovely? Why, it's one o' those sand rivers. Don't you ever go into it if we get down there; you'd be sucked into the quicksands before you knew where you were. I don't think much of this place, Master Bart."

"I do," cried the lad, stooping to pick up a rough fragment of stone, and then, as it was long and thin, breaking it against the edge of a piece of rock, when the newly-fractured end shone brightly in the sun with a metallic sheen.

"Why, there is plenty of silver up here, Joses," he said, examining the stone intently. "This is silver, is it not?"

Joses took the piece of stone in an ill-used way, examined it carefully, and with a sour expression of countenance, as if he were grieved to own the truth, and finally jerked it away from him so that it might fall into the canyon.

"Yes," he growled; "that's silver ore, but it's very poor."

"Poor, Joses?"

"Yes; horrid poor. There wasn't above half of that silver; all the rest was stone. I like to see it in great solid lumps that don't want any melting. That's what I call silver. Don't think much of this."

"Well, it's a grand view, at all events, Joses," said Bart.

"It's a big view, and you can see far enough for anything," he growled. "You can see so far that you can't see any farther; but I don't see no good in that. What's the good of a view that goes so far you can't see it? Just as well have no view at all."

"Why, you are never satisfied, Joses," laughed Bart.

"Never satisfied! Well, I don't see nothing in this to satisfy a man. You can't eat and drink a view, and it won't keep Injun off from you. Pshaw! views are about no good at all."

"Bart!"

It was the Doctor calling, and on the lad running to him it was to find that he was standing by a great chasm running down far into the body of the mountain, with rough shelving slopes by which it was possible to descend, though the task looked risky except to any one of the firmest nerve.

"Look down there, Bart," said the Doctor, rather excitedly; "what do you make of it?"

Bart took a step nearer so as to get a clearer view of the rent, rugged pit, at one side of which was a narrow, jagged slit where the sunshine came through, illumining what would otherwise have been gloomy in the extreme.

How far the chasm descended it was impossible to see from its irregularity, the sides projecting in great buttresses here and there, all of grey rock, while what had seemed to be the softer portions had probably crumbled away. Here and there, though, glimpses could be obtained of what looked like profound depths where all was black and still.

"What should you think this place must have been?" said the Doctor, as if eager to hear the lad's opinion.

"Wait a minute, sir," replied Bart, loosening a great fragment of rock, which with some difficulty he pushed to the edge, and then, placing his foot to it, thrust it over, and then bent forward to hear it fall.

The distance before it struck was not great, for there was a huge mass of rock projecting some fifty feet below upon which the stone fell, glanced off, and struck against the opposite side, with the effect that it was again thrown back far down out of sight; but the noise it made was loud enough, and as Bart listened he heard it strike heavily six times, then there was a dead silence for quite a minute, and it seemed that the last stroke was when it reached the bottom.

Bart was just about turning to speak to the Doctor when there came hissing up a horrible echoing, weird sound, like a magnified splash, and they knew that far down at an immense depth the great stone had fallen into water.

"Ugh!" ejaculated Bart, involuntarily imitating the Indians. "What a hole! Why, it must be ten times as deep as this place is high. I shouldn't care about going down."

"Horrible indeed, Bart; but what should you think? Is this place natural or dug out?"

"Natural, I should say, sir," replied Bart. "Nobody could dig down to such a depth as that."

"Yes, natural," said the Doctor, carefully scanning the sides of the place with a small glass. "Originally natural, but this place has been worked."

"Worked? What, dug out?" said Bart. "Why, what for—to get water?"

"No," said the Doctor, quietly; "to get silver. This has been a great mine."

"But who would have dug it?" said Bart, eagerly. "The Indians would not."

"The people who roughly made the zigzag way up to the top here, my boy."

"But what people would they be, sir? The Spaniards?"

"No, Bart. I should say this was dug by people who lived long before the Spaniards, perhaps thousands of years. It might have been done by the ancient peoples of Mexico or those who built the great temples of Central America and Yucatan—those places so old that there is no tradition of the time when they were made. One thing is evident, that we have come upon a silver region that was known to the ancients."

"Well, I am disappointed," cried Bart. "I thought, sir, that we had made quite a new find."

"So did I at first, Bart," replied the Doctor; "but at any rate, save to obtain a few scraps, the place has not been touched, I should say, for centuries; and even if this mine has been pretty nearly exhausted, there is ample down below there in the canyon, while this mount must be our fortress and our place for furnaces and stores."

They descended cautiously for about a couple of hundred feet, sufficiently far for the Doctor to chip a little at the walls, and find in one or two places veins that ran right into the solid mountain, and quite sufficient to give ample employment to all the men without touching the great lode in the crack of the canyon side; and this being so, they climbed back to meet Joses, who had been just about to descend after them.

"You'll both be killing of yourselves before you're done, master," he said, roughly. "No man ought to go down a place like that without a rope round his waist well held at the end."

"Well, it would have been safer," said the Doctor, smiling.

"Safer? Yes," growled Joses; "send down a greaser next time. There's plenty of them, and they aren't much consequence. We could spare a few."

The Doctor smiled, and after continuing their journey round the edge of the old mine, they made their way to the zigzag descent, whose great regularity of contrivance plainly enough indicated that human hands had had something to do with it; while probably, when it was in use in the ancient ages, when some powerful nation had rule in the land, it might have been made easy of access by means of logs and balks of wood laid over the rifts from side to side.

Chapter Twenty Two.: Preparations for Safety.

The descent was almost more arduous than the ascent, but there was no danger save such as might result from a slip or wrench through placing a foot in one of the awkward cracks, and once more down in the plain, where the camp was as busy as an ant hill, the Doctor called the principal Englishmen about his waggon, and formed a sort of council, as he proceeded to lay his plans before them.

The first was—as they were ready to defy the Indians, and to fight for their position there, to make the mountain their fortress, and in spite of the laborious nature of the ascent, it was determined that the tents should be set up on the top, while further steps were taken to enlarge the interior of the opening as soon as the narrow entrance was passed, so as to allow of a party of men standing ready to defend the way against Indians who might force themselves in.

This was decided on at once, and men told off to do the work.

Then it was proposed to build three or four stout walls across the sloping path, all but just room enough for a man to glide by. These would be admirable means of defence to fight behind, if the enemy forced their way in past the first entry, and with these and a larger and stronger barrier at the top of the slope by the first turn, it was considered by the Doctor that with ordinary bravery the place would be impregnable.

So far so good; but then there were the horses and cattle, the former in the cavern-like stable, the latter in their stonewalled corral or enclosure.

Here was a difficulty, for now, however strong their defence might be, they were isolated, and it would be awkward in case of attack to have two small parties of men detailed for the guarding of these places, which the Indians would be sure to attack in force, in place of throwing their lives away against the well-defended mountain path.

"Couldn't we contrive a gallery along the face of the mountain, right along above the ravine and the stables, sir?" said Bart. "I think some stones might be loosened out, and a broad ledge made, too high for the Indians to climb up, and with a good wall of stones along the edge we could easily defend the horses."

"A good idea, Bart, if it can be carried out," said the Doctor. "Let's go and see!"

Inspection proved that this could easily be done so as to protect the horses, but not the corral, unless its position were altered and it were placed close alongside of the cavern stable.

After so much trouble had been taken in rearing this wall it seemed a great pity, but the men willingly set to work, while some loosened stones from above, and levered them down with bars, these fallen stones coming in handy for building up the wall.

Fineness of finish was not counted; nothing but a strong barrier which the cattle could not leap or throw down, if an attempt was made to scare them into a stampede, was all that was required, and so in a few days not only was this new corral strongly constructed, and the ledge projected fifty feet above it in the side of the mountain had been excavated, and edged with a strong wall of rock.

There was but little room, only advantage was taken of holes in the rock, which were enlarged here and there so as to form a kind of rifle-pit, in which there was plenty of space for a man to creep and kneel down to load and fire at any enemy who should have determined to carry off the cattle. In fine, they had at last a strong place of defence, only to be reached from a spot about a hundred feet up the sloping way to the summit of the mountain; and the road to and from the bastion, as the Doctor called it, was quite free from observation in the plain, if the defenders crept along on hands and knees.

Beneath the entrance to this narrow gallery a very strong wall was built nearly across the slope; and at Bart's suggestion a couple of huge stones were loosened in the wall just above, and a couple of crowbars were left there ready to lower these still further, so that they would slip down into the narrow opening left in case of emergency, and thus completely keep the Indians out.

All these matters took a great deal of time, but the knowledge of the danger from the prowling bands of Indians always on the war-path on the plains, and also that of the large treasure in silver that was within their reach, made the men work like slaves.

Water had been found in a spring right at the top of the mountain, and after contriving a basin in the rock that it should fill, it was provided with an outlet, and literally led along a channel of silver down to where it could trickle along a rift, and then down by the side of the sloping paths to a rock basin dug and blasted out close to the entrance in the plain.

This was a good arrangement, for the water was deliciously pure, and gave an ample supply to the camp, and even to the cattle when necessary, a second overflow carrying the fount within the corral, where a drinking-place was made, so that they were thus independent of the lake upon the plain, or the necessity for contriving a way down to the river in the canyon. Attention had then to be given to the food supply, and this matter was mentioned to the Beaver.

For Bart had suggested that no doubt the Indians would find buffalo for them, instead of passing their time playing the part of mountain scouts and herdsmen when the cattle were driven to feed down in the rich pastures by the lake.

Chapter Twenty Three.: Off on a Hunt.

The Beaver did not often smile, but when Bart tried to explain his wishes to him that he should lead a little party out into the plains to shoot buffalo for the party, his stolid, warlike countenance began slowly to expand; there was a twinkle here and a crease there; his solemn, watchful eyes sparkled; then they flashed, and at last a look of joy overspread his countenance, and he said a few words eagerly to the interpreter.

"The Beaver-with-Sharp-Teeth," began the latter slowly, "says that it is good, and that we will go and hunt bison, for it is men's work, while minding the grazing cattle here is only fit for squaws."

The Indians immediately began their preparations, which were marked by their brevity. Rifles and ammunition were examined, girths were tightened, and small portions of dried meat tied to the pad saddles ready for use if required, though it was hoped that a sufficiency of fresh meat would soon be obtained.

Then it was reported to Dr Lascelles that all was ready.

At that moment it seemed as if there were two boys in the camp, and that these two were sun-blackened, toil-roughened Joses, and Bart.

For these two could not conceal their eagerness to be of the hunting party, and every now and then Joses kept stealing a quick, animal-like glance at Bart, while the latter kept glancing as sharply at the frontiersman.

Neither spoke, but their looks said as plainly as could be:

"What a shame it will be if he goes, and I have to stay in camp."

The Indians had mounted, and were sitting like so many bronze statues, waiting for the Doctor's permission to go; for military precision and discipline had of late been introduced, and regular guards and watches kept, much to the disgust of some of the Englishmen, who did not scruple to say that it was quite unnecessary.

Meanwhile the Doctor seemed to have been seized with a thoughtful fit, and stood there musing, as if he were making some plan as to the future.

Bart kept on trying to catch his eye, but in vain. Then he glanced towards where the Beaver was seated upon his horse, with his keen black eyes fixed upon the youth, and his look seemed to Bart to say: "Are not you coming?"

"I don't like to ask leave to go," thought Bart; "but oh, if I could only have permission! What a gallop! To be at the back of a drove of bison as they go thundering over the plain! It will be horrible if I have to stay."

He looked towards where Joses stood frowning heavily, and still the Doctor gave no orders. He seemed regularly absorbed in his thoughts. The Beaver was growing impatient, and his men were having hard work to quiet their fiery little steeds, which kept on snorting and pawing up the sand, giving a rear up by way of change, or a playful bite at some companion, which responded with a squeal or a kick.

At last Joses began making signs to Bart that he should come over to his side, but the lad did not see them, for his eyes were fixed upon the Doctor, who at last seemed to start out of his musing fit.

"Ah!" he said; "yes, you men had better go. Tell them, Bart, to drive the bison as near camp as they can before they kill them. It will save so much trouble."

"Yes, sir," replied Bart, drawing in his breath in a way that sounded like a sigh. "Any other orders?"

"No, my boy, no. Or, stop; they ought to have an Englishman with them perhaps. Better let Harry go; we can spare him. Or, stay, send Joses."

The frontiersman uttered a snort, and was about turning to go to the spot where his horse was tethered, when he stopped short, to stand staring at Bart, with a look full of commiseration, and Bart read it truly— "I'll stop, my lad, if you can get leave to go instead."

Then came fresh words from the Doctor's lips—words that sent the blood galloping through Bart's veins, and made his nerves thrill and his eyes flash with delight.

"I suppose you would not care to go upon such a rough expedition as this, Bart?" the Doctor said.

"Oh, but I should, sir," the lad exclaimed. "I'd give anything to go—if you could spare me," he added.

The Doctor looked at him in a half-thoughtful, half-hesitating way, and remained silent for a time, while Bart felt upon the tiptoe of expectation, and in a horrible state of dread lest his guardian should alter his mind.

"Better stop, Bart," he said at last. "Bison-hunting is very difficult and dangerous work. You might be run or trampled down, or tossed, or goodness knows what beside."

"I'd take the greatest care to be out of danger, sir," said Bart, deprecatingly.

"By running into it at every turn, eh, my boy?" said the Doctor, good-humouredly. "Then I'll ask the opinion of Joses, and see what he says. Here, Joses!"

The frontiersman came up at a trot, and then stood leaning upon his rifle.

"What do you think?" asked the Doctor. "Would it be safe to allow Bart here to go with you after the bison?"

"You mean buffler, don't you?" said Joses, in a low, growling tone.

"No; I mean bison," replied the Doctor, sharply. "You people call them buffalo. I say, do you think it safe for him to go with you?"

"Safe? Course it is," growled Joses. "We shall want him too. He's so light, and his Black Boy is so swift, that the hunting party will get on better and cut out more buffalo meat if he comes."

"Well, then, according to that, Bart," said the Doctor, good-humouredly, "I suppose I must let you go."

"If you please, sir," said Bart, quietly; and then, with a gush of boyish enthusiasm, "I'd give anything to go, sir—I would indeed."

"Then I suppose you must go, Bart. Be off!"

The lad rushed off, followed by Joses, who seemed quite as much excited and as overjoyed, for he kept on slapping Bart upon the shoulder, and giving vent to little "hoorays" and "whoops", and other inhuman cries, indicative of his delight; while no sooner did the Beaver realise that Joses and Bart would be of the party than he began to talk quickly to the interpreter, then to his followers, and at last sat there motionless, in dignified silence, waiting for what was to come.

Stolid Indian as he was, though, he could not keep it up, but dashed his heels into his pony's ribs after a few moments, and cantered to where Joses and Bart were making their preparations, and, leaping to the ground, he eagerly proffered his services.

They were not needed, and he stood looking on, talking eagerly in his own language, putting in an English word wherever he could think of one, or fancied that it would fit, till all seemed ready, and Bart stood patting his little arch-necked black cob, after slinging his rifle over his shoulder.

Just then the Doctor waved his hand as a signal to him of farewell, and reading it also as a sign that they might set off, Bart leaped into his saddle, Joses followed suit, and saying something to his pony which started it off, the Beaver seemed to swing himself out into a horizontal position over his steed's back, and then dropped into his place, and they all then cantered up to where the rest of the Indians were impatiently waiting.

"All ready?" cried Bart.

"Ready we are, Master Bart," growled Joses.

"Off, then," cried Bart, waving his hand, when, amidst a ringing cheer from the little crowd of lookers-on, the bison-hunters went off at full speed over the sandy plain, making for the left of the lake; and as Bart turned in his saddle to gaze back, the camp, with its round-topped waggons, the flat mountain, and the faintly shown track up to its summit, looked like some beautiful panorama, above which the great flag blew out in the brisk breeze, and flapped and waved its folds merrily as if flaunting defiance to every Indian on the plain. But as Bart gazed up at the flag, he could not help thinking what a mere scrap of coloured cloth it was, and what a very little the Indians would think of it if they determined to come down and attack the camp in their might.

Chapter Twenty Four.: Hints on Bison-hunting.

"Ease off a bit, Master Bart," cried Joses, after they had all been riding at full gallop for a couple of miles over the plains. "Whoo—hoop, my Injun friends! Whoo—hoop!"

"Whoo-hoop! whoo-hoop! whoo-hoop!" yelled back the Indians, excitedly; and taking it as an incentive to renewed exertion, they pressed the flanks of their horses, which responded freely, and they swept on more swiftly still.

"Tell Beaver to stop a bit," cried Joses; "you're nighest to him, my lad." And Bart was about to shout some words to the chief, who was on his other side, riding with eyes flashing with excitement, and every nerve on the throb, thoroughly enjoying the wild race after so long a time of inaction in the camp. And it was not only the riders who enjoyed the racing; the horses seemed to revel in it, all tossing their massive manes and snorting loudly with delight, while swift as they went they were always so well-prepared that they would try to kick each other whenever two were in anything like close proximity.

Bart shouted to the Beaver to check his pace, but he was misunderstood, and the party swept on, whooping with delight, for all the world like a pack of excited schoolboys just let loose for a holiday.

"We shall have our nags regularly blown, my lad," panted Joses;—"and then if we come upon unfriendly Injuns it'll be the worse for us. Let's you and me draw rein, then they'll stop."

A pause in the mad gallop came without the inciting of Bart and his follower, for all at once one of the Indians' horses planted his hoof in a gopher hole, cunningly contrived by the rat-like creature just in the open part of the plain; and unable to recover itself or check its headlong speed, the horse turned a complete somersault, throwing his rider right over his head quite twenty feet away, and as the rest drew rein and gathered round, it seemed for the time as if both pony and rider were killed.

Bart leaped down to go to the poor fellow's help, but just as the lad reached him, the Indian, who had been lying flat upon his back, suddenly sat up, shook his head, and stared round in bewilderment. The next moment he had caught sight of his steed, and leaped to his feet to run and catch the rein just as the pony was struggling up.

As the pony regained its feet the Indian leaped upon its back, while the sturdy little animal gave itself a shake that seemed to be like one gigantic quiver, beginning at its broad inflated nostrils, and ending with the rugged strands of its great thick uncombed tail.

Just then the Beaver uttered a yell, and away the whole party swept again, the Indian who had fallen seeming in no wise the worse for his encounter with the sandy earth.

"That's where the Indian gets the better of the white man, Master Bart. A fall like that would have about knocked all the life out of me. It's my belief them Injuns likes it, and so you see they can bear so much that they grow hard to clear away; and in spite of our being so much more knowing, they're often too much for us."

"But had we not better pull up, Joses?" cried Bart, for they were tearing along over the plain once more at a tremendous gallop.

"It's no use to try, my lad; the horses won't stop and leave them others galloping on. You may train horses as much as you like, but there's a lot of nature left in them, and that you can't eddicate out."

"What do you mean?" panted Bart, for it was hard work riding so fast.

"What do I mean, my boy? why, that horses is used to going in big droves together, and this puts 'em in mind of it, and they like it. You try and pull Black Boy in. There, I told you so. See how he gnaws at his bit and pulls. There's no stopping him, my lad, no more than there is mine. Let 'em go, my lad. Perhaps we mayn't meet any one we don't want to meet after all."

Hardly had he spoken before the Beaver raised his arm, and his followers pulled up as if by magic, forming in quite a small circle close to him, with their horses' heads almost touching him.

The Beaver signed to Bart and Joses to approach, and room was made for them to join in the little council which was to be held, and the result was that being now well out in the plains far north of where they had originally travelled to reach the mountain, they now headed off to the west, the Indians separating, and opening out more and more so as to cover wider ground with their keen eyes, while every little eminence was climbed so that the horizon could be swept in search of bison.

"Do you think we shall meet with any, Joses?" asked Bart.

"What, buffler, my lad? Well, I hope so. There's never no knowing, for they're queer beasts, and there's hundreds here to-day, and to-morrow you may ride miles and miles, and not see a hoof. Why, I've known times when I've come upon a drove that was miles long."

"Miles, Joses?"

"Yes, Master Bart, miles long. Bulls, and cows, and calves, of all kinds, from little bits o' things, right up to some as was nearly as big as their fathers and mothers, only not so rough and fat; and they'd go on over the plain in little bands. If you was looking at 'em from far off, it seemed like one great long drove that there was no counting, but when you rode nearer to see, you found that what you took for one big drove was only made up of hundreds of other droves— big families like of fathers, and mothers, and children, which always kept themselves to themselves and didn't mix with the others. Then all along outside the flanks of the great drove of droves you'd see the wolves hanging about, half-starved, fierce-looking vermin, licking their bare chops, and waiting their chance to get something to eat."

"But wolves wouldn't attack the great bison, would they?" asked Bart.

"Only when they're about helpless—wounded or old, you know, then they will. What they wolves is waiting for is for the young calves—little, helpless sort of things that are always being left behind as the great drove goes feeding on over the plains; and if you watch a drove, you'll every now and then find a calf lying down, and its mother trying to coax it to get up and follow the others, while the old cow keeps mooing and making no end of a noise, and cocking up her tail, and making little sets of charges at the wolves to drive them back whenever they get too near. Ah, it's a rum sight to see the lank, fierce, hungry beasts licking their chops, and thinking every now and then that they've got the calf, for the old mother keeps going off a little way to try and make the stupid cow baby get up and follow. Then the wolves make a rush, and so does the buffalo, and away go the hungry beggars, for a wolf is about as cowardly a thing as ever run on four legs, that he is."

"I should like to see a sight like that, Joses," said Bart; "how I would shoot at the wolves!"

"What for?" said Joses.

"What for? Why, because they must be such cowardly, cruel beasts, to try and kill the calves."

"So are we cowardly, cruel beasts, then," said Joses, philosophically. "Wolves want to live same as humans, and it's all their nature. If they didn't kill and keep down the buffler, the country would be all buffler, and there wouldn't be room for a man to walk. It's all right, I tell you; wolves kills buffler for food, and so do we. Why, you never thought, praps, how bufflers fill up the country in some parts. I've seen droves of 'em miles upon miles long, and if it wasn't for the wolves and the Injun, as I said afore, there wouldn't be room for anything else."

"Are there so many as you say, Joses?" asked Bart.

"Not now, my lad. There used to be, but they've been killed down a deal. You see the Injun lives on 'em a'most. He cuts up and dries the beef, and he makes himself buffler robes of the skins, and very nice warm things they are in cold parts up in the mountains. I don't know what the Injun would do if it wasn't for the buffler. He'd starve. Not as that would be so very much consequence, as far as some tribes goes—Comanches and Apachés, and them sort as lives by killing and murdering every one they sees. Halloa! what's that mean?"

He pulled up, and shaded his eyes with his hand, to gaze at where one of the Indians was evidently making some sign with his spear as he sat in a peculiar way, right on their extreme left, upon an eminence in the plain.

Bart looked eagerly on, so as to try and learn what this signal meant.

"Oh, I know," said Joses directly, as he saw the Beaver make his horse circle round. "He can see a herd far out on the plain, and the Beaver has just signalled him back; so ride on, my lad, and we may perhaps come across a big run of the rough ones before the day is out."

Chapter Twenty Five.: Bart's first Bison.

Joses was wrong, for no sign was seen of buffalo that day, and so the next morning, after a very primitive kind of camp out in the wilderness, the Beaver took them in quite a different direction, parallel to the camp, so as to be within range, for distance had to be remembered in providing meat for so large a company.

It was what Joses called ticklish work.

"You must keep your eyes well skinned, Master Bart," he said, with a grim smile, as they left the plain for an undulating country, full of depressions, most of which contained water, and whose gentle hills were covered with succulent buffalo-grass. "If you don't, my lad, you may find yourself dropping down on to a herd of Apachés instead of buffaloes; and I can tell you, young fellow, that a buck Injun's a deal worse thing to deal with than a bull buffler. You must keep a sharp look-out."

"I'll do the best I can, Joses, you may be sure; but suppose I should come upon an Indian party—what am I to do?"

"Do, my lad? Why, make tracks as sharp as ever you can to your friends—that is, if you are alone."

"But if I can't get away, and they shoot at me?"

"Well, what do you mean?" said Joses, dryly.

"I mean what am I to do if I am in close quarters, and feel that they will kill me?"

"Oh," said Joses, grimly, "I should pull up short, and go up to them and give them my hatchet, and rifle, and knife, and say to 'em that you hope they won't be so wicked as to kill you, for you are very fond of Injun, and think 'em very nice; and then you'll see they'll be as pleased as pleased, and they'll make such a fuss over you."

"Do you mean that, Joses?"

"Mean it, my lad? to be sure I do. A friend of mine did so, just as I've told you, for he was afraid to fight."

"And did the Indians make a fuss over him?" asked Bart.

"To be sure they did, my lad; they took his weppuns, and then they set him on his knees, and pulled all the hair off his head to make an ornament for one of their belts, and then, because he hollered out and didn't like it, they took their lariats and tethering pegs, and after fixing the pegs in the ground, they put a rope round each of his ankles and his wrists, and spread-eagled him out tight, and then they lit a fire to warm themselves, for it was a very cold day."

"What!" cried Bart, looking aghast at his companion, who was evidently bantering him.

"Oh no, not to roast him," said Joses, laughing; "they didn't mean that. They lit the fire on purpose to warm themselves; and where do you think they lit it?"

"In a hole in the ground," said Bart.

"No, my boy; they lit it on that poor fellow's chest, and kept it burning there fiercely, and sat round it and warmed themselves; and the more that poor wretch shrieked for mercy, the more they laughed."

"Joses, it's too horrid to believe," cried Bart.

"Well, it does sound too horrid; don't it, eh? But it's the simple, honest truth, my boy, for some of they Injuns is regular demons, and stop at nothing. They do any mortal thing under the sun to a white."

"Then you would not surrender?" said Bart.

"Surrender? What! to an Indian? Not till I hadn't got a bit o' life in my body, my lad. Not before."

"But would you have me turn upon them and shoot them, Joses?" said the lad, with all a boy's horror of shedding blood.

"Bart, my lad," said Joses, holding out his rough hand, which the boy readily grasped, "if you ask me for a bit of advice, as one who knows pretty well what unfriendly Injun is, I'll give it to you."

"I do ask it, Joses, for it horrifies me to think of trying to take a man's life."

"Of course it does, my lad; so it used to me. But here's my bit of advice for you:—Whenever you meet Injun, don't trust 'em till they're proved to be of the right grit. Don't hurt a hair of any one of their heads, and always be honest in dealing with them. But if it comes to fighting, and you see they mean your life, fight for it like a man. Show 'em that an English boy has got a man's heart, only it's young, and not full growed. Never give up, for recklect that if the Injuns get hold of you it means death—horrible death—while if you fight you may beat 'em, and if you don't it's only death all the same."

"But it seems so dreadful to shoot at a man, knowing that you may kill him."

"So it does, my lad, but it's ever so much more dreadful for them to shoot at you. They've only got to leave you alone and it's all right."

Just then the Beaver came cantering up to them, gently lying right down upon his horse.

"Jump off, Master Bart," cried Joses; "there's buffler in sight, and we don't want to scare 'em."

Setting the example, he slid from his horse, and stood behind it, Bart imitating his acts, and they waited there till the Beaver came up, and pointed towards an opening in the distance, where, for the moment, Bart could see nothing; but watching attentively, he soon made out what seemed to be a dark patch moving slowly towards them.

"Are those bison?" he whispered to Joses; though the objects at which he gazed were miles away.

"No, they aren't," growled Joses; "them's buffler, and they're a feeding steadily on in this way, so that we shall be able to get a good few, I hope, and p'r'aps drive two or three a long way on towards the camp, so as to save carrying them there."

"May we ride up to them now?" cried Bart.

"I ain't going to have anything to do with the hunt," cried Joses, grimly. "Let the Beaver do it all; he's used to it. I haven't had anything to do with buffler-hunting for a many years."

"Are the bulls very dangerous?" said Bart then. "I mean may I ride pretty close up to one without getting gored?"

"They ain't half so dangerous as our own bulls used to be down at the ranche, my lad, and not a quarter so dangerous as them that have taken to a wild life after jumping out of the corral."

By this time the Beaver had signalled his followers to approach, and after giving them some instructions, they all rode off together into a bit of a valley, the Beaver and his English companions following them, so that in a few minutes they were out of sight of the approaching herd of buffalo, which came steadily on in profound ignorance of there being enemies in their neighbourhood.

The country was admirably adapted for a hunt, the ground being unencumbered by anything larger than a scrubby kind of brush, while its many shallow valleys gave the hunters ample opportunity for riding unseen until they had reached a favourable situation for their onslaught.

The Beaver was evidently a thorough expert in such a hunt as this, for he kept on dismounting and making observations, directing his followers here and there, and often approaching pretty near, making retrograde movements, so as to bring them forward again in a more satisfactory position.

His last arrangement was to place his following in couples about a hundred yards apart, parallel with the line of march of the herd, which was still invisible to Bart, though on the other side of the ridge in whose valley he sheltered he could hear a strange snorting noise every now and then, and a low angry bellow.

"We're to wait his signal, Master Bart, and then ride up the slope here, and go right at the buffler. Don't be afraid, my lad, but pick out the one you mean to have, and then stick to him till you've brought him down with a bullet right through his shoulder."

"I'll try not to be afraid, Joses," said Bart; "but I can't help feeling a bit excited."

"You wouldn't be good for much if you didn't, my boy," said the frontiersman. "Now then, be ready. Is your rifle all right?"

"Yes."

"Mind then: ride close up to your bull, and as he gallops off you gallop too, till you reach out with your rifle in one hand and fire."

"But am I to ride right up to the herd, Joses?"

"To be sure you are, my boy. Don't you be afraid, I tell you. It's only getting over it the first time. Just you touch Black Boy with your heels, and he'll take you right in between a couple of the bulls, so that you can almost reach them on each side. Then you'll find they'll begin to edge off on both sides, and get farther and farther away, when, as I told you before, you must stick to one till you've got him down."

"Poor brute!" said Bart, gently.

"Poor stuff!" cried Joses. "We must have meat, mustn't we? You wouldn't say poor salmon or poor sheep because it had to be killed. Look out. Here we go."

For the Beaver had made a quick signal, and in a moment the hunting party began to ascend the slope leading to the ridge, beyond which Bart knew that the bison were feeding, and most probably in a similar depression to the one in which the horsemen had been hidden.

"Look out for yourself," said Joses, raising his rifle; and nerving himself for the encounter, and wondering whether he really was afraid or no, Bart pressed his little cob's sides with his heels, making it increase its pace, while he, the rider, determined to dash boldly into the herd just as he had been told.

At that moment Bart's courage had a severe trial, for it seemed as if by magic that a huge bull suddenly appeared before him, the monster having trotted heavily to the top of the ridge, exactly opposite to Bart, and, not ten yards apart, the latter and the bull stopped short to gaze at each other.

"What a monster!" thought Bart, bringing his rifle to bear upon the massive head, with the tremendous shoulders covered with long coarse shaggy hair, while the short curved horns and great glowing eyes gave the bull so ferocious an aspect that upon first acquaintance it was quite excusable that Bart's heart should quail and his hands tremble as he took aim, for the animal did not move.

Just then Bart remembered that Joses had warned him not to fire at the front of a bison.

"He'd carry away half-a-dozen balls, my lad, and only die miserably afterwards in the plain. What you've got to do is to put a bullet in a good place and bring him down at once. That's good hunting. It saves powder and lead, makes sure of the meat, and don't hurt the buffler half so much."

So Bart did not fire, but sat there staring up at the bull, and the bull stood above him pawing the ground, snorting furiously, and preparing himself for a charge.

Truth must be told. If Bart had been left to himself on this his first meeting with a bison, especially as the beast looked so threatening, he would have turned and fled. But as it happened, he was not left to himself, for Black Boy did not share his rider's tremor. He stood gazing warily up at the bull for a few moments, and then, having apparently made up his mind that there was not much cause for alarm, and that the bison was a good deal of a big bully without a great deal of bravery under his shaggy hide, he began to move slowly up the slope, taking his master with him, to Bart's horror and consternation.

"He'll charge at and roll us over and over down the slope," thought Bart, as he freed his feet from the stirrups, ready to leap off and avoid being crushed beneath his nag.

Nine yards—eight yards—six yards—closer and closer, and the bison did not charge. Then so near that the monster's eyes seemed to flame, and still nearer and nearer, with the great animal tossing its head, and making believe to lower it and tear up the earth with one horn.

"If he don't run we must," thought Bart, at last, as Black Boy slowly and cautiously took him up to within a yard of the shaggy beast, whose bovine breath Bart could smell now as he tossed his head.

Then, all at once, the great fellow wheeled round and thundered down the slope, while, as if enjoying the discomfiture, Black Boy made a bound, cleared the ridge, and descended the other slope at full gallop close to the bison's heels.

All Bart's fear went in the breeze that swept by him. He felt ready to shout with excitement, for the valley before him seemed to be alive with bison, all going along at a heavy lumbering gallop, with Joses and the Indians in full pursuit, and all as much excited as he.

His instructions were to ride right in between two of the bison, single out one of them, and to keep to him till he dropped; and Bart saw nothing but the huge drove on ahead, with the monstrous bull whose acquaintance he had made thundering on between him and the main body.

"I must keep to him," thought Bart; "and I will, till I have shot him down."

"If I can," he added a few minutes later, as he kept on in the exciting chase.

How long it lasted he could not tell, nor how far they went. All he knew was that after a long ride the bull nearly reached the main body; and once mingled with them, Bart felt that he must lose him.

But this did not prove to be the case, for Black Boy had had too good a training with cattle-driving. He had been a bit astonished at the shaggy hair about the bison's front, but it did not trouble him much; and without being called upon by spur or blow, no sooner did the bison plunge into the ranks of his fellows as they thundered on, than the gallant little horse made three or four bounds, and rushed close up to his haunch, touching him and the bison on his left, with the result that both of the shaggy monsters edged off a little, giving way so that Bart was carried right in between them, and, as Joses had suggested, there was one moment when he could literally have kicked the animals on either side of his little horse.

That only lasted for a moment, though; for both of the bison began to edge away, with the result that the opening grew wider and wider, while, remembering enough of his lesson, Bart kept close to the bull's flank, Black Boy never flinching for a moment; and at last the drove had scattered, so that the young hunter found himself almost all alone on the plain, going at full speed beside his shaggy quarry, the rest of the herd having left him to his fate.

And now the bull began to grow daring, making short rushes at horse and rider, but they were of so clumsy a nature that Black Boy easily avoided them, closing in again in the most pertinacious manner upon the bull's flanks as soon as the charge was ended.

All at once Bart remembered that there was something else to be done, and that he was not to go on riding beside the bison, but to try and shoot it.

Easier said than done, going at full gallop, but he brought his rifle to bear, and tried to get a good aim, but could not; for it seemed as if the muzzle were either jerked up towards the sky or depressed towards the ground.

He tried again and again, but could not make sure of a shot, so, checking his steed a little, he allowed the bison to get a few yards ahead, and then galloped forward till he was well on the right side, where he could rest the rifle upon his horse's withers, and, waiting his time, get a good shot.

It might have been fired into the earth for all the effect it had, save to produce an angry charge, and it was the same with a couple more shots. Then, all at once, as Bart was re-loading, the poor brute suddenly stood still, panting heavily, made an effort to charge the little horse, stopped, ploughed up the ground with its right horn, and then shivered and fell over upon its flank—dead.

Bart leaped from his horse in his excitement, and, running to the bison, jumped upon its shaggy shoulder, took off his cap, waved it above his head, and uttered a loud cheer.

Then he looked round for some one to echo his cry, and he saw a widespread stretch of undulating prairie land, with some tufts of bush here, some tall grass there, and beneath his feet the huge game beast that he had fairly run down and shot, while close beside him Black Boy was recompensing himself for his long run by munching the coarse brown grass.

And that was all.

Chapter Twenty Six.: Alone in the Plains.

Where were the hundreds of buffalo that had been thundering over the plain?

Where was Joses?

Where were the Indians?

These were the questions Bart asked as he gazed round him in dismay. For the excitement of his gallop was over now, and, though they wanted meat so badly, he felt half sorry that he had shot the poor beast that lay stiffening by his side for he had leaped down, and had, as if by instinct, taken hold of Black Boy's rein, lest he should suddenly take it into his head to gallop off and leave his master in the solitude by himself.

For a few minutes there was something novel and strange in the sensation of being the only human being in that vast circle whose circumference was the horizon, seen from his own centre.

Then it began to be astonishing, and Bart wondered why he could not see either hunters or buffaloes.

Lastly, it began to be painful, and to be mingled with a curious sensation of dread. He realised that he was alone in that vast plain—that he had galloped on for a long while without noticing in which direction he had gone, and then, half-stunned and wondering as he fully realised the fact that he was lost, he mounted his horse and sat thinking.

He did not think much, for there was a singular, stupefied feeling in his head for a time. But this passed off, and was succeeded by a bewildering rush of thought—what was to become of him if he were left here like this—alone—without a friend—hopeless of being found?

This wild race of fancies was horrible while it endured, and Bart pressed the cold barrel of his rifle to his forehead in the hope of finding relief, but it gave none.

The relief came from his own effort as he tried to pull himself together, laughing at his own cowardice, and ridiculing his fears.

"What a pretty sort of a hunter I shall make!" he said aloud, "to be afraid of being left alone for a few minutes in broad daylight, with the sun shining down upon my head, and plenty of beef to eat if I like to light myself a fire."

It was ridiculous, he told himself, and that he ought to feel ashamed; for he was ignorant of the fact that even old plainsmen and practised hunters may lose their nerve at such a time, and suffer so from the horror of believing themselves lost that some even become insane.

Fortunately, perhaps, Bart did not know this, and he bantered himself until he grew cooler, when he began to calculate on what was the proper thing to do.

"Let me see," he said; "they are sure to begin looking for me as soon as I am missed. What shall I do? Fire my rifle—make a fire—ride off to try and find them?"

He sat upon his horse thinking.

If he fired his rifle or made a fire, he might bring down Indians upon him, and that would be worse than being lost, so he determined to wait patiently until he was able to see some of his party; and no sooner had he come to this determination than he cheered up, for he recollected directly that the Beaver, or some one or other of his men, would be sure to find him by his trail, even though it had been amongst the trampling hoof-marks of the bison. The prints of a well-shod horse would be unmistakable, and with this thought he grew more patient, and waited on.

It was towards evening, though, before he had the reward of his patience in seeing the figure of a mounted Indian in the distance; and even then it gave no comfort, for he felt sure that it might be an enemy, for it appeared to be in the very opposite direction from that which he had come.

Bart's first idea was to go off at a gallop, only he did not know where to go, and after all, this might be a friend.

Then another appeared, and another; and dismounting, and turning his horse and the bison into bulwarks, Bart stood with his rifle resting, ready for a shot, should these Indians prove to be enemies, and patiently waited them as they came on.

This they did so quickly and full of confidence that there was soon no doubt as to who they were, and Bart at last mounted again, and rode forward to meet them.

The Indians came on, waving their rifles above their heads, and no sooner did they catch sight of the prize the lad had shot than they gave a yell of delight; and then, forgetting their customary stolidity, they began to chatter to him volubly in their own tongue, as they flung themselves from their horses and began to skin the bison as it lay.

Bart could not help thinking how thoroughly at home these men seemed in the wilds. A short time before he had been in misery and despair because he felt that he was lost. Here were these Indians perfectly at their ease, and ready to set to work and prepare for a stay if needs be, for nothing troubled them—the immensity and solitude had no terrors for their untutored minds.

They had not been at work above an hour before a couple more Indians came into sight, and soon after, to his great delight, Bart recognised Joses and the Beaver coming slowly over a ridge in the distance, and he cantered off to meet them at once.

"Thought we lost you, Master Bart," cried Joses, with a grim smile. "Well, how many bufflers did you shoot?"

"Only one," replied Bart, "but it was a very big fellow."

"Calf?" asked Joses, laughing.

"No; that great bull that came over the ridge."

"You don't mean to say you ran him down, lad, and shot him, do you?" cried Joses, excitedly.

"There he lies, and the Indians are cutting him up," said Bart quietly.

Joses pressed his horse's sides with his heels, and went off at a gallop to inspect Bart's prize, coming back in a few minutes smiling all over his face.

"He's a fine one, my lad. He's a fine one, Master Bart—finest shot to-day. I tell you what, my lad, if I'd shot that great bull I should have thought myself a lucky man."

As he spoke he pointed to the spot, and the Beaver cantered off to have his look, and he now came back ready to nod and say a few commendatory words to the young hunter, whom they considered to have well won his spurs.

The result of this first encounter with the bison was that nine were slain, and for many hours to come the party were busy cutting up the meat into strips, which were hung in the sun to dry.

Then four of the Indians went slowly off towards the miners' camp at the mountain, their horses laden with the strips of meat, their instructions being to come back with a couple of waggons, which Joses believed they would be able to fill next day.

"How far do you think we are from the camp?" asked Bart.

"'Bout fifteen miles or so, no more," replied Joses. "You see the run after the bison led us down towards it, so that there isn't so far to go."

"Why, I fancied that we were miles upon miles away," cried Bart; "regularly lost in the wilderness."

"Instead of being close at home, eh, lad? Well, we shall have to camp somewhere out here to-night, so we may as well pick out a good place."

"But where are the other Indians?" asked Bart.

"Cutting up the buffler we killed," replied Joses.

"Faraway?"

"Oh, no; mile or so. We've done pretty well, my lad, for the first day, only we want such a lot to fill so many mouths."

A suitable place was selected for the camp, down in a well-sheltered hollow, where a fire was lit, and some bison-meat placed upon sticks to roast. The missing Indians seemed to be attracted by the odour, for just as it was done they all came straight up to camp ready to make a hearty meal, in which their white companions were in no wise behind hand.

"Not bad stuff," said Joses, after a long space, during which he had been too busy to speak.

"I never ate anything so delicious," replied Bart, who, upon his side, was beginning to feel as if he had had enough.

"Ah, there's worse things than roast buffler hump," said Joses; "and now, my lad, if I was you I'd take as big and as long a sleep as I could, for we must be off again before daylight after the herd."

"Shall we catch up to them again, Joses?" asked Bart.

"Catch up to 'em? why, of course, they haven't gone far."

A quarter of an hour later Bart was fast asleep, dreaming that he was hunting a bull bison ten times as big as the one he had that afternoon shot, and that after hunting it for hours it suddenly turned round and began to hunt him, till he became so tired that he lay down and went off fast asleep, when, to his great disgust, when he was so weary, Joses came and began to shake him by the shoulder, saying:

"Come, Master Bart, lad, wake up. The buffer's been coming close in to camp during the night."

Chapter Twenty Seven.: More Food for the Camp.

For it was nearly day, and Bart jumped up, astonished that he could have slept so long—that is to say, nearly since sundown on the previous evening.

A good fire was burning, and buffalo steaks were sizzling and spurting ready for their repast, while the horses were all standing together beneath a little bold bluff of land left sharp and clear by the action of a stream that doubtless flowed swiftly enough in flood time, but was now merely a thread of water.

The party were settling down to their meal, for which, in spite of the previous evening's performance, Bart felt quite ready, when the horses suddenly began to snort and show a disposition to make a stampede, for there was a rushing noise as of thunder somewhere on ahead, and as the Indians rushed to their horses' heads, and he made for Black Boy, thinking that there must be a flood rolling down from the hills, he caught a glimpse of what was amiss.

For, as Bart stood up, he could see over the edge of the scarped bank beneath which they had made their fire, that the plain was literally alive with bison, which, in some mad insensate fit of dread, were in headlong flight, and their course would bring them right over the spot where the party was encamped.

The Beaver saw it, and, prompt in action, he made his plans:— Signing to several to come to his side, while the rest held the horses, he leaped upon the edge of the stream bed just as the bison were within a hundred yards, and Bart and Joses followed him. Then altogether, as the huge herd was about to sweep over them, they uttered a tremendous shout, and all fired together right in the centre of the charging herd.

Bart set his teeth, feeling sure that he would be run down and trampled to death; but the effect of the sudden and bold attack was to make the herd separate. It was but a mere trifle, for the bison were so packed together that their movements were to a great extent governed by those behind; but still they did deviate a little, those of the front rank swerving in two bodies to right and left, and that saved the little party.

Bart had a sort of confused idea of being almost crushed by shaggy quarters, of being in the midst of a sea of tossing horns and dark hair, with lurid eyes glaring at him; then the drove was sweeping on—some leaping down into the stream bed and climbing up the opposite side, others literally tumbling down headlong, to be trampled upon by those which followed; and then the rushing noise began to die away, for the herd had swept on, and the traces they had left were the trampled ground and a couple of their number shot dead by the discharge of rifles, and lying in the river bed, while another had fallen a few hundred yards farther on in the track of the flight.

Fortunately the horses had been held so closely up to the bluff that they had escaped, though several of the bison had been forced by their companions to the edge, and had taken the leap, some ten feet, into the river bed below.

It had been a hard task, though, to hold the horses—the poor creatures shivering with dread, and fighting hard to get free. The worst part of the adventure revealed itself to Bart a few moments later when he turned to look for Joses, whom he found rubbing his head woefully beside the traces of their fire, over which the bison had gone in enormous numbers, with the result that the embers had been scattered, and every scrap of the delicious, freshly-roasted, well-browned meat trampled into the sand.

"Never mind, Joses," cried Bart, bursting out laughing; "there's plenty more meat cut up."

"Plenty more," growled Joses; "and that all so nicely done. Oh, the wilful, wasteful beasts! As if there wasn't room enough anywhere else on the plain without their coming right over us!"

"What does the Beaver mean?" said Bart just then.

"Mean? Yes; I might have known as much. He thinks there's Injun somewhere; that they have been hunting the buffler and made 'em stampede. We shall have to be off, my lad. No breakfast this morning."

It was as Joses said. The Beaver was of opinion that enemies must be near at hand, so he sent out scouts to feel for the danger, and no fire could be lighted lest it should betray their whereabouts to a watchful foe.

A long period of crouching down in the stream bed ensued, and as Bart waited he could not help thinking that their hiding-place in the plain was, as it were, a beginning of a canyon like that by the mountain, and might, in the course of thousands of years, be cut down by the action of flowing water till it was as wide and deep.

At last first one and then another scout came in, unable to find a trace of enemies; and thus encouraged, a fire was once more made and meat cooked, while the three bison slain that morning were skinned and their better portions cut away.

The sun was streaming down with all its might as they once more went off over the plain in search of the herd; and this search was soon rewarded, the party separating, leaving Bart, and Joses together to ride after a smaller herd about a mile to their left.

As they rode nearer, to Bart's great surprise, the herd did not take flight, but huddled together, with a number of bulls facing outwards, presenting their horns to their enemies, tossing and shaking their shaggy heads, and pawing up the ground.

"Why don't they rush off, Joses?" asked Bart.

"Got cows and calves inside there, my boy," replied the frontiersman. "They can't go fast, so the bulls have stopped to take care of them."

"Then it would be a shame to shoot them," cried Bart. "Why, they are braver than I thought for."

"Not they," laughed Joses. "Not much pluck in a bison, my lad, that I ever see. Why, you might walk straight up to them if you liked, and they'd never charge you."

"I shouldn't like to try them," said Bart, laughing.

"Why not, my lad?"

"Why not? Do you suppose I want to be trampled down and tossed?"

"Look here, Master Bart. You'll trust me, won't you?"

"Yes, Joses."

"You know I wouldn't send you into danger, don't you?"

"Of course, Joses."

"Then look here, my lad. I'm going to give you a lesson, if you'll learn it."

"A lesson in what?" asked Bart.

"In buffler, my lad."

"Very well, go on; I'm listening. I want to learn all I can about them," replied Bart, as he kept on closely watching the great, fierce, fiery-eyed bison bulls, as they stamped and snorted and pawed the ground, and kept making feints of dashing at their approaching enemies, who rode towards them at a good pace.

"I don't want you to listen, my lad," said Joses; "I want you to get down and walk right up to the buffler bulls there, and try and lay hold of their horns."

"Walk up to them?" cried Bart. "Why, I was just thinking that if we don't turn and gallop off, they'll trample us down."

"Not they, my lad," replied Joses. "I know 'em better than that."

"Why, they rushed right over us at the camp."

"Yes, because they were on the stampede, and couldn't stop themselves. If they had seen us sooner they'd have gone off to the right, or left. As for those in front, if they charge, it will be away from where they can see a man."

"But if I got down and walked towards them, the bulls would come at me," cried Bart.

"Not they, I tell you, my lad; and I should like to see you show your pluck by getting down and walking up to them. It would be about the best lesson in buffler you ever had."

"But they might charge me, Joses," said Bart, uneasily.

"Did I tell you right about 'em before," said Joses, "or did I tell you wrong, my lad?"

"You told me right; but you might be wrong about them here."

"You let me alone for that," replied Joses, gruffly. "I know what I'm saying. Now, then, will you get down and walk up to 'em, or must I?"

"If you'll tell me that I may do such a thing, I'll go up to them," said Bart, slowly.

"Then I do tell you, my lad, and wouldn't send you if it wasn't safe. You ought to know that. Now, then, will you go?"

For answer Bart slipped off his horse and cocked his rifle.

"Don't shoot till they're turning round, my lad," said Joses; "and then give it to that big young bull in the middle there. He's a fine one, and we must have meat for the camp."

"But it seems a pity; he looks such a brave fellow," said Bart.

"Never mind; shoot him. All the other bulls will be precious glad, for he's the tyrant of the herd, and leads them a pretty life. Now then, on you go."

They were now some sixty yards from the herd, and no sooner did Bart take a step forward than Joses leaped lightly from his horse, and rested his rifle over the saddle ready for a sure shot when he should see his chance.

Bart tried to put on a bold front, but he felt very nervous, and walked cautiously towards the herd, where ten or a dozen bulls faced him, and now seemed to be furious, snorting and stamping with rage.

But he walked on, gaining courage as he went, but ere he had gone half-a-dozen steps six of the bulls made a headlong charge at him, and Bart stood still, ready to fire.

"How stupid I was," he said to himself. "They'll go right over me;" and with his heart beating heavily he felt that he must turn and run.

"Go on, my lad, go on," shouted Joses, encouragingly; and in spite of himself, and as if bound to obey orders, the lad took a step forward again, when, to his utter amazement, the bison bulls, now not twenty yards away, stopped short, shook their heads at him, made some impotent tosses in the air, pawed up a little grass, and then turned altogether, and trotted back to take up their old position in front of the herd.

"Ha! ha! ha!" laughed Joses, behind him. "What did I tell you? Go on, my lad. You've got more heart than a bison."

This emboldened Bart, who went steadily on, reducing the distance between him and the herd; and it was a curious sensation that which came upon the lad as he walked nearer and nearer to the furious-looking beasts.

Then his heart gave a tremendous throb, and seemed to stand still, for, without warning, and moved as if by one impulse, the bison charged again, but this time not half the distance; and as Bart did not run from them, they evidently thought that some one ought to flee, so they galloped back.

Bart was encouraged now, and began to feel plenty of contempt for the monsters, and walking more swiftly, the beasts charged twice more, the last time only about the length of their bodies, and this was when Bart was so near that he could almost feel their hot moist breath.

This was the last charge, for as they turned the leading bull evidently communicated his opinion that the young visitor was a stupid kind of being, whom it was impossible to frighten, and the whole herd set off at a lumbering gallop, but as they did so two rifle-shots rang out, and two bulls hung back a little, evidently wounded.

Joses led up Bart's horse as the lad reloaded, and put the rein in his hand.

"There, off after your own bull, my lad. It was bravely done. I'm off after mine."

Then they separated, and after a short, gallop Bart reached his quarry, and better able now to manage his task, he rode up on its right side, and a well-placed bullet tumbled the monstrous creature over on the plain dead.

Joses had to give two shots before he disabled his own bison, but the run was very short; and when Bart and he looked round they were not above a couple of hundred yards apart, and the Beaver and a couple of Indians were cantering towards them.

That evening their messengers returned with a couple of the white men and two waggons, which were taken in triumph next morning to the camp, heavily laden with bison-meat; and as they came near the mountain, Bart drew rein to stay and watch the curious sight before him, for, evidently in pursuance of the Doctor's idea to make the top of the mountain the stronghold of the silver adventurers, there was quite a crowd of the people toiling up the path up the mountain, all laden with packages and the various stores that had been brought for the adventure.

"Been pretty busy since we've been gone, Master Bart," said Joses, grimly. "Won't they come scuffling down again when they know there's meat ready for sharing out."

But Joses was wrong, for the meat was not shared out down in the plain, but a second relay of busy hands were set to work to carry the store of fresh food right up the mountain-side to a tent that had already been pitched on the level top, while as soon as the waggons were emptied they were drawn up in rank along with the others close beneath the wall-like rock.

Chapter Twenty Eight.: Down in the Silver Canyon.

The Doctor had not lost any time. Tents had been set up, and men were busy raising sheds of rough stone which were to be roofed over with poles. But at the same time, he had had men toiling away in opening up a rift that promised to yield silver pretty bounteously, for the ancient mine seemed hardly a likely place now, being dangerous, and the principal parts that were easy of access apparently pretty well worked out.

This was something of a disappointment, but a trifling one, for the mountain teemed with silver, and then there was the canyon to explore.

This the Doctor proposed to examine on the day following Bart's return, for the services of the chief would be required to find a way down unless the descent was to be made by ropes.

The Beaver and his interpreter were brought to the Doctor's tent, and the matter being explained, the Indian smiled, and expressed his willingness to show them at once; so a few preparations having been made, and some provisions packed in case that the journey should prove long, Bart, the Doctor, Joses, and the interpreter started, leaving the Beaver in front to lead the way.

He started off in a line parallel to the canyon, as it seemed to Bart, and made for a patch of good-sized trees about half a mile from the mountain, and upon reaching this they found that the great river chasm had curved round, so that it was not above a hundred yards away, and Bart began to think that perhaps it would not prove to be so precipitous there.

The Beaver, seeing his eagerness, smiled and nodded, and thrusting the bushes aside, he entered the patch of dense forest, which was apparently about half a mile in length, running with a breadth of half that distance along the edge of the canyon.

The interpreter followed, and after a few minutes they returned to say that no progress could be made in that direction, so they re-entered the forest some fifty yards lower, and where it looked less promising than before.

The chief, however, seemed to be satisfied, and drawing his knife, he hacked and chopped at the projecting vines and thorns so as to clear a way for those who followed; till after winding in and out for some time, he came at length to what seemed little more than a crack in the ground about a yard wide, and pretty well choked up with various kinds of growth.

At the first glance it seemed impossible for any one to descend into this rift, but the interpreter showed them that it was possible by leaping down, and directly after there was a loud, rattling noise, and an extremely large rattlesnake glided out of the rift on to the level ground. It was making its escape, when a sharp blow from the chief's knife divided it nearly in two, and he finished his task by crushing its head with the butt of his rifle.

"We must be on the look-out, Bart," said the Doctor, "if these reptiles are in any quantity;" and as the Beaver leaped down he followed, then came Bart, and Joses closed up the rear.

"I shall get all the sarpents," he grumbled. "You people will disturb them all, and they'll do their stinging upon me."

Then the descent became so toilsome that conversation ceased, and nothing was heard but the crackling of twigs, the breaking off of branches, and the sharp, rustling noise that followed as the travellers forced their way through the bushes.

This lasted for about fifty yards, and then the descent became very rapid, and the trees larger and less crowded together. The rift widened, too, at times, but only to contract again; and then its sides so nearly approached that their path became terribly obscure, and without so energetic a guide as they possessed it would have required a stout-hearted man to proceed.

Every here and there they had to slide down the rock perhaps forty or fifty feet; then there would be a careful picking of the way over some rugged stones, and then another slide down for a while.

Once or twice it seemed as if they had come to a full stop, the rift being closed up by fallen masses of earth and stones; but the Beaver mounted these boldly, as if he knew of their existence, and lowered himself gently down the other side, waiting to help the Doctor, for Bart laughingly declined, preferring as he did to leap from stone to stone, and swing himself over cracks that seemed almost impassable.

"This is nature's work, Bart," the Doctor said, as he paused to wipe his streaming face. "No former inhabitants ever made this. It is an earthquake-split, I should say."

"But it might be easily made into a good path, sir," replied Bart.

"It might be made, Bart, but not easily, and it would require a great deal of engineering to do it. How dark it grows! You see nothing hardly can grow down here except these mosses and little fungi."

"Is it much farther, sir?" cried Bart.

"What! are you tired, my lad?"

"No, sir; not I. Only it seems as if we must be near the bottom of the canyon."

"No, not yet," said the Beaver in good English, and both the Doctor and Bart smiled, while the chief seemed pleased at his advance in the English tongue being noticed. "Long down—long down," he said in continuation.

"The Beaver-with-Sharp-Teeth tells the English chief and the little boy English chief that it is far yet to the bottom of the way to the rushing river of the mountain," said the interpreter, and the chief frowned at him angrily, while Bart felt as if he should like to kick him for calling him a "little boy English chief;" but the stoical Indian calmly and indifferently allowed the angry looks he received to pass, and followed the party down as they laboriously stepped from stone to stone.

"There's a pretty good flush o' water here in rainy times, master," shouted Joses. "See how all the earth has been washed out. Shouldn't wonder if you found gold here."

"I ought to have thought of that, Joses," replied the Doctor, as he proceeded to examine the crevices of the rock over which he was walking as well as he could for the gloom and obscurity of the place, and at the end of five minutes he uttered a cry of joy. "Here it is!" he exclaimed, holding up two or three rounded nodules of metal. "No; I am wrong," he said. "This light deceives me; it is silver."

To his surprise, the Beaver took them from his hand with a gesture of contempt, and threw the pieces away, though they would have purchased him a new blanket or an ample supply of ammunition at Lerisco or any other southern town.

"Wait," he said, airing his English once more. "Plenty! plenty!" and he pointed down towards the lower part of the narrow crevice or crack in the rock along which they were passing.

"Go on, then," said the Doctor; and once more they continued their descent, which grew more difficult moment by moment, and more dark, and wild, and strange.

For now the rock towered up on either side to a tremendous height, and the daylight only appeared as a narrow streak of sky, dappled with dark spots where the trees hung over the rift. Then the sky was shut out altogether, and they went on with their descent in the midst of a curious gloom that reminded Bart of the hour just when the first streaks of dawn are beginning to appear in the morning sky.

This went on for what seemed to be some time, the descent growing steeper and more difficult; but at last there came a pleasant rushing sound, which Bart knew must be that of the river. Then there was the loud song of a bird, which floated up from far below, and then all at once a pale light appeared on the side of the rocks, which were now so near together that the sides in places nearly touched above their heads.

Five minutes' more arduous descent, and there was glistening wet moss on the rock, and the light was stronger, while the next minute the pure, clear light of day flashed up from an opening that seemed almost at their feet—an opening that was almost carpeted with verdant green, upon which, after dropping from a rock some ten feet high, they stood, pausing beneath an arch of interweaving boughs that almost hid the entrance to the rift, and there they stood, almost enraptured by the beauty of the scene.

For the bottom of the canyon had been reached, and its mighty verdure-decked, rocky walls rose up sheer above their heads, appearing to narrow towards the top, though this was an optical delusion. All was bright and glorious in the sunshine. The trees and shrubs were of a vivid green, the grass was brilliant with flowers; and running in serpentine waves through the middle of the lovely prairie that softly sloped down to it on either side, and whose sedges and clumps of trees dipped their tips in its sparkling waters, ran the river, dancing and foaming here over its rocky bed, there swirling round and forming deep pools, while in its clear waters as they approached Bart could see the glancing scales of innumerable fish on its sun-illumined shallows.

Hot and weary with their descent, the first act of all present was to dip their cups into the pure clear water, and then, as soon as their feverish thirst was allayed, the Doctor proceeded to test the sand of the river to see if it contained gold, while Bart, after wondering why a man who had discovered a silver mine of immense wealth could not be satisfied, went wandering off along the edge of the river, longing for some means of capturing the fish, whose silver scales flashed in the sunshine whenever they glided sidewise over some shallow ridge of yellow sand that would not allow of their swimming in the ordinary way.

Sometimes he was able to leap from rock to rock that stood out of the river bed, and formed a series of barriers, around which the swift stream fretted and boiled, rushing between them in a series of cascades; and wherever one of these masses of water-worn stone lay in the midst of the rapid stream, Bart found that there was always a deep still transparent pool behind; and he had only to approach softly, and bend down or lie upon his chest, with his head beyond the edge, to see that this pool was the home of some splendid fish, a very tyrant ready to pounce upon everything that was swept into the still water.

"I wish we were not bothering about gold and silver," thought Bart, as after feasting his eyes upon the fish he turned to gaze upon the beauties of the drooping trees, and spire-shaped pines that grew as regular in shape as if they had been cast in the same mould; while, above all, the gloriously coloured walls of the canyon excited his wonder, and made him long to scale them, climbing into the many apparently inaccessible places, and hunting for fruit, and flower, and bird.

Bart had rambled down the river, so rapt in the beauties around him that he forgot all about the Doctor and his search for the precious metals. All at once, as he was seated out upon a mass of stone by the river side, it struck him that, though he had watched the fish a good deal, it would be very pleasant to wade across a shallow to where a reef of rocks stood out of the water, so placed that as soon as he reached them he could leap from the one to the other, and settle himself down almost in the very middle of the river; and when there he determined to wait his chance and see if he could not shoot two or three of the largest trout for their meal that night.

The plan was no sooner thought of than Bart proceeded to put it in execution.

He waded the shallow pretty easily, though he could not help wondering at the manner in which his feet sank down into the soft sand, which seemed to let them in right up to the knees at once, and then to close so tightly round them that, to use his own words, he seemed to have been thrusting his legs into leaden boots. However, he dragged them out, reached the first rock of the barrier or reef, and stood for a few minutes enjoying the beauty of the scene, while the stream rushed by on either side with tremendous force.

The next stone was a good five feet away, with a deep glassy flood rushing around. Bart leaped over it, landed safely, and found the next rock quite six feet distant, and a good deal higher than the one he was upon.

He paused for a moment or two to think what would be the consequences if he did not reach this stone, and judged that it meant a good ducking and a bit of a swim to one of the shallows below.

"But I should get my rifle and cartridges wet," he said aloud, "and that would never do. Shall I? Shan't I?"

Bart's answer was to gather himself up and leap, with the result that he just reached the edge of the rock, and throwing himself forward managed to hold on, and then scramble up in safety.

Going back's easy enough, thought Bart, as he prepared to bound to the next rock, a long mass, like the back of some monstrous alligator just rising above the flood. Along this he walked seven or eight yards, jumped from block to block of a dozen more rugged pieces, and then bounded upon a roughly semi-circular piece that ended the ridge like a bastion, beyond which the water ran deep and swift, with many an eddy and mighty curl.

"This is grand!" cried Bart, whose eyes flashed with pleasure; and settling himself down in a comfortable position, he laid his rifle across his knees with the intention of watching the fish in a shallow just above him, but only to forget all about them directly after, as he sat enjoying the beauties of the scene, and wished that his sisterly companion Maude were there to see how wonderfully grand their mother Nature could be.

"If there were no Indians," thought Bart, "and a good large town close by, what a lovely place this would be for a house. I could find a splendid spot; and then one could hunt on the plains, and shoot and fish, and the Doctor could find silver and gold, and—good gracious! What's that?"

Chapter Twenty Nine.: A Narrow Escape.

Bart laid down his rifle as he uttered this very feminine exclamation, and shading his eyes, gazed before him up the river.

For as he had been dreamily gazing before him at the shallow where the water ran over a bed of the purest sand for about a hundred yards, it seemed to him that he had seen a dark something roll over, and then for a moment a hand appeared above the water, or else it was the ragged leaf of some great water-plant washed out from its place of growth in the bank.

"It looks like—it must be—it is!" cried Bart. "Somebody has fallen in, and is drowning."

As he thought this a chill feeling of horror seemed to rob him of the power of motion. And now, as he gazed at the glittering water with starting eyes, he knew that there was no mistake—it was no fancy, for their was a body being rolled over and over by the stream, now catching, now sweeping along swiftly, and nearer and nearer to where the lad crouched.

The water before him was shallow enough, and all clear sand, so without hesitation Bart lowered himself down from the rock, stepped on to the sand with the water now to his knees, and was then about to wade towards the body, when he turned sharply and clutched the rough surface of the rock, clinging tightly, and after a brief struggle managed to clamber back panting, and with the perspiration in great drops upon his brow.

He knew now what he had only partly realised before, and that was the fact that these beautiful, smooth sands, over which the swift current pleasantly glided, were quicksands of the most deadly kind, and that if he had not struggled back there would have been no chance of escape. Another step would have been fatal, and he must have gone down, for no swimming could avail in such a strait.

But Bart, in spite of the shock of his narrow escape, had not forgotten the object for which he had lowered himself from the rock, and gazing eagerly towards the shallows, he saw that it was just being swept off then into the deep water that rushed round the buttress upon which he stood.

It was the work of moments. Reaching out as far as he could, he just managed to grip the clinging garment of the object sweeping by, and as he grasped it tightly, so great was the power of the water, that he felt a sudden snatch that threatened to tear the prize from his hand. But Bart held on fiercely, and before he could fully comprehend his position he found that he had overbalanced himself, and the next moment he had gone under with a sullen plunge.

Bart was a good swimmer, and though encumbered with his clothes, he felt no fear of reaching the bank somewhere lower down; and, confident in this respect, he looked round as he rose to the surface for the body of him he had tried to save, for as he struck the water he had loosened his hold.

There was just a glimmer of something below the surface, and taking a couple of sturdy strokes, Bart reached it before it sank lower, caught hold, and then guiding his burden, struck out for the shore.

The rocks from which he had come were already a hundred yards above them, the stream sweeping them down with incredible swiftness, and Bart knew that it would be folly to do more than go with it, striving gently the while to guide his course towards some projecting rocks upon the bank. There was the possibility, too, of finding some eddy which might lead him shoreward; and after fighting hard to get a hold upon a piece of smooth stone that promised well, but from which he literally seemed to be plucked by the rushing water, Bart found himself in a deep, still pool, round which he was swept twice, and, to his horror, nearer each time towards the centre, where, with an agonising pang, he felt that he might be sucked down.

Dreading this, he made a desperate effort, and once more reached the very edge of the great, calm, swirling pool just as the bushes on the bank were parted with a loud rush, and the Beaver literally bounded into the water, to render such help that when, faint and exhausted, they all reached a shallow, rocky portion of the stream a quarter of a mile below where Bart had made his plunge, the chief was ready to lift out the object the lad had tried to save, and then hold out his hand and help the lad ashore.

The next minute they were striving all they knew to try and resuscitate him whom Bart had nearly lost his life in trying to save, the interpreter joining them to lend his help; and as they worked, trying the plan adopted by the Indians in such a case, the new-comer told Bart how the accident had occurred.

His words amounted to the statement that while the speaker and the chief had been collecting sticks for a fire to roast a salmon they had speared with a sharp, forked stick, they had seen the Doctor busily rinsing the sand in a shallow pool of the rocks, well out, where the stream ran fast. They had not anticipated danger, and were busy over their preparations, when looking up all at once, they found the Doctor was gone.

Even then they did not think there was anything wrong, believing that while they were busy their leader had gone to some other part among the rocks, till, happening to glance down the stream some minutes later, the Beaver's quick eyes had caught sight of the bright tin bowl which the Doctor had been using to rinse the sand in his hunt for gold, floating on the surface a hundred yards below, and slowly sailing round and round in an eddy.

This started them in search of the drowning man, with the result that they reached Bart in time to save both.

For after a long and arduous task the Doctor began to show signs of returning life, and at last opened his eyes and stared about him like one who had just awakened from a dream.

"What—what has happened?" he asked. "Did—did I slip from the rocks, or have I been asleep?"

He shuddered, and struggled into a sitting position, then thoroughly comprehending after a few minutes what had passed:

"Who saved me?" he asked quickly.

The Beaver seemed to understand the drift of the question, for he pointed with a smile to Bart.

"You?" exclaimed the Doctor.

"Oh, I did nothing," said Bart modestly. "I saw you floating down towards me, and tried to pull you on a rock; instead of doing which, you pulled me in, and we swam down together till I got near the shore, and then I could do no more. It was the Beaver there who saved us."

The Doctor rose and grasped the chief's hand, wringing it warmly.

"Where's Joses?" he said sharply.

No one knew.

"Let us go back," said the Doctor; "perhaps we shall meet him higher up;" and looking faint and utterly exhausted, he followed the two Indians as they chose the most easy part of the valley for walking, the Doctor's words proving to be right, for they came upon Joses toiling down towards the passage leading to the plain with six heavy fish hanging from a tough wand thrust through their gills.

They reached the chimney, as Bart christened it, just about the same time as Joses, who stared as he caught sight of the saturated clothes.

"What! been in after the fish?" he said with a chuckle. "I got mine, master, without being wet."

"We've had a narrow escape from drowning, Joses," said the Doctor, hoarsely.

"That's bad, master, that's bad," cried Joses. "It all comes o' my going away and leaving you and Master Bart, there; but I thought a few o' these salmon chaps would be good eating, so I went and snared 'em out with a bit o' wire and a pole."

"I shall soon be better, Joses," replied the Doctor. "The accident would have happened all the same whether you had been there or no. Let us get back to the camp."

"Are we going to leave them beautiful fish the Beaver and old Speechworks here have caught and cooked?" asked Joses, regretfully.

"No," said the Doctor, sinking down upon a stone, "let us rest and eat them. We shall not hurt out here in this bright sunshine, Bart, and we'll wring some of the water out of our clothes, and have less weight to carry."

This speech gave the greatest of satisfaction, for the party were ravenously hungry, and the halt was not long enough to do any one hurt, for the broiled salmon was rapidly eaten. Then they started, and after a rather toilsome climb, ascended once more to the level of the plain, and reaching the waggons learned that all was well, before proceeding to the Doctor's quarters in his tent at the top of the mountain.

Chapter Thirty.: The Beaver sniffs Danger.

"There's something wrong, Master Bart," said Joses that evening, as Bart, rejoicing in the luxury of well-dried clothes, sat enjoying the beauty of the setting sun, and thinking of the glories of the canyon, longing to go down again and spend a day spearing trout and salmon for the benefit of the camp.

"Wrong, Joses!" cried Bart, leaping up. "What's wrong?"

"Dunno," said Joses, gruffly, "and not knowing, can't say."

"Have you seen anything, then?"

"No."

"Have you heard of anything?"

"No."

"Has anybody brought bad news?"

"No."

"Then what is it?" cried Bart. "Why don't you speak."

"'Cause I've nothing to say, only that I'm sure there's something wrong."

"But why are you sure?"

"Because the Beaver's so busy."

"What is he doing?"

"All sorts of things. He hasn't said anything, but I can see by his way that he sniffs danger somewhere. He's getting all the horses into the cavern stable, and making his men drive all the cattle into the corral, and that means there's something wrong as sure as can be. Injun smells danger long before it comes. There's no deceiving them."

"Let's go and see him, Joses," cried Bart; and, shouldering their rifles, they walked past the drawn-up rows of empty waggons, whose stores were all high up on the mountain.

As they reached the entrance to the corral the Indians had driven in the last pair of oxen, while the horses and mules were already in their hiding-place.

"Did the Doctor order this?" asked Bart.

"Not he, sir: he's busy up above looking at the silver they dug out while we were down in the canyon. It's all the Beaver's doing, Master Bart, and you may take it for granted there's good cause for it all."

"Ah, Beaver," said Bart, as the chief came out of the corral, "why is this?"

"Indian dog. Apaché," said the chief, pointing out towards the plain.

Bart turned sharply round and gazed in the indicated direction, but he could see nothing, neither could Joses.

The Beaver smiled with a look of superior wisdom.

"The Beaver-with-Sharp-Teeth," said the interpreter, coming up, "hears the Indian dog, the enemies of his race, on the wind; and he will not stampede the horses and cattle, but leave the bones of his young men upon the plain."

"But where are the Apachés?" cried Bart. "Oh, he means, Joses, that they are out upon the plain, and that it is wise to be ready for them."

"Yes; he means that they are out upon the plain, and that they are coming to-night, my lad," said Joses. Then, turning to the chief, he patted the lock of his rifle meaningly, and the chief nodded, and said, "Yes."

"Come," he said directly after, and he led the frontiersman and Bart to the entrance of the stable, where his followers were putting the last stones in position. Then he took them to the corral, which was also thoroughly well secured with huge stones; and the Indians now took up their rifles, and resuming their ordinary sombre manner, stood staring indifferently about them.

Just then there was a loud hail, and turning quickly round, Bart saw the Doctor waving his hand to them to join him.

"Indians are on the plains," exclaimed the Doctor. "I saw them from the top of the castle,"—he had taken to calling the mountain rock "the castle,"—"with the glass. They are many miles away, but they may be enemies, and we must be prepared. Get the horses secured, Joses; and you, interpreter, ask the Beaver to see to the cattle."

"All safely shut in, sir," said Bart, showing his teeth; "the Beaver felt that there was danger an hour ago, and everything has been done."

"Capital!" cried the Doctor; "but how could he tell?"

"That's the mystery," replied Bart, "but he said there were Indian dogs away yonder on the plains."

"Indian dog, Apaché," said the Beaver, scowling, and pointing towards the plain.

"Yes, that's where they are," said the Doctor, nodding; "he is quite right, and this being so, we must get up into our castle and man the walls. Let me see first if all is safe."

He walked to both entrances, and satisfied himself, saying:

"Yes; they could not be better, but, of course, all depends upon our covering them from above with our rifles, for the Apachés could pull those rocks down as easily as we put them there. Now then, let us go up; the waggons are fortunately empty enough."

The Doctor led the way, pausing, however, to mount a waggon and take a good look-out into the plain, which he swept with his glass, but only to close it with a look of surprise.

"I can see nothing from here," he said, "but we may as well be safe;" and entering the slit in the rock they called the gateway, he drew aside for the last few "greasers," who had been tending the cattle, to mount before him; then Joses, Bart, the Beaver, and his followers came in. The strong stones kept for the purpose were hauled into place, and the entry thoroughly blocked, after which the various points of defence were manned, the Doctor, with several of the Englishmen, taking the passage and the gate, while the Beaver, with Joses, Bart and the Indians, were sent to man the ramparts, as the Doctor laughingly called them; that is to say, the ingeniously contrived gallery that overlooked the stable cavern and the great corral.

"You must not spare your powder if the cattle are in danger," said the Doctor for his last orders. "I don't want to shed blood, but these savages must have another severe lesson if they mean to annoy us. All I ask is to be let alone."

Bart led the way, and soon after was ensconced in his rifle-pit, with Joses on one side and the

Beaver on the other, the rest of the party being carefully arranged. Then the Doctor spread the alarm up above, and the men armed and manned the zigzag way, but all out of sight; and at last, just as it was growing dark, the great plain fortress looked as silent as if there was not a man anywhere upon its heights, and yet in their various hiding-places there were scores, each with his deadly rifle ready to send a return bullet for every one fired by an enemy.

"No firing unless absolutely necessary," was the Doctor's whispered order; and then all was silent while they waited to see if any enemy would really come.

They were not long kept in doubt, for just as the heavens had assumed that peculiar rich grey tint that precedes darkness, and a soft white mist was rising from the depths of the canyon, there was seen, as if arising from out of the plain itself, a dark body moving rapidly, and this soon developed itself into a strong band of Indians, all well-mounted in their half-naked war costume, their heads decked with feathers, and each armed with rifle and spear.

They were in their war-paint, but still they might be disposed to be friendly; and the Doctor was willing to believe it till he saw through his glass that they wore the skull and cross-bones painted in white upon their broad, brown chests, and he knew that they were of the same tribe as had visited them before, and gone off after so severe a lesson.

Still he hoped that they might be friendly, and he was determined that they should not be fired upon without good reason.

A few minutes later he changed his opinion, for, evidently well-drilled by their chief, the Indians charged towards where the tilted waggons were drawn up in the shade of the rock, riding with as much precision as a well-drilled body of cavalry. Then, at a sign, they drew rein in a couple of ranks, about fifty yards from the waggons, and presenting their rifles, without word of warning, fired a volley.

Another volley followed, and another, the thick smoke rising on the evening air, and then, apparently surprised at there being no replying shot, about twenty galloped up with lowered spears, thrust two or three times through the canvas tilts, and galloped back, the whole band sweeping off the next moment as swiftly and as silently as they came, gradually becoming fainter and more shadowy, and then quite disappearing from the watchers' sight.

"They're gone, then?" whispered Bart, drawing a breath of relief.

"Yes; they're a bit scared by the silence," said Joses; "but they'll come back again."

"When?" said Bart.

"Sneaking about in the dark, to stampede the horses and cattle, as soon as ever they know where they are, my boy."

"Yes—come back," said the Beaver in a low tone, and he whispered then to the interpreter.

"Apaché dogs will come back in the night when the moon is up," said the interpreter. "They will steal up to the camp like wolves, and die like dogs and wolves, for they shall not have the horses and oxen."

And just then the Beaver, who seemed to comprehend his follower's English, said softly:

"It is good."

Chapter Thirty One.: In the Watches of the Night.

The hours went by, but no sound or sign came from the plain; the stars started out bright and clear, and in the east there was a faint, lambent light that told of the coming of the moon ere long, but still all seemed silent in the desert.

The Englishmen of the party seemed to grow weary, and began talking so loudly that the Doctor sent sternly-worded messages to them to be silent; and once more all was still, save when some one fidgeted about to change his position.

"Why can't they keep still?" growled Joses, softly, as he lay perfectly motionless, listening to every sound. "They don't understand how a man's life—ah, all our lives—may depend on their being still. Look at them Injuns. They never move."

Joses was quite right. Each Indian had taken his place where appointed, and had not moved since, saving to settle down into a part of the rock. The swarthy, muscular fellows might have been part of the stone for any sign they gave of life.

At last the moon rose slowly above the edge of the vast plain, sending a flood of light to bring into prominence every bush and tree, striking on the face of the mountain, and casting its shadow right away over the plain. From where Bart crouched he could not see the moon, for he and his companions were behind rocks, but there was the heavy shadow of the mountain stretching to an enormous distance; and as he watched it, and saw how boldly it was cut, and how striking was the difference between the illumined portions of the plain and those where the shadow fell, he could not help thinking how easily the Indians might creep right up to them and make a bold assault, and this idea he whispered to Joses.

"'Taint much in their way, my lad," he whispered. "Injun don't care about night-fighting, it's too risky for them. They don't mind a sneak up—just a few of them to scare the horses and cattle and make 'em stampede, and they don't mind doing a bit o' spy of the enemy's camp in the dark; but it isn't often they'll fight at night."

"But you expect them to come, don't you?"

"I don't," said Joses; "but the Beaver does, and I give in. He knows best about it, having been so much more among the Injun than I have, and being Injun himself. I daresay they will come, but they won't stampede our horses, I'm thinking, and they won't get the cattle. They may get to know where the ways are into the corral and the horse 'closure, and perhaps find out the path up to the castle, as the master calls it."

"But they couldn't unless they came close up, Joses."

"Well, what's to hinder 'em from coming close up? They'll crawl through the grass, and from stone to stone in the dark there, and who's to see 'em? My eyes are sharp enough, but I don't know as I should see them coming. Let's ask the Beaver what he says."

"The Beaver-with-Sharp-Teeth has heard all you said," whispered the interpreter, "and he says that the Apachés will come before long to find the way into the camp, and then they will go away again if they do not die."

A curious silence seemed to fall after this, and Bart felt, as he crouched there watching the plains, that something very terrible was going to happen ere long. At another time he would have been drowsy, but now sleep was the last thing of which he thought, all his nerves being overwrought; and as his eyes swept the wide flat plain, he kept on fancying that sooner or later he would see the Apachés coming up to them with the slow, silent approach of so many shadows.

And now it suddenly struck Bart that the shadow of the mountain was shorter than when the moon first rose, and that its edges were more boldly defined, and by this he knew, of course, that the moon was getting higher. At the same time though, soft fleecy clouds began to hide the stars, and at times the shadow of the mountain was blotted out, for the moon was from time to time obscured, and the peculiar indistinctness of the earth seemed to Bart as exactly suited for an enemy's approach.

A slight movement at his side told him that this was the Indians' idea as well, and that to a man they were eagerly scanning the plain and the rugged patches of rock beneath.

Every here and there the fallen masses were piled-up into buttresses, and it was amongst these that, after failing to keep his attention upon the misty plain, Bart let his gaze wander till at last he became convinced that he could see some dark patch in slow motion, and it was long enough before he could satisfy himself that it was only a stone.

He was deceived in this way so often—the various little prominences below him seeming to waver and move, and assume form in accordance with his ideas—that he grew tired of watching, feeling sure at last that there would be nothing to trouble them that night, when suddenly a soft firm hand glided gently and silently as a snake to his wrist, took firm hold of it and pressed it, before rising and pointing down below them into the plain.

Bart followed the direction of the pointing hand, but he could see nothing, and he was about to say so, when gradually sweeping past, a few light clouds must have left the moon partially clear, and with the sudden access of light, Bart could make out two somethings close beside the piled-up rocks, and for some moments he could not be sure that they were men prostrated on their chests crawling towards the entrance to the cattle corral, for they seemed to assimilate with the colour of the earth; and though he strained his eyes, not a trace of motion could he detect.

By degrees though it seemed to him that one of the figures was a man, the other some shaggy kind of crouching beast, till his eyes grew more educated, and he decided that one was an Indian naked to the waist, while the other was wearing his buffalo robe as an additional means of protection.

Bart watched them attentively, and still the figures did not move. At last, however, he saw that they had changed their position, creeping closer to the piled-up rocks, and at last, evidently encouraged by the fact that when the firing took place that evening there was no response, the two savages suddenly rose erect, and went to the piled-up stones that blocked the corral entry.

"How did they know the cattle were there?" said Bart, putting his lips close by Joses' ear.

"Nose!" whispered back the frontiersman, laconically.

"But how could they tell that this was the entrance?" whispered Bart again.

"Eyes!" replied Joses; and he then laid his hand upon Bart's lips, as a sign that he must refrain from speaking any more.

Bart rather chafed at this, and he was growing excited as well, for it troubled him that Joses and the Beaver should have let these two spies go right up to such a treasure as the cattle corral unchallenged; and though he would not have thought of firing at the savages, he could not help thinking that something ought to be done—what he could not say—for the low grating noise he now heard was certainly the Indians moving one of the blocks of stone that had so carefully been placed there that afternoon.

"They're opening the corral, my lad," said Joses just then, in a hoarse whisper; "and if we don't stop 'em we shall be having 'em drive the whole lot of bullocks and cows right away into the plains, and never see a hoof again."

"What's to be done, then?" whispered Bart, whose face was covered with a cold dew, while his cheeks were at fever heat.

"Well, my lad, they seem to have found out the way easy enough by crawling over the cattle trail, and it's a very unpleasant thing to do, but I suppose we shall either have to be robbed, or else we must stop 'em; so as the Doctor won't like all our cattle to go, I'm going to stop 'em."

"It's very horrible," whispered Bart.

"Horrid, my lad; so's having your cattle and horses stole, for if they get one they're bound to have t'other; so is being starved to death; and the worsest of all is being scalped, and that's sure to come if we let them brutes go."

"But it is so horrible to shoot them, Joses," panted Bart.

"'Tis, my lad, so don't you do it. Leave it to us. Hah! that's a big stone down, and the cattle's beginning to fidget. Now, Beaver, what do you say?"

The Beaver answered with his rifle, which gave a sharp report, just as the moon shone out a little more clearly.

"Hit!" said Joses, laconically, as they saw quite plainly the two Indians start back from the rocks right out into the clear moonlight, one of them uttering a fierce, hoarse yell, and staggering as if about to fall, when the other sprang forward and caught him by the chest, holding him up, and, as it was plain to see, forming of the body of his wounded companion a shield to protect himself from the bullets of their unseen assailants.

"They must not go away and tell tales," muttered Joses, as he took aim; but just then the interpreter's rifle rang out, and the half-nude Indian turned partly round, so that they could see in white paint upon his breast, seeming to gleam horribly in the moonlight, the ghastly skull and cross-bones that seemed to have been adopted as the badge of the tribe. Then he fell back into the arms of his friend, who clasped his arms round him, and backed slowly, keeping the wounded man's face to the firing party, while, as if mechanically, the injured savage kept step.

Crack went the Beaver's rifle again, and there was a dull thud telling of a hit, but still the two Indians retreated slowly.

Crack! went Joses' rifle, and he uttered a low growl.

"I'll swear I hit him, but I dunno whether it touched the t'other one—a cowardly skunk, to sneak behind his fellow like that."

Crack—crack—crack—crack! four rifles uttered their reports, which seemed to reverberate from the face of the mountain; and as the smoke rose slowly, and Bart could gaze at the moonlit plain, and try to read the meaning of the fierce yell of defiance that he had heard arise, he saw that the first Indian lay upon his back with the moon shining upon his ghastly, painted breast, while his companion was rapidly disappearing as he ran swiftly over the plain.

The Beaver's rifle rang out again, and he started up into a kneeling position, gazing after the object at which he had fired, while his fingers mechanically reloaded his piece. Then he uttered a low guttural cry of anger, and sank down into his former position.

"Missed him, Beaver," said Joses, quietly.

"No," was the sharp retort. "He was hit, but he will escape to his dogs of people."

This was a tremendous speech for the chief, who, however, seemed to be acquiring the English tongue with remarkable rapidity, the fact being that he had long known a great deal of English, but had been too proud to make use of it till he could speak sufficiently well to make himself understood with ease, and therefore he had brought up the interpreter as a medium between him and his English friends.

They watched through the rest of the night, after communicating to the Doctor the reason for the firing, but there was no fresh alarm. The moon rose higher, and shed a clear effulgence that seemed to make the plain as light as day, while the shadow of the mountain appeared to become black, and the ravines and cracks in its sides to be so many dense marks cut in solid silver.

Daylight at last, with the silvery moon growing pale and the stars fading out. First a heavy grey, then a silvery light, then soft, roseate tints, followed by orange flecks far up in the east, and then one glorious, golden blaze to herald the sun, as the great orb slowly seemed to roll up over the edge of the plain, and bring with it life, and light, and hope.

"Hurrah!" shouted Bart, as he rose from his cramped position in the rifle-pit. "Oh, Joses! my back! my legs! Ah, ah! Oh my! Do rub me! I'm so stiff I can hardly move."

"That'll soon go off, my lad. There, I suppose most of us may go off duty now, for I can't see any Injun out on the plains."

"Yes: hundreds!" said the Beaver, who had been shading his eyes and gazing attentively over the sunlit expanse of rocky landscape dotted with trees.

"Where, Beaver?" said Joses.

For answer the chief pointed right away, and both Joses and Bart tried to make out what he meant, but in vain.

"Your eyes are younger than mine, Bart," said Joses at last, gruffly. "I can't see nothing—can you?"

"No, Joses," replied Bart. "I can see nothing but trees."

The Beaver smiled.

"Ah, it's all very well for you to laugh," said Joses, bluntly, "but you've got eyes that see round corners of hills, and through clumps of wood and bits of mountain. I never saw such eyes in my life."

"My eyes will do," said the Beaver, quietly. "The Apachés are over yonder. They will be on the watch to carry off the cattle or to kill us if they can."

"Yes, that's it," said Joses; "if they can."

Without another word, the Beaver and half-a-dozen of his followers went down the slope, and climbed the stone gateway, to leap into the plain, where, without a word of instruction, they bore off the body of the fallen Indian, and buried it down in the rift where the other two had been laid, after which they returned to partake of the morning meal that had been prepared—fires being lit in various crevices and chasms off the zigzag way; and this meal being partaken of in the bright morning sunshine, seemed to make the dangers of the night appear trifling, and the spirits of the people rose.

In fact, there was no time for despondency. Every man knew when he came out to adventure for silver that he would have to run the risk of encounters with the Indians, and nothing could be more satisfactory than their position. For they had a stronghold where they could set half the Indian nations at defiance, while the savages could not hinder their mining operations, which could be continued on the mountain if they were invested, and at the edge of the canyon or down below, where there was nothing to fear.

The greatest danger was with respect to the cattle, which had to be drawn out to pasture along near the side of the lake, and this was done at once, every available man mounting his horse and forming guard, so as to protect the cattle and pasture his horse at the same time.

This was carried on for some days, and a careful watch was kept out towards the plain; but though bodies of Indians were seen manoeuvring in the distance, none approached the mountain, whose flag waved out defiance; and as night after night passed without alarm, there were some of the party sanguine enough to say that the Indians had had their lesson and would come no more.

"What do you say to that, Beaver?" said Joses, laying his hand upon the chiefs shoulder, and looking him in the face.

"Indian dog of Apaché never forgives," he replied quietly. "They may come to-day—to-morrow—next moon. Who can tell when the Apaché will come and strike? But he will come."

"There, Master Bart, hear that!" said Joses. "How about going down into the canyon to spear salmon now?"

"The young chief, Bart, can go and spear salmon in the river," said the Beaver, whose face lit up at the prospect of engaging in something more exciting than watching cattle and taking care that they did not stray too far. "The Beaver and his young men will take care the Apachés do not come without warning."

Chapter Thirty Two.: Spearing Salmon under Difficulties.

The undertaking of the chief was considered sufficient, and as a change of food would be very acceptable to the little mining colony, the Doctor made no difficulty about the matter, so the Beaver sent out scouts into the plain to give the earliest notice of the appearance of danger, and to supplement this, the Doctor posted Harry, their English follower, in the best position on the mountain, with the powerful glass, so that he might well sweep the plain, and give an earlier notice of the enemy's coming than even the Indians could supply.

The Beaver looked very hard at the telescope, and said that it was very great medicine, evidently feeling for it a high degree of respect. Then certain other arrangements having been made, including the choice of half-a-dozen of the Mexican greasers to carry the salmon that Bart said laughingly they had not yet caught, the fishing party, which included Bart, Joses, the Beaver, the interpreter, and six more Indians, all started for the patch of forest.

They were all well-armed, and, in addition to their weapons, the Indians had contrived some ingeniously formed three-pronged spears, keen as lancets, and well barbed, ready for use in the war against the fish.

The deep rift leading down to the canyon was soon found, and this time Bart approached cautiously, lest there should be another of the rattle-tailed snakes lurking in a crevice of the rock; but this time they had nothing of the kind to encounter. A magnificent deer, though, sprang from a dense thicket, and Bart's rifle, like that of Joses, was at his shoulder on the instant.

"No, no!" cried the Beaver, eagerly; and they lowered the pieces.

"Ah!" cried Bart, in a disappointed tone, "I had, just got a good sight of him. I know I should not have missed."

"The Beaver's right, Master Bart," said Joses, quietly. "If we fired, the sound might travel to the Apachés, and bring 'em down upon us. Best not, my lad. We'll get the salmon without our guns."

They entered the "chimney," and, acquainted now with its peculiarities, the party descended much more quickly than on the previous occasion. The way was clearer, too, the vines and tangled growth having been cleared at the first descent, when pieces of rock were removed, and others placed in clefts and cracks to facilitate the walking, so that, following the same plan again, there was a possibility of the slope becoming in time quite an easy means of communication between the canyon and the plain.

They reached the bottom in safety, and probably to make sure that there should be no such accident as that to the Doctor occur unseen, the chief took the precaution of planting the party on rocks out in the stream well in view one of the other, and just where the fish would pass. He then set a couple of his men to watch for danger, and the spearing began.

"Now, Master Bart," said Joses, "sling your rifle as I do, and let's see what you can do in spearing salmon."

"Hadn't we better leave our rifles ashore there, under the trees?" replied Bart.

"Yes, my lad, if you want to be taken at a disadvantage. Why, Master Bart, I should as soon think of leaving an arm or a leg ashore as my rifle. No, my lad, there's no peace times out here; so no matter how inconvenient it may be, sling your piece, and be always prepared for the worst."

"Oh, all right, Joses," replied Bart, pettishly, and he slung his rifle.

"Oh, it's of no use for you to be huffy, my lad," growled Joses. "You never know when danger's coming. I knowed a young fellow once up in the great north plains. He'd been across the Alkali Desert in a bad time, and had been choked with the heated dust and worried with the nasty salty stuff that had filled his eyes and ears, so that when he got to a branch of one of the rivers up there that was bubbling over rocks and stones just as this may be, and—ah, stoopid! Missed him!" cried Joses, after making a tremendous stab at a salmon.

"Well, Joses?"

Well! no, it wasn't well. He thought he must have a good swim, and so he took off his clothes, laid his rifle up against the trunk of a big pine-tree, and in he went, and began splashing about in the beautiful cool clear water, which seemed to soften his skin, and melt off quite a nasty salt crust that had made him itchy and almost mad for days.

Well, this was so good that he swam farther and farther, till he swam right across to where the stream ran fast right under the steep rock, not so big as this, but still so big and steep that a man could not have climbed up it at the best of times, and—"Got him, my lad?" he exclaimed, as he saw Bart make a vigorous thrust with his spear.

"Yes, I have him," cried Bart, excitedly, as he struggled with the vigorous fish, a large one of fourteen or fifteen pounds' weight, one which he successfully drew upon the rocks, and after gloating over its silvery beauty, carried to the shore, returning just in time to see Joses strike down his fish-spear, and drag out a fish a little larger than the first one caught.

"That's a fine one, Master Bart," growled Joses, as he set off to step from stone to stone to the bank, while Bart, eager and excited, stood with poised spear, gazing intently down into the clear depths for the next beauty that should come within his reach.

Just then one came up stream, saw the danger impending, and went off like a flash through the water, turning slightly on his side and showing his great silvery scales.

"Too late for him, Joses," cried Bart.

"Ah, you must be sharp with them, my lad, I can tell you," cried his companion. "Well, as I was telling of you, the rock on the opposite side of the river rose up like a wall, and there was just a shelf of stone big enough for a man to land on before he tried to swim back. Those stones, too, were right in the sunshine, and the wall behind them was just the same, and they'd be nice and warm."

"How do you know, Joses?"

"How do I know? because I've swum across that river often, and it's very cold—so cold that you're glad to get out and have a good warm on the rocks before you try to swim back. Got him again?"

"Yes," replied Bart, who had made a successful thrust. "Only a small one though."

"Not so bad, my lad; not so bad. He's a good eight or nine pounds. Well, as I was telling you, this young man got out on the bit of a shelf, and was warming himself, when his eyes nearly jumped out of his head, for he saw half-a-dozen Injuns come from among the pine-trees, and one of them, when he saw that young man there, ran loping towards where the gun stood, caught it up, and took a quick aim at him. Now, then—Ah, I've got you this time," cried Joses, spearing the largest fish yet caught, dragging it out of the water, and taking it ashore.

"Fine one, Joses?" cried Bart.

"Yes; he's a pretty good one. Ah, you missed him again. It wants a sharp poke, my lad. Well, now then," he added, as Bart, recovered himself after an ineffectual thrust, "what ought that young man to have done, Master Bart?"

"Taken a header into the river, dived, and swum for his life."

"Right, boy; but he was so scared and surprised that he sat there staring at the Injun, and gave him a chance to fire at him, being so near that the shot whistled by his ear and flattened on the rock behind, and fell on the shelf where he was sitting."

"That woke him up, I suppose?" said Bart.

"It just did, my lad; and before the Indians knew where he was, he went plop into the river and disappeared, and the Injun ran down to catch him as he came up again."

"And," said Bart, quickly, "they didn't catch sight of his head when he came above the water, because he swam up with the eddy into a dark pool among some rocks, and squatted there, with only his nose above the water, till they thought he was drowned, and went, and then he crept out."

"Why, how did you know?" growled Joses.

"Because you've told me half-a-dozen times before. I recollect now," said Bart, "only you began it in a different way, so that I thought it was a new story; and you were that young man, Joses."

"Course I was," growled the other; "but hang me if I tell you a story again."

"Never mind, Joses; here's another," cried Bart, laughing.

"And here's a bigger one, Master Bart," said Joses, chuckling.

"What splendid sport!" cried Bart, as he followed Joses ashore with his prize, and added it to the silvery heap.

"Ay, it ain't amiss. We shall give them a reg'lar treat in the camp, that we shall."

"Look, Joses, the Beaver's got a monster. He has let it go. What's he bounding ashore for like that?"

"Quick, Master Bart—danger!" cried Joses, excitedly, as a warning cry rang along the river. "Look out! This way!"

"What's the danger?" cried Bart, leaping ashore and un-slinging his rifle.

"Injun, my lad; don't you see 'em? they're coming down the canyon. This way. Never mind the fish; make straight for the chimney. We can hold that again 'em anyhow."

Crack—crack! went a couple of rifles from some distance up the river, and the bullets cut the boughs of the trees above their heads.

Bart's immediate idea was to sink down amongst the herbage for cover and return the shot, but the Beaver made a rush at him, shouting, "No, no, no!" and taking his place, began to return the fire of the approaching Indians, bidding Bart escape.

"I don't like leaving all that fish after all, Master Bart," said Joses; "they'd be so uncommon good up yonder. Go it, you skunks! fire away, and waste your powder! Yah! What bad shots your savages are! I don't believe they could hit our mountain upstairs there! Hadn't we better stop and drive them back, Beaver, and let the greasers carry away the fish?"

Crack—crack—crack! rattled the rifles; and as the faint puffs of smoke could be seen rising above the bushes and rocks high up the canyon, the sounds of the firing echoed to and from the rocky sides till they died away in the distance, and it seemed at last, as the firing grew a little hotter, and was replied to briskly by Joses and the Indians, that fifty or sixty people were firing on either side.

The attack was so fairly responded to that the Apachés were checked for the time, and Joses raised himself from the place he had made his rifle-pit, and called to the Mexican greasers to run and pick up the fish, while he and the Indians covered them; but though he called several times, not one responded.

"What's come of all them chaps, Master Bart?" he cried.

"I think they all got to the chimney, and began to climb up," replied Bart.

"Just like 'em," growled Joses. "My word, what a brave set o' fellows they are! I don't wonder at the Injun looking down upon 'em and making faces, as if they was an inferior kind of beast. Ah, would you?"

Joses lowered himself down again, for a bullet had whizzed by in unpleasant proximity to his head.

"Are you hurt, Joses?" cried Bart, half rising to join him.

"Keep down, will you, Master Bart! Hurt me? No. They might hit you. I say, have you fired yet?"

"Yes, three times," replied Bart; "but I fired over their heads to frighten them."

"Hark at that!" cried Joses; "just as if that would frighten an Injun. It would make him laugh and come close, because you were such a bad shot. It does more harm than good, my lad."

Crack!

Joses' rifle uttered its sharp report just then, and the firing ceased from a spot whence shot after shot had been coming with the greatest regularity, and the rough fellow turned grimly to his young companion.

"I don't like telling you to do it, Master Bart, because you're such a young one, and it seems, of course, shocking to say shoot men. But then you see these ain't hardly like men; they're more like rattlesnakes. We haven't done them no harm, and we don't want to do them no harm, but all the same they will come and they'll kill the lot of us if they can; so the time has come when you must help us, for you're a good shot, my lad, and every bullet you put into the Injun means one more chance for us to save our scalps, and help the Doctor with his plans."

"Must I fire at them then, Joses?" said Bart, sadly.

"Yes, my lad, you must. They're five or six times as many as we are, and they're coming slowly on, creeping from bush to bush, so as to get a closer shot at us. There, I tell you what you do; fire at their chests, aim right at the painted skull they have there. That'll knock 'em down and stop 'em, and it'll comfort you to think that they may get better again."

"Don't talk foolery, Joses," cried Bart, angrily, "Do you think I'm a child?"

Joses chuckled, and took aim at a bush that stood above a clump of rocks, one from which another Indian was firing regularly; but just then the Beaver's rifle sent forth its bullet, and Bart saw an Indian spring up on to the rocks, utter a fierce yell, shake his rifle in the air, and then fall headlong into the river.

"Saved my charge," said Joses, grimly. "There, I won't fool about with you, Master Bart, but tell you the plain truth. It's struggle for life out here; kill or be killed; and you must fight for yourself and your friends like a man. For it isn't only to serve yourself, lad, but others. It's stand by one another out here, man by man, and make enemies feel that you are strong, or else make up your mind to go under the grass."

Bart sighed and shuddered, for he more than once realised the truth of what his companion said. But he hesitated no longer, for these savages were as dangerous as the rattlesnakes of the plains, and he felt that however painful to his feelings, however dreadful to have to shed human blood, the time had come when he must either stand by his friends like a man, or slink off like a cur.

Bart accepted the stern necessity, and watching the approach of the Indians, determined only to fire when he saw pressing need.

The consequence was that a couple of minutes later he saw an Indian dart from some bushes, and run a dozen yards to a rock by the edge of the swift river, disappear behind it, and then suddenly his head and shoulders appeared full in Bart's view; the Indian took quick aim, and as the smoke rose from his rifle the Beaver uttered a low hissing sound, and Bart knew that he was hit.

Not seriously apparently, for there was a shot from his hiding-place directly after, and then Bart saw the Indian slowly draw himself up into position again, partly over the top of the rock, from whence he was evidently this time taking a long and careful aim at the brave chief, who was risking his life for the sake of his English friends.

Bart hesitated no longer. Joses had said that he was a good shot. He was, and a quick one; and never was his prowess more needed than at that moment, when, with trembling hands, he brought his rifle to bear upon the shoulders of the savage. Then for a moment his muscles felt like iron; he drew the trigger, and almost simultaneously the rifle of the savage rang out. Then, as the smoke cleared away, Bart saw him standing erect upon the rock, clutching at vacancy, before falling backwards into the river with a tremendous splash; and as Bart reloaded, his eyes involuntarily turned towards the rushing stream, and he saw the inanimate body swept swiftly by.

"What have I done!" he gasped, as the cold sweat broke out upon his brow. "Horrible! What a deed to do!" and his eyes seemed fixed upon the river in the vain expectation of seeing the wretched savage come into sight again.

Just then he felt a touch upon his arm, and turning sharply found himself face to face with the

Beaver, whose shoulder was scored by a bullet wound, from which the blood trickled slowly down over his chest.

As Bart faced him he smiled, and grasped the lad's hand, pressing it between both of his.

"Saved Beaver's life," he said, softly. "Beaver never forgets. Bart is brave chief."

Bart felt better now, and he had no time for farther thought, the peril in which they were suddenly appearing too great.

For the Beaver pointed back to where the chimney offered the way of escape.

"Time to go," the Beaver said. "Come."

And, setting the example, he began to creep from cover to cover, after uttering a low cry, to which his followers responded by imitating their leader's actions.

"Keep down low, Master Bart," whispered Joses. "That's the way. The chimney's only about three hundred yards back. We shall soon be there, and then we can laugh at these chaps once we get a good start up. We must leave the fish though, worse luck. There won't be so many of 'em to eat it though as there was at first. Hallo! How's that?"

The reason for his exclamation was a shot that whizzed by him—one fired from a long way down the canyon in the way they were retreating, and, to Bart's horror, a second and a third followed from the same direction, with the effect that the savages who had attacked first gave a triumphant yell, and began firing quicker than before.

"Taken between two fires, Master Bart," said Joses, coolly; "and if we don't look out they'll be up to the chimney before we can get there, and then—"

"We must sell our lives as dearly as we can, Joses," cried Bart.

"Good, lad—good, lad!" replied Joses, taking deadly aim at one of the Indians up the river, and firing; "but my life ain't for sale. I want it for some time to come."

"That's right; keep up the retreat. Well done, Beaver!"

This was an account of the action of the chief, who, calling upon three of his men to follow him, dashed down stream towards the chimney, regardless of risk, so as to hold the rear enemies in check, while Bart, Joses, and the other three Indians did the same by the party up stream, who, however, were rapidly approaching now.

"I want to know how those beggars managed to get down into the canyon behind us," growled Joses, as he kept on steadily firing whenever he had a chance. "They must have gone down somewhere many miles away. I say, you mustn't lose a chance, my lad. Now then; back behind those rocks. Let's run together."

Crack—crack—crack! went the Indians' rifles, and as the echoes ran down the canyon, they yelled fiercely and pressed on, the Beaver's men yelling back a defiance, and giving them shot for shot, one of which took deadly effect.

There was a fierce yelling from down below as the savages pressed upwards, and the perils of the whole party were rapidly increasing.

"Didn't touch you, did they, Master Bart?" cried Joses from his hiding-place.

"No."

"Keep cool, then. Now, Injuns! Another run for it—quick!"

A dash was made after the Beaver to a fresh patch of cover, and the firing from above and below became so fierce that the position grew one of dire extremity.

"Look out, my lads!" cried the frontiersman; "they're getting together for a rush. You must each bring down your man."

There was no mistaking the plan of the Indians now, and Bart could see them clustering into some bushes just at the foot of the mountain where it ran perpendicularly down, forming part of the canyon wall. They seemed to be quite thirty strong, and a bold rush must have meant death to the little party, unless they could reach the chimney; and apparently the savages coming up from below had advanced so far that the Beaver had not been able to seize that stronger point.

"Keep cool, Master Bart. We must stand fast, and give 'em such a sharp fire as may check them. As soon as we've fired, you make a run for it, my lad, straight for the chimney. Never mind anybody else, but risk the firing, and run in and climb up as fast as you can."

"And what about you, Joses?" asked Bart.

"I'll stop and cover your retreat, my lad; and if we don't meet again, tell the Doctor I did my best; and now God bless you! good-bye. Be ready to fire."

"I'm ready, Joses, and I shan't go," replied Bart firmly.

"You won't go? But I order you to go, you young dog!" cried Joses, fiercely.

"Well, of all the—look out, Beaver! Fire, Master Bart! Here they come!"

Quite a volley rang out as some five-and-twenty Indians came leaping forward, yelling like demons, and dashing down upon the little party. Two of this number fell, but this did not check them, and they were within fifty yards of Bart, who was rapidly re-charging, when Joses roared out: "Knives—knives out! Don't run!"

The bravery of the Indians, of Joses, and Bart would have gone as nothing at such a time as this, for they were so terribly outnumbered that all they could have done would have been to sell their lives as dearly as they could. In fact, their fates seemed to be sealed, when help came in a very unexpected way, and turned the tide of affairs.

The savage Apachés had reduced the distance to thirty yards now, and Bart felt quite dizzy with excitement as he fired his piece and brought down one of the enemy, whose ghastly, painted breasts seemed to add to the horror of the situation.

Another moment or two, and then he knew that the struggle would come, and dropping his rifle, he wrenched his knife from its light sheath, when suddenly there was a fierce volley from on high—a fire that took the Indians in the rear. Six fell, and the rest, stunned by this terrible attack from a fresh quarter, turned on the instant, and fled up the canyon, followed by a parting fire from which a couple more fell.

"Hurray!" shouted Joses; "now for the chimney. Come, Master Bart! Now, Beaver—now's your time!"

They ran from cover to cover, meeting shot after shot from below, and in a minute were close up with the Beaver and his three men, who were hard pressed by the advancing party.

"Now, Beaver," cried Joses, finishing the re-loading of his piece, "what do you say to a bold rash forward—right to the mouth of the chimney?"

"Yes," said the chief; "shoot much first."

"Good," cried Joses. "Now, Master Bart, fire three or four times wherever there's a chance, and then re-load and forward."

These orders were carried out with so good an effect that the Apachés below were for the moment checked, and seemed staggered by this accession of strength, giving the little party an opportunity to make their bold advance, running from bush to bush and from rock to rock until they were well up to the mouth of the chimney, but now in terribly close quarters with their enemies, who held their fire, expecting that the advance would be continued right on to a hand-to-hand encounter.

Then there was a pause and a dead silence, during which, in obedience to signs made by the Beaver, first one and then another crept behind the bushes to the mouth of the chimney, entered it, and began to ascend. There was a bit of a fight between Bart and Joses as to which should be first, with the result that the latter went first, then Bart followed, and the Beaver came last.

So close was it, though, that as they climbed up the steep narrow rocky slope there was a fierce yell and a rush, and they saw the light slightly obscured as the Apachés dashed by the entrance in a fierce charge, meant to overwhelm them.

Directly after the canyon seemed to be filled with yells of disappointment and rage, as the Apachés found that their intended victims had eluded them just as they had vowed their destruction.

This gave a minute's grace, sufficient for the fugitives to get some little distance up the narrow rock passage, the Beaver and Bart pausing by the top of the steepest piece of rock about a hundred feet above the entrance, which, overshadowed as it was by trees, had a beautifully peaceful appearance as seen against the broad light of day.

All at once there was a loud yell, betokening the fact that the entrance to the chimney had been seen, and directly after a couple of Indians leaped in and began to climb.

Bart's and the Beaver's rifles seemed to make but one report, when the narrow chasm was filled with the vapour of exploded gunpowder, and the two Indians fell back.

"Climb," whispered the Beaver; and Bart led the way, the chief keeping close behind him, till they were on the heels of the rest of the party, who had halted to see if they could be of use.

The entry was now hidden, and they stopped to listen, just as the successive reports of three rifles came echoing up in company with the curious pattering noise made by the bullets, which seemed as if they glanced here and there against the stones, sending fragments rattling down, but doing no farther harm, for the fugitives were not in the line of the shooters' sight.

The retreat went on, with the Beaver and Joses taking it in turn to remain behind at a corner of the rift or some barrier of rock to keep the Apachés in check, for they kept coming fiercely on. Now and then they were checked by a shot, but in that dark narrow pass there was but little opportunity for firing, and the chief thing aimed at was retreat.

The top was reached at last, and as they neared it, to Bart's great delight, he found that there was a strong party there, headed by the Doctor, who had heard the firing, and came to his followers' relief.

The main thing to decide now was how to hold the Apachés in check while a retreat was made to the mountain, where all was right, the horses and cattle being in their strong places, and every one on the alert.

The Beaver decided the matter by undertaking, with one of his men, to keep the Apachés from getting to the top till their friends had reached the rock, where they were to be ready to cover his retreat.

The Doctor made a little demur at first, but the chief insisted, and after an attempt on the part of the Apachés at fighting their way up had been met by a sharp volley, the whole party, saving the Beaver and one follower, retreated to the rock fortress, where they speedily manned all the points of defence, and waited eagerly for the coming of the chief. But to Bart's horror he did not come, while simultaneously there was a shout from the Doctor and another from Joses, the one giving warning that a very strong body of mounted men was appearing over the plains, the other that the savages from the canyon had fought their way up the chimney, and were coming on to the attack.

Chapter Thirty Three.: Mourning lost Friends.

The failure of the Beaver and his follower to put in an appearance made Bart's heart sink down like lead, while Joses turned to him with a dull look of misery in his eye.

"It's bad, Master Bart," he said; "it's very bad. I hates all Indians as hard as ever I can hate 'em, but somehow the Beaver and me seemed to get on well together, and if I'd knowed what was going to happen, it isn't me as would have come away and left him in the lurch."

"No, Joses, neither would I," said Bart, bitterly. "But do you think—"

"Do I think he has escaped, my lad?" said Joses, sadly, for Bart could not finish his speech; "no, I don't. The savage creatures came upon him sudden, or they knocked him over with a bullet, and he has died like an Indian warrior should."

"No," said a sharp voice behind them; and the interpreter stood there with flashing eyes gazing angrily at the speakers. "No," he cried again, "the Beaver-with-Sharp-Teeth is too strong for the miserable Apaché. He will come back. They could not kill a warrior like that."

"Well, I hope you're right, Mr Interpreter," growled Joses. "I hope you are right, but I shall not believe it till I see him come."

There was no time for further conversation, the approach of the enemies being imminent. On the one side, far out on the plain, were scattered bodies of the Apachés, evidently in full war-paint, riding about in some kind of evolution; and, as the Doctor could see with his glass, for the most part armed with spears.

Some of the men bore the strong short bow that had been in use among them from time immemorial, and these could be made out by the thick quiver they had slung over their backs. But, generally speaking, each Indian carried a good serviceable rifle, pieces of which they could make deadly use.

At present there seemed to be no intention of making an immediate attack, the Indians keeping well out in the plain beyond the reach of rifle-ball, though every now and then they gathered together, and as if at the word of command, swept over the ground like a whirlwind, and seemed bent upon charging right up to the mountain.

This, however, they did not do, but turned off each time and rode back into the plain.

"Why do they do that, Joses?" said Bart, eagerly.

"To see all they can of our defences, my lad. They'll come on foot at last like the others are doing, though I don't think they'll manage a very great deal this time."

For the party from the canyon, now swollen to nearly fifty men, were slowly approaching from the direction of the chimney, and making use of every tuft, and bush, and rock, affording Bart a fine view from the gallery of the clever and cunning means an Indian will adopt to get within shot of an enemy.

They had crept on and on till they were so near that from the hiding-place in the gallery which protected the cattle Joses could have shot them one by one as they came along, the men being quite ignorant of the existence of such a defence, as nothing was visible from the face of the rock.

"I shan't fire so long as they don't touch the horses or the cattle," said Joses, "though perhaps I ought to, seeing how they have killed our best friend. Somehow, though, I don't feel to like shooting a man behind his back as it were. If they were firing away at us the thing would be different. I could fire them it back again then pretty sharply, I can tell you!"

Joses soon had occasion to use his rifle, for, finding themselves unmolested, the Indians took advantage of every bit of cover they could find; and when this ceased, and there was nothing before them but a patch of open plain, they suddenly darted forward right up to the cattle corral, the tracks of the animals going to and fro plainly telling them the entrance, as the odour did the men who had crept up by night.

Reaching this, they made a bold effort to get an opening big enough for the cattle to be driven out; but without waiting for orders, the Indians in the rock gallery opened fire, and Joses and Bart caught the infection, the latter feeling a fierce kind of desire to avenge his friend the Beaver.

The rifle-shots acted like magic, sending the Apachés back to cover, where they began to return the fire briskly enough, though they did no more harm than to flatten their bullets, some of which dropped harmlessly into the rifle-pits, and were coolly appropriated by the Beaver's followers for melting down anew.

"Don't shoot, my lads," said Joses before long; "it is only wasting ammunition. They are too well under cover. Let them fire away as long as they like, and you can pick up the lead as soon as they are gone."

The interpreter told his fellows Joses' words, and they ceased firing without a moment's hesitation, and crouched there with their white friends, listening to the loud crack of the Apachés' rifles, and the almost simultaneous fat! of the bullet against the rock.

Not a man in the gallery was injured in the slightest degree, while, as soon as he had got over a sort of nervous feeling that was the result of being shot at without the excitement of being able to return the fire, Bart lay watching the actions of the Apachés, and the senseless way in which they kept on firing at the spots where they fancied that their enemies might be.

The cover they had made for was partly scrubby brush and partly masses of stone lying singly in the plain, and it was curious to watch an Indian making his attack. First the barrel of his rifle would be protruded over some rugged part of the stone, then very slowly a feather or two would appear, and then, if the spot was very closely watched, a narrow patch of brown forehead and a glancing eye could be seen. Then where the eye had appeared was shut out by the puff of white smoke that suddenly spirted into the air; and as it lifted, grew thin, and died away, Bart could see that the barrel of the rifle had gone, and its owner was no doubt lying flat down behind the piece of rock, which looked as if no Indian had been near it for years.

Five minutes later the muzzle of the rifle would slowly appear from quite a different part, and so low down that it was evident the Apaché was lying almost upon his face. This time perhaps Bart would note that all at once a little patch of dry grass would appear, growing up as it were in a second, as the Indian balanced it upon the barrel of his piece, making it effectually screen his face, while it was thin and open enough for him to take aim at the place from whence he had seen flashes of fire come.

Bart saw a score of such tricks as this, and how a patch of sage-brush, that looked as if it would not hide a prairie dog began to send out flashes of fire and puffs of smoke, telling plainly enough that there was an Indian safely ensconced therein.

The Apachés' attitudes, too, excited his wonder, for they fired face downwards, lying on their sides or their backs, and always from places where there had been no enemy a minute before; while, when he was weary of watching these dismounted men at their ineffective toil, there were their friends out in the plain, who kept on swooping down after leaving their spears stuck in the earth a mile away. They would gallop to within easy range, and then turning their horses' heads, canter along parallel with the mountain, throw themselves sidewise on the flank of their horse farthest from the place attacked, take aim and fire beneath the animal's neck, their own bodies being completely hidden by the horse. It is almost needless to say that the shots they fired never did any harm, the position, the bad aim, and the motion of the horse being sufficient to send the bullets flying in the wildest way, either into the plain or high up somewhere on the face of the rock.

All at once this desultory, almost unresisted attack came to an end, as a fresh body of Indians cantered up; many of the latter leading horses, to which the attacking party from the canyon now made their way; and just at sundown the whole body galloped off, without so much as giving the beleaguered ones a farewell shot.

Bart watched them go off in excellent order right away out into the plain, the orange rays of the setting sun seeming to turn the half-nude figures into living bronze. Then the desert began to grow dim, the sky to darken, a few stars to peep out in the pale grey arch, and after a party had been deputed to keep watch, this intermission in the attack was seized upon as the time for making a hearty meal, the sentries not being forgotten.

"And now, Bart," said the Doctor, "I shall keep the gate myself to-night with half a dozen men. I should like you and Joses to watch in the gallery once more with the Beaver's men. These Apachés will be back again to-night to try and drive off the capital prize, if they could get it, of our cattle."

"Very good, sir," said Bart, cheerily; "I'll watch."

"So will I," growled Joses.

"I wish you had the Beaver to help you. Poor fellow!" said the Doctor, sadly; "his was a wonderful eye. The interpreter will become chief now, I suppose."

"Perhaps so, sir," said Bart; "but he says that the Beaver is not dead, but will come back."

"I would he spoke the truth," said the Doctor, sadly. "The poor fellow died that we might be saved, like a hero. But there, we have no time for repining. Let us get well into our places before dark. Joses, can you be a true prophet?" he added.

"What about, master?" said the frontiersman.

"And tell me when I may be allowed to mine my silver in peace?"

"No, master, I'm not prophet enough for that. If you killed off all these Injun, you might do it for a time, but 'fore long a fresh lot would have sprung up, and things would be as bad as ever. Seems to me finding silver's as bad as keeping cattle. Come along, Master Bart. I wish we had some of them salmon we speared."

"Never mind the salmon," said Bart, smiling; "we escaped with our lives;" and leading the way, they were soon ensconced in their places, watching the darkness creep over the plain like a thick veil, while the great clusters of stars came out and shone through the clear air till the sky was like frosted gold.

"Do you think the Apachés will come again to-night?" said Bart, after an hour's silence.

"Can't say, my lad. No, I should say. Yes, I should say," he whispered back; "and there they are."

As he spoke, he levelled his rifle at the first of two dusky figures that had appeared out in the plain, rising as it were out of the earth; but before he could fire, there was a hand laid upon his shoulder, and another raised the barrel of his piece.

"Treachery!" shouted Joses. "Bart, Master Bart, quick—help!"

There was a fierce struggle for a few moments, and then Joses loosened his hold and uttered an exclamation full of vexed impatience.

"It's all right, Master Bart," he cried. "Here, give us your hand, old Speak English," he added, clapping the interpreter on the shoulder, "it's of no use for us English to think of seeing like you, Injun."

"What does all this mean, Joses?" whispered Bart, excitedly, for it seemed marvellous that two Indians should be allowed to come up to their stronghold unmolested.

"Why, don't you see, my lad," cried Joses, "Beaver and his chap arn't dead after all. There they are down yonder; that's them."

Bart leaped up, and forgetful of the proximity of enemies, waved his cap and shouted: "Beaver, ahoy! hurrah!"

The two Indians responded with a cheery whoop, and ran up to the rocks, while Bart communicated the news to the Doctor and his fellow-guardians of the gate, where the lad pushed himself to the front, so as to be the first to welcome the chief back to their stronghold—a welcome the more warm after the belief that had been current since his non-return.

The Doctor's grasp was so friendly that the chief seemed almost moved, and nodding quietly in his dignified way, he seated himself in silence to partake of the refreshments pressed upon him by his friends.

"The Apaché dogs must live longer and learn more before they can teach the Beaver-with-Sharp-Teeth," said the interpreter scornfully to Joses.

"I'm very glad of it," said the latter, heartily. "I hate Injun, but somehow I don't hate the Beaver and you, old Speak English, half—no, not a quarter—so much as I do some of 'em. I say, how could you tell in the dark that it was the Beaver?"

"Speak English has eyes," said the Indian, accepting the nickname Joses gave him without a moment's hesitation. "Speak English uses his eyes. They see in the dark, like a puma or panther, as much as yours see in the sunshine."

"Well, I suppose they do," said Joses, with a sigh. "I used to think, too, that I could see pretty well."

They were back now in the gallery, keeping a steady watch out towards the plain, Bart being with them, and all were most anxiously waiting till the Beaver and his companion should come; for they were steadily endeavouring to make up for a very long fast to an extent that would astound an Englishman who saw a half-starved Indian eating for the first time. Joses and Bart made no scruple about expressing their wonder as to how it was that the Beaver had managed to escape; but the interpreter and his fellows hazarded no conjecture whatever. They took it for granted that their clever chief would be sure to outwit the Apachés, and so it had proved.

At last the Beaver came gliding softly into their midst, taking his place in the watch as if nothing whatever had happened; and in reply to Bart's eager inquiries, he first of all raised himself up and took a long and searching survey of the plain.

This done, he drew the interpreter's attention to something that had attracted his own notice, and seemed to ask his opinion. Then the Indian changed his position, and sheltering his eyes from the starlight, also took a long searching look, ending by subsiding into his place with a long, low ejaculation that ended like a sigh.

"That means it is all right," whispered Joses.

"Yes; all right," said the Beaver, turning his dark face toward them, and showing his white teeth, as if pleased at being able to comprehend their speech.

"Then now tell us, Beaver, how it was you managed to get away."

Without following the chief's halting delivery of his adventures in English, it is sufficient to say that he and his follower kept the Apachés back as they made attempt after attempt to ascend the chimney, shooting several, and so maddening the rest that they forgot their usual cautious methods of approach, and at last gathered together, evidently meaning to make a headlong rush.

This, the Beaver knew, meant that he and his man must be overpowered or shot down before they could reach the pathway of the natural fort, so cunning was brought to bear to give them time.

He knew that the Apachés would be sure to spend some few minutes in firing, partly to distract their enemies and partly to give them the cover of abundant smoke for their approach before they made their final rush; and taking off his feather head-gear, he secured it with a couple of stones so near the top of the rock which sheltered him and his companion that the eagle plumes could be seen by the Apachés as they gathered below.

His companion did the same, and as soon as this was done, they broke away from their hiding-place, and ran a few yards over the soft, sandy soil at the edge of the patch of forest, to some rocks, making deep impressions with their moccasins. Then, taking a few bounds along the hard rock, they found a suitable place, and there the Beaver bent down, his follower leaped upon his shoulders, and he walked quickly backward into the forest.

"And so made only one trail!" cried Bart, excitedly.

"And that one coming from the trees if the Apachés should find it," said Joses, grinning. "Well, you are a clever one, Beaver, and no mistake."

To put the chiefs words in plain English:

"We had only just got into cover when we heard the firing begin very sharply, and knowing that there was not a moment to lose, we backed slowly in among the trees till it grew stony, and our moccasins made no sign, and then my young man stepped down, and we crept from cover to cover, stopping to listen to the yelling and howling of the dogs, when they found only our feathers; and then we seemed to see them as they rushed off over the plain, meaning to catch us before we were in safety. But the dogs are like blind puppies. They have no sense. They could not find our trail. They never knew that we were behind them in the forest; and there we hid, making ourselves a strong place on the edge of the canyon, where we could wait until they had gone; and when at last they had gone, and all was safe, we came on, and we are here."

"They wouldn't have escaped you like that, would they, Beaver?" said Bart, after shaking hands once more warmly, and telling him how glad he was to see him back.

"Escaped me?" said the Beaver, scornfully; "there is not one of my young men who would have been trifled with like that."

This he said in the Indian tongue, and there was a chorus of assenting ejaculations.

"But the Apachés are blind dogs, and children," he went on, speaking with bitter contempt. "They fight because they are so many that one encourages the other, but they are not brave, and they are not warriors. The young men of the Beaver-with-Sharp-Teeth are all warriors, and laugh at the Apachés, for it takes fifty of them to fight one of my braves."

He held up his hand to command silence after this, and then pointed out into the plain.

"Can you see anything, Joses?" whispered Bart.

"Not a sign of anything but dry buffler grass and sage-brush. No; it's of no use, Master Bart, I've only got four-mile eyes, and these Injun have got ten-mile eyes. Natur's made 'em so, and it's of no use to fight again it. 'Tis their natur to, and it arn't our natur to, so all we can do is to use good medicine."

"Why, you don't think that physic would do our eyes any good, do you, Joses?" whispered Bart.

"Physic, no! I said medicine," chuckled Joses.

"Well, what's the difference?" replied Bart.

"Difference enough. I meant Injun's medicine, as they call it. Didn't the Beaver say that the master's glass was all good medicine? He thought it was a sort of conjuring trick like their medicine-men do when they are making rain come, or are driving out spirits, as they call it. No; we can't help our eyes being queer, my lad, but we can use medicine spy-glasses, and see farther than the Injun. Hold your tongue; he's making signs."

For the Beaver had held up his hand again to command silence. Then he drew Bart towards him, and pointed outwards.

"Apaché dogs," he whispered. "Young chief Bart, see?"

"No," replied the lad, after gazing intently for some time; and then, without a word, he glided off along the narrow, rocky, well-sheltered path, and made his way to the Doctor, who, with his men, was upon the qui vive.

"Well, Bart, what is it?" he said, eagerly.

"The Beaver can see Apachés on the plain."

"A night attack, eh?" said the Doctor. "Well, we shall be ready for them. Why have you come—to give us warning?"

"I came first for the glass," replied Bart. "I'll send you notice if they appear likely to attack, sir."

"Then I hope you will not have to send the notice, my lad," said the Doctor, "for I don't like fighting in the dark."

As he spoke he handed the glass, and Bart returned to the gallery.

"Are they still there?" he whispered.

"Yes; Apaché dogs," was the reply. "Good medicine."

"They won't find it so," growled Joses, "if they come close up here, for my rifle has got to be hungry again. I'm 'bout tired of not being left peaceable and alone, and my rifle's like me—it means to bite."

As he crouched there muttering and thinking of the narrow escapes they had had, Bart carefully focussed the glass, no easy task in the deep gloom that surrounded them; and after several tries he saw something which made him utter an ejaculation full of wonder.

"What is it, my lad?" whispered Joses.

"The young chief sees the Apaché dogs?" said the interpreter.

"Yes," exclaimed Bart; "the plain swarms with them."

"Then they're gathering for a big attack in the morning," said Joses. "Are they mounted?"

"Yes, all of them. I can just make them out crossing the plain."

"Well, their horses are only good to run away on," growled Joses; "they can't ride up this mountain. Let me have a look, my lad."

Bart handed the glass, and Joses took a long, eager look through, at the gathering of Apaché warriors.

"I tell you what," he said, "we shall have to look out or they'll drive off every head of cattle and every leg of horse. They're as cunning as cunning, I don't care what any one says, and some of these days we shall open our eyes and find ourselves in a pretty mess."

"The Apaché dogs shall not have the horses," said the Beaver fiercely.

"That's right; don't let 'em have them," cried Joses. "I don't want 'em to go; but here's one thing I should like answered—How are we going to find 'em in pasture with all these wild beasts hanging about, ready to swoop down and make a stampede of it, and drive them off?"

"The Beaver's young men will drive the horses and cattle out," said the Beaver, in tones of quiet confidence, "and bring them back again quite safe."

"If you can do that," said Joses, "perhaps we can hold out; but it don't seem likely that we shall get much salmon from down in the canyon yonder, which is a pity, for I've took to quite longing for a bit of that; and if the Apaché don't take care, I shall have some yet."

Chapter Thirty Four.: Hard Pressed.

Day broke, and the sun rose, displaying a sight that disheartened many of the occupants of the rock; for far out on the plain, and well beyond the reach of rifle-bullets, there was troop after troop of Indian warriors riding gently here and there, as if to exercise their horses, but doubtless in pursuance of some settled plan.

The Doctor inspected them carefully through his glass, to try and estimate their numbers, and he quite came to the conclusion that they intended to invest the rock fortress, and if they could make no impression in one way, to try and starve out its occupants.

"We must make sure, once for all, Bart, that we have no weak points—no spot by which these Indian wretches can ascend and take us in the rear. Suppose you take the Beaver and two of his men with you, ascend the mountain, and make a careful inspection."

"But that would hardly be so satisfactory, sir, as if we went all round the base first to make sure that there is no way up from the plain."

"No, I know that," replied the Doctor; "but that is too dangerous a task."

"I'm beginning to like dangerous tasks now, sir," said Bart; "they are so exciting."

"Well, go then," said the Doctor; "but you must be mounted, or you will have no chance of retreat; and of course you will all keep a sharp look-out in case the Indians swoop down."

Bart promised, and went at once to the Beaver and Joses.

"I'm to come too, ain't I?" said the latter.

"No, you are to help keep guard," was the reply; and very sulkily Joses resumed his place, while the Beaver descended with Bart and four of his men to enter the rock stable and obtain their horses, the rest having to remain fasting while their companions were mounted and ridden out; the Indian ponies in particular resenting the indignity of being shut up again behind the stones by turning round and kicking vehemently.

The Apachés were so far distant that Bart was in hopes that they would not see the reconnaissance that was being made, as he rode out at the head of his little Indian party, after fully explaining to the Beaver that which they were to do.

His first step was to inspect the part of the mountain on the side that was nearest to the chimney, and the chasm into which they had descended to see the silver on their first coming.

This was the shortest portion by far, and it had the advantage of a good deal of cover in the shape of detached rocks, which sheltered them from the eyes of those upon the plain; but all the same, the Beaver posted two of his men as scouts in good places for observing the movements of the foe and giving warning should they approach; the plan being to take refuge beneath the gallery, where they would be covered by the rifles of Joses and their friends.

It was not at all a difficult task to satisfy the most exacting that ascent from the plain anywhere from the gallery to the precipice at the edge of the canyon was utterly impossible; and after carefully examining every crack and rift that ran upwards, the little party cantered back, said a few words to Joses, and then prepared for their more risky task, that of examining the mountain round by its northern and more open side, for there was no cover here, and their path would be more fully in view of any watchful eye upon the plain.

They drew up by the gateway, and had a few minutes' conversation with the Doctor, who said at parting:

"You can soon satisfy yourself, Bart; but give a good look up as you come back, in case you may have missed anything in going."

"I'll be careful," said Bart eagerly.

"Mind that scouts are left. I should leave at least three at different points on the road. They can give you warning at once. Then gallop back as if you were in a race. We shall be ready to cover you with our rifles if they come on. Now lose no time. Go!"

Bart touched Black Boy with his heels, and went off at a canter, but checked his speed instantly, so that he might the more easily gaze up at the mountain-side, while, thoroughly intent upon his task, the Beaver left scouts at intervals, each man backing close in to the rock, and sitting there like a statue watching the plain.

No Indians were in sight as far as Bart could see, and he rode slowly on, inspecting every opening in the face of the mountain, and so intent upon his task that he left the care of his person to the chief, whose watchful eyes were everywhere, now pointing out rifts in the rock, now searching the plain.

It was a much longer distance, and the importance of the task and its risk gave a piquancy to the ride that made the blood dance through Bart's veins. He could not help a little shudder running through him from time to time, though it was almost more of a thrill, and he could not have told, had he been asked, whether it was a thrill of dread or of pleasure. Perhaps there may have been more of the former, for he kept glancing over his right shoulder from time to time to see if a body of Indians might be sweeping at full gallop over the plain.

Half the distance was ridden over, and this gave confidence to the adventurer, who rode more steadily on, and spared no pains to make sure of there being no possibility of the Indians reaching the top from that side.

On went Bart, and three-fourths of the way were passed with nothing overhead but towering perpendicular rocks, impossible for anything but a fly to scale. The Indians had been left one after the other as scouting sentries, and at last, when no one was in company with the young adventurer but the Beaver, the edge of the canyon on this side was well in sight, and only a few hundred yards of the rock remained to be inspected.

"We will do this, at all events," said Bart, pressing his cob's sides with his heels; and he cantered on, for the face of the mountain was now so perpendicular and smooth that there was no difficulty in determining its safety at a glance.

Only about three hundred yards more and then there was the canyon, presenting a barrier of rock so steep, as well as so much higher, that there was nothing to fear on that side. Only these three hundred yards to examine, and the dangerous enterprise was almost as good as done, for every step taken by the horses then would be one nearer to safety. Bart had ridden on, leaving the Beaver, who had drawn rein, looking back at the plain, when suddenly there was a warning cry, and the lad looked over his shoulder to see the Beaver signalling to him.

"A minute won't make much difference," thought Bart excitedly, and instead of turning, he pressed his horse's flanks and galloped on to finish his task, rejoicing in the fact as he reached the canyon edge that he had seen every yard of the mountain-side, and that it was even more perpendicular than near the gateway.

"Now for back at a gallop," said Bart, who was thrilling with excitement; and turning his steed right on the very edge of the canyon, he prepared to start back, when, to his horror, he saw a party of dismounted Indians rise up as it were from the canyon about a hundred yards away, the place evidently where they had made their way down on the occasion of the attack during the salmon-fishing. With a fierce yell they made for the young horseman, but as Black Boy bounded forward they stopped short. A score of bullets came whizzing about Bart's ears, and as the reports of the pieces echoed from the face of the mountain, the cob reared right up and fell over backwards, Bart saving himself by a nimble spring on one side, and fortunately retaining his hold of the bridle as the cob scrambled up.

Just then, as the Indians came yelling on, and Bart in his confusion felt that he must either use rifle or knife, he could not tell which, there was a rush of hoofs, a quick check, and a hand gripped him by the collar.

For a moment he turned to defend himself, but as he did so he saw that it was a friend, and his hand closed upon the Indian pony's mane, for it was the Beaver come to his help; and spurring hard, he cantered off with Bart, half running, half lifted at every plunge as the pony made towards where their first friend was waiting rifle in hand.

"Let me try—draw him in," panted Bart, gripping his own pony's mane hard as it raced on close beside the Beaver's; and with a hand upon each, he gave a bound and a swing and landed in his saddle, just as the Apachés halted to fire another volley.

Black Boy did not rear up this time, and Bart now saw the reason of the last evolution, feeling thankful that the poor beast had not been more badly hit. His hurt was painful enough, no doubt, the rifle-ball having cut one of his ears right through, making it bleed profusely.

But there was no time to think of the pony's hurts while bullets were whistling about them from behind; and now Bart could see the cause of the Beaver's alarm signal, and bitterly regretted that he had not responded and turned at once, the few minutes he had spent in continuing his inspection having been a waste of time sufficient to place all of them in deadly peril.

For there far out on the plain was a very large body of the Apachés coming on at full gallop, having evidently espied them at last, and they were riding now so as to cut them off from their friends, and drive them back into the corner formed by the mountain and the canyon, a spot where escape would have been impossible even without the presence of a second hostile party of Indians to make assurance doubly sure.

"Ride! ride!" the Beaver said hoarsely; and in his excitement his English was wonderfully clear and good. "Don't mind the dogs behind; they cannot hit us as we go."

All the same, though, as Bart listened to their yells and the reports of their rifles, he shuddered, and thought of the consequences of one bullet taking effect on horse or man.

Every moment, though, as they rode on, the cries of the Apachés behind sounded more faint, but the danger in front grew more deadly.

They picked up first one Indian of their party, and then another, the brave fellows sitting motionless in their saddles like groups cut in bronze, waiting for their chief to join them, even though the great body of enemies was tearing down towards them over the plain. Then as the Beaver reached them, a guttural cry of satisfaction left their lips, and they galloped on behind their leader without so much as giving a look at the dismounted Indians who still came running on.

A tremendous race! Well it was that the little horses had been well fed and also well-rested for some time past, or they would never have been able to keep on at such a headlong speed, tearing up the earth at every bound, and spurning it behind them as they snorted and shook their great straggling manes, determined apparently to win in this race for life or death, and save their riders from the peril in which they were placed.

Another Indian of their scouts reached, and their party increased to five, while two more were ahead waiting patiently for them to come.

The wind whistled by their ears; the ponies seemed to have become part of them, and every nerve was now strained to the utmost; but Bart began to despair, the Apachés were getting to be so near. They were well-mounted, too, and it was such a distance yet before the gateway could be reached, where the first prospect of a few friendly shots could be expected to help them to escape from a horrible death. Mercy, Bart knew, there would certainly be none, and in spite of all their efforts, it seemed as if they must lose the race.

How far away the next sentry seemed! Try how they would, he seemed to be no nearer, and in very few minutes more Bart knew that the Indians would be right upon them.

Involuntarily he cocked his rifle and threw it to the left as if getting ready to fire, but the Beaver uttered an angry cry.

"No; no; ride, ride," he said; and Bart felt that he was right, for to fire at that vast body would have been madness. What good would it do him to bring down one or even a dozen among the hundreds coming on, all thirsting for their blood?

In response Bart gripped his pony more tightly, rising slightly in the stirrups, and the next moment they were passing their scout like a flash, and he had wheeled his pony and was after them.

One more scout to reach, and then a race of a few hundred yards, and rifles would begin to play upon their pursuers; but would they ever reach that next scout?

It seemed impossible; but the ponies tore on, and Bart began in his excitement to wonder what would be done if one should stumble and fall. Would the others stop and defend him, or would they gallop away to save their own lives? Then he asked himself what he would do if the Beaver were to go down, and he hoped that he would be brave enough to try and save so good a man.

Just then a rifle-shot rang out in their front. It was fired by the scout they were racing to join.

It was a long shot, but effective, for an Apaché pony fell headlong down, and a couple more went over it, causing a slight diversion in their favour—so much, trifling as it was, that the

Beaver and his party gained a few yards, and instead of galloping right down upon them, the Apachés began to edge off a little in the same direction as that in which the fugitives were rushing.

And still they tore on, while at last the Apachés edged off more and more, till they were racing on about a hundred yards to their left, afraid to close in lest their prey should get too far ahead; and they were all tearing on in this fashion when the last scout was reached, already in motion to retreat now and lose no time, setting spurs to his pony as the Beaver passed, and then came the final gallop to the gateway for life or death.

For now came the question—would the firing of their friends check the Apachés, or would they press on in deadly strife to the bitter end?

"Ride close up to the rock below Joses," shouted the Beaver; "then jump off on the right side of your horse, turn and fire;" and with these words, spoken in broken English, ringing in his ears, Bart felt his spirits rise, and uttering a cheer full of excitement, he rose in his stirrups and galloped on.

The endurance of the little horses was wonderful, but all the same the peril was of a terrible nature; for the ground which they were forced to take close in under the perpendicular mountain walls was strewn with blocks of stone, some of a large size, that had to be skirted, while those of a smaller size were leaped by the hardy little animals, and Bart felt that the slightest swerve or a fall meant death of the most horrible kind.

Twice over his cob hesitated at a monstrous piece of rock. And each time Bart nearly lost his seat; but he recovered it and raced on.

Faster and faster they swept along, the Indian followers of the Beaver urging their horses on by voice and action, while the yells of the Apachés acted like so many goads to the frightened beasts.

Would they hear them on the rocks? Would Joses be ready? Would the Doctor give their enemies a salutation? Would they never reach the gateway?

These and a dozen other such questions passed like lightning through Bart's brain in those moments of excitement; for the rocky gateway, that had seemed so near to the first scout when they set out that morning and cantered off, now appeared at an interminable distance, and as if it would never be reached; while the Apachés, as if dreading that their prey might escape, were now redoubling their efforts, as Bart could see when he glanced over his left shoulder.

But on the little band of fugitives swept, so close together that their horses almost touched; and, unless some unforeseen accident occurred—a slip, a stumble, or a fatal shot—they would soon be in comparative safety.

The Beaver saw this, and, forgetting his ordinary calm, he rose in his stirrups, half turned and shook his rifle at the great body of Apachés, yelling defiantly the while, and drawing a storm of vengeful cries from the pursuers that rose loud above the thunder of the horses' hoofs.

Another two hundred yards, and the gateway would be reached, but it seemed as if that short distance would never be passed; while now the Apachés, taking advantage of the fact that their prey was compelled to swerve to the left, began to close in, bringing themselves in such close proximity that Bart could see the fierce, vindictive faces, the flashing eyes, and eager clutching hands, ready to torture them should they not escape.

Another fierce race for the last hundred yards, with the Apachés closing in more and more, and the fate of the fugitives seemed sealed, when, just as the enemy gave a fierce yell of triumph, rising in their stirrups to lash their panting little steeds into an accelerated pace, the rock suddenly seemed to flash, and a sharp sputtering fire to dart from the zigzag path. Some of the pursuing horses and their riders fell, others leaped or stumbled over them; and as Bart and his companions drew rein close in beneath the gallery, forming a breastwork of their blown horses, and began firing with such steadiness as their excitement would allow, a regular volley flashed from above their heads, and Joses and his companions followed it up with a triumphant shout.

The effect was marvellous,—the great body of Apachés turning as upon a pivot, and sweeping off at full gallop over the plain, leaving their dead and wounded behind, and pursued by many a deadly shot.

This was the result of their surprise, however; for before they had gone far, they turned and charged down again, yelling furiously.

"Don't fire till they're close in, Master Bart," Joses shouted from above; "they've come back for their wounded. Give 'em some more to take."

Joses was right, for the charge was not pushed home, the savages galloping only sufficiently near to come to the help of their friends; and doubtless they would have carried off their dead, but they encountered so fierce a fire from the rock that they were glad to retreat, leaving several of their number motionless upon the plain.

Then they rode on right away, and Bart threw himself down, completely overcome, to lie there panting and exhausted, till the Doctor and Joses came and led him up, the Beaver and his followers staying behind to safely enclose the cavern stable with stones, after they had placed their own ponies and Black Boy within.

Chapter Thirty Five.: How Joses fed the Cattle.

The Apachés seemed to have had so severe a lesson that they kept right away in the plain for the rest of the day; and as it appeared to be safe, the Indians went out with the Beaver to hide the ghastly relics of the attack, returning afterwards to the Doctor to sit in council upon a very important point, and that was what they were to do about the cattle and horses.

This was a terrible question; for while the occupants of the rock fortress could very well manage to hold out for a considerable time if they were beleaguered, having an ample store of meal and dried meat, with an abundant supply of water, the horses and cattle must have food, and to have driven them out to the lake grazing-grounds meant to a certainty that either there must be a severe battle to save them or the Apachés would sweep them off.

"The Beaver and his men will watch and fight for the cattle," said the chief, quietly.

"I know that, my brave fellow; but if they were yours, would you let them go out to graze?" said the Doctor.

"No," replied the chief, smiling; "because the Apaché dogs would carry all away."

"Well," said the Doctor, "we must not risk it. Let us go out and cut as much grass as we can to-day, for the poor brutes are in great distress."

The chief nodded, and said that it was good; and while strict watch was kept from the rock, three parts of the men were hurried down to the nearest point where there was an abundance of buffalo-grass really in a state of naturally-made hay, and bundles of this were cut and carried to the starving cattle.

It was a terribly arduous job in the hot sun; and it made the Doctor think that if matters went on in this way, the silver procured from the mine would be very dearly bought.

Even with all their efforts there was but a very scanty supply obtained, and of that Joses declared the mules got by far the best share, biting and kicking at the horses whenever they approached, and driving the more timid quite away.

Strict watch was kept that night, but no Apachés came, and as soon as it was light the next morning the horizon was swept in the hope of finding that they were gone; but no such good fortune attended the silver-miners, and instead, to the Doctor's chagrin, of their being able to continue their toil of obtaining the precious metal, it was thought advisable to go out and cut more fodder for the starving beasts.

The next day came, and no Apachés were visible.

"We can drive the cattle out to-day, Beaver," said the Doctor; "the enemy are gone."

"The Apaché dogs are only hiding," replied the chief, "and will ride down as soon as the cattle are feeding by the lake."

The Doctor uttered an impatient ejaculation and turned to Joses.

"What do you say?" he asked.

"Beaver's right, master."

"Well, perhaps he is; but we can't go on like this," cried the Doctor, impatiently. "No silver can be dug if the men are to be always cutting grass. Here! you and Harry and a dozen greasers, drive out half the cattle to feed. Bart, you take the glass, and keep watch from high up the path. The signal of danger directly you see the Indians is the firing of your piece. If you hear that fired, Joses, you are to drive in the cattle directly, and we will cover your return."

"Good!" said Joses; and without a word he summoned Harry and a dozen men, going off directly after through the gateway to the corral, saying to Bart, as he went, "Of course, I do as master tells me, but you keep a sharp look-out, Master Bart, or we shan't get them bullocks and cows back."

Bart promised, and took his station, rifle across his knee and glass in hand, to look out for danger, while before he had been there long the Beaver came and sat beside him, making Bart hurriedly apologise for the risk he had caused on the day of their adventure, he never having been alone since with the chief.

"Master Bart, brave young chief," was all the Indian said; and then he sat silently gazing out over the plain, while no sooner were the cattle released than they set off lowing towards the pastures at a long lumbering gallop, Joses and his followers having hard work to keep up with them, for they needed no driving.

In less than half an hour they were all munching away contentedly enough, with Joses and his men on the far side to keep the drove from going too far out towards the plain, and then all at once the Beaver started up, pointing right away.

"Apaché dogs!" he shouted.

Bart brought the glass to bear, and saw that the chief was right.

In an instant he had cocked and fired his piece, giving the alarm, when the garrison ran to their places ready to cover the coming in of the cattle-drivers and their herd, Bart, seeing that Joses had taken the alarm, and with his men was trying to drive the feeding animals back.

But the Doctor had not calculated upon hunger and bovine obstinacy. The poor brutes after much fasting were where they could eat their fill, and though Joses and his men drove them from one place, they blundered back to another, lowing, bellowing, and getting more and more excited, but never a step nearer to their corral.

And all this while the Apachés were coming on at full speed, sweeping over the level plain like a cloud.

The Doctor grew frantic.

"Quick!" he cried; "we must go out to help Joses and his men. No, it would be madness. Good heavens! what a mistake!"

"Let me go with the Beaver and his men to his help," cried Bart excitedly.

"My dear Bart, the Indians will be upon them before you could reach the horses, let alone saddle and bridle and mount."

"It is true," said the Beaver, sternly. "Chief Joses must fight the Apaché dogs himself."

Bart knew they could do nothing, and just then he saw that the Mexican greasers had left the cattle, and were coming at full speed as hard as they could run towards the shelter of the rock.

"The cattle must go," cried the Doctor, bitterly. "It is my fault. Why does not Joses leave them? Harry is running with the others."

"Because poor Joses is too brave a fellow," cried Bart in despair. "I must go to his help; I must indeed," he cried piteously.

"Young chief Bart must stay," said the Beaver, sternly, as he seized the lad's arm. "He would be killed. Let chief Joses be. He is wise, and can laugh at the Apaché dogs."

It was an exciting scene, the Mexican labourers fleeing over the plain, the cattle calmly resuming their grazing, and the cloud of Indian horsemen tearing along like a whirlwind.

The occupants of the rock were helpless, and the loss of the cattle was forgotten in the peril of Joses, though murmurs long and deep were uttered by the Englishmen against him who had sent them out to graze.

In spite, too, of the terrible loss, there was something interesting and wonderfully exciting in the way in which the Apachés charged down with lowered lances, the cattle calmly grazing till they were near; then lifting up their heads in wonder, and as the Indians swooped round, they wheeled about, and went off at a gallop, but only to be cleverly headed and driven back; and then with the Apachés behind, and forming a crescent which partly enclosed the lumbering beasts, they were driven off at full speed fight away towards the plain, gradually disappearing from their owners' eyes.

"Only half as many to feed," said the Doctor, bitterly.

"Poor Joses!" groaned Bart with a piteous sigh.

"Chief Joses coming," said the Beaver pointing; and to the delight of all they could see Joses in the distance, his rifle shouldered, marching quietly towards them, and evidently making himself a cigarette as he came.

Half an hour later he was in their midst.

"Couldn't save the obstinate beasts, master," he said quietly; "they were worse than buffler."

"But how did you manage to escape?" cried the Doctor and Bart in a breath.

"Oh! when I see it was all over, I just crept under a bush, and waited till the Indian dogs had gone."

"Chief Joses too wise for Apaché dog," said the Beaver, with a calm smile. "Beaver-with-Sharp-Teeth told young chief Bart so."

"Yes," said Bart; "and I can't tell you how glad I am."

"Just about as glad as I am, Master Bart," said Joses, gruffly. "I did my best, master, and I couldn't do no more."

"I know, Joses," replied the Doctor. "It was my fault; and the greasers ran away?"

"Lord, master, if we'd had five hundred thousand greasers there it would have been all the same. Nothing but a troop of horse would have brought the obstinate cattle back to their corral. You won't send out no more?"

"No, Joses, not a hoof," said the Doctor, gloomily; and he went to his tent on the top of the mountain to ponder upon the gloomy state of their affairs.

Chapter Thirty Six.: Another Friend comes back.

Watch was set that night as usual, but it came on so pitchy dark that nothing could be made out distinctly a yard away. Bart was with the Beaver and Joses in their old place in the gallery, fortunately well-sheltered by the rock overhead, for the rain came down in torrents, and gurgled loudly as it rushed in and out of the crevices of the rock, finding its way to the plains.

"How uneasy the cattle seem!" said Bart once, as they could be heard lowing down below in the darkness.

"'Nough to make 'em," said Joses, with a chuckle; "they'll have got wet through to-night, and I daresay there'll be water enough in the stable for the horses to nearly swim."

"What a night for the Apachés!" said Bart after a pause, as they crouched there listening to the hiss and roar of the falling waters. "Suppose they were to come; we would never see them."

"But they wouldn't in a night like this," replied Joses. "Would they, Beaver?"

"Beaver don't know. Beaver think much," replied the chief. "He and his men would come if they wanted their enemies' horses; but perhaps the Apachés are dogs and cowards, and would fear the rain."

Towards morning the rain ceased, and with the rising sun the clouds cleared away, the sun shining out brilliantly; and as the Beaver strained over the stones to get a good look into the corral, he uttered a hoarse cry.

"What's wrong?" cried Bart and Joses, starting up from their wearying cramped position.

"Cattle gone!" cried the Beaver; and a moment later, "Horses are gone!"

It was too true; for, taking advantage of the darkness and the heavy rain, the Apachés had sent in a party of their cleverest warriors, who had quietly removed the barriers of rock, and the cattle had followed their natural instinct, and gone quietly out to the last hoof, the horses the same, making their way down to the pastures, where, at the first breaking of day, there was a strong band of mounted men ready to drive them right away into the plain, where the Beaver pointed them out miles away, moving slowly in the bright sunshiny morning.

The alarm was given, but nothing could be done, and the Doctor looked with dismay at the lowering faces of the men who had agreed to follow his fortunes out there into the wilderness.

"You never said that we should meet with enemies like this," said one man, threateningly. "You said you'd bring us where silver was in plenty, that was all."

"And have I not?" cried the Doctor, sharply. "There, now, get to your work; we have plenty of food and water, and we are relieved of the care of our horses and cattle. The Apachés will not interfere with us perhaps now, and when they have gone, we must communicate with Lerisco, and get more cattle. Have we not silver enough to buy all the cattle in the province?"

This quieted the complainers, and they went quietly to their tasks, getting out the ore in large quantities, though it was, of course, impossible to touch the vein in the canyon. That had to be reserved for more peaceful times.

It almost seemed as if the Doctor was right, and that the Apachés would go away contented now; but when Bart asked the Beaver for his opinion, he only laughed grimly.

"As long as we are here they will come," he said. "They will never stay away."

"That's pleasant, Joses," said Bart; and then he began to bemoan the loss of his little favourite, Black Boy.

"Ah! it's a bad job, my lad," said Joses, philosophically; "but when you go out into the wilderness, you never know what's coming. For my part, I don't think I should ever take to silver-getting as a trade."

It was a serious matter this loss of the horses and cattle, but somehow the Indians seemed to bear it better than the whites. Whatever they felt they kept to themselves, stolidly bearing their trouble, while the Englishmen and Mexicans never ceased to murmur and complain.

"How is it, Joses?" asked Bart one day, as they two were keeping guard by the gate. "One would think that the Indians would feel it more than any one else."

"Well, yes, my lad, one would think so; but don't you see how it is? An Indian takes these things coolly, for this reason; his horse is stolen to-day, to-morrow his turn will come, and he'll carry off perhaps a dozen horses belonging to some one else."

Their task was easy, for the Apachés seemed to have forsaken them in spite of the Beaver's prophecy, and several days went by in peace, not a sign being discovered of the enemy. The little colony worked hard at getting silver, and this proved to be so remunerative, that there was no more murmuring about the loss of the cattle and horses; but all the same, Bart saw that the Doctor went about in a very moody spirit, for he knew that matters could not go on as they were. Before long they must have fresh stores, and it was absolutely necessary for communications to be opened up with Lerisco if they were to exist at the mountain.

"I don't know what is to be done, Bart," the Doctor said one day. "I cannot ask the Indians to go without horses, and if a message is not conveyed to the governor asking him for help, the time will come, and is not far distant, when we shall be in a state of open revolution, because the men will be starving."

"Not so bad as that, sir," cried Bart.

"Yes, my dear boy, it is as bad as that I begin to repent of coming upon this silver expedition, for I am very helpless here with these wretched savages to mar all my plans."

It was the very next morning that, after being on guard at the gate all night, Bart was thinking of the times when, for the sake of protecting the cattle, they had kept guard in the gallery over the corral and by the cavern stable, when, out in the bright sunshine at the foot of the mountain, he saw a sight which made him rub his eyes and ask himself whether he was dreaming.

For there, calmly cropping what herbage he could find, was his old favourite who had carried him so often and so well—Black Boy.

"He must have escaped," cried Bart excitedly, "or else it is a trap to get us to go out, and the Indians are waiting for us."

With this idea in his mind he called Joses and the Beaver, showing them the little horse, and they both agreeing that it was no trap or plan on the Indians' part, Bart eagerly ran out and called the docile little steed, which came trotting up and laid its soft muzzle in his hand.

"If he could only have coaxed the others into coming with him," said Bart, "we should have been all right;" and leading his favourite up to the gateway, he coaxed it to enter and climb carefully up over the rugged stones till it was well in a state of safety, for he felt that he dared not risk leaving it outside.

It was almost absurd to see the curious way in which the little horse placed one foot before another, pawing at the road to make sure of its being safe before he trusted it and planted it firmly down, and so on with the others; but Bart's word seemed to give him confidence, and step by step he climbed up till he was in the spot where his master intended him to stay, when he gave a loud snort as if of relief, and stood perfectly still while he was haltered to a peg.

Chapter Thirty Seven.: A wild Night-ride.

"Yes, Bart," said the Doctor, "we have a horse now for a messenger, but I dare not send you; and if you lent Black Boy to the Beaver and sent him, I am sure the governor would never respond to my appeal for help. I should be doubtful even if I sent Joses."

"Black Boy would not let Joses mount him, sir," replied Bart; "he never would."

"I dare not send you," said the Doctor again.

"Why not, sir? I could find my way," replied Bart excitedly. "Trust me, and I will go and tell the governor such a tale that you will see he will send us a squadron or two of lancers, and horses and cattle for our help."

"I do not like sending you, Bart," said the Doctor again, shaking his head. "No, we will wait and see how matters turn out."

The silver-mining went on merrily, and universal satisfaction was felt by the people, who were too busy to think of the rate at which provisions were failing; but the Doctor thought of it deeply, and he knew that help must be sent for if they were to exist.

They had made two or three excursions into the canyon and brought up large quantities of salmon, and what was dearer to the hearts of all, large pieces of virgin silver; and after the last excursion it had been determined to risk the coming of the Indians, and work the rich deposits of silver below, when, the very next morning at daybreak, the Beaver announced the coming of the Apachés.

"And now," he said quietly to Bart and Joses, "the Beaver's young men will get back many horses."

"Yes, I thought that," said Joses, "and I'm willing; but take care of yourselves, my lads; there is danger in the task."

The Beaver nodded and smiled and went his way, while Bart joined the Doctor, who was eagerly watching the coming savages as they rode slowly across the distant plains.

"Bart," he said at last, shutting up his glass, "you are very young."

Bart nodded.

"But I find myself compelled to send you on a very dangerous errand."

"To ride on to Lerisco, sir?" said Bart promptly. "I'm ready, sir; when shall I go?"

"Not so fast," said the Doctor, smiling at the lad's bravery and eagerness. "You must make some preparations first."

"Oh, that will soon be done, sir; a few pieces of dried bison-meat and a bag of meal, and I shall be ready."

"I was thinking," said the Doctor, "that I ought to have sent you off before the Indians came, but I have since thought that it is better as it is, for we know now where our enemies are. If I had sent you yesterday, you might have ridden right into their midst."

"That's true, sir. But when shall I go?"

"If I send you, Bart, it must be to-night, with a letter for the governor, one which, I am sure, he will respond to, when he hears from you of the enormous wealth of the canyon and the mine.

Now go and consult with the Beaver as to the track you had better follow so as to avoid the Indians. I must take a few precautions against attack, for they seem to be coming straight on, and I sadly fear that they mean to invest us now."

Bart found the Beaver, who was watching his natural foes, the Apachés, along with Joses, as they talked together in a low tone.

"I am going to ride back to Lerisco for help," said Bart suddenly.

"You are, my lad?" cried Joses. "I shall go too."

"But you have no horse, Joses," said Bart smiling, and the rough fellow smote himself heavily on the chest.

"It is good," said the Beaver in his calm way. "My young men would like to ride with you, but it cannot be."

"Tell me, Beaver, how I had better go so as to escape the Apachés."

"The young chief must ride out as soon as it is dark, and go straight for the lake, and round its end, then straight away. The Apaché dogs will not see him; if they do, they will not catch him in the dark. Ugh!" he ejaculated with a look of contempt, "the Apaché dogs are no match for the young chief."

Bart could not help feeling very strangely excited as the evening approached, the more especially that the Apachés had come close on several hundred strong, and they could see them from the rock lead their horses down into the lake for water, and then remount them again, while a couple of small parties remained on foot, and it seemed possible that they intended to make an attack upon the fortress, for they were all well-armed.

"I shouldn't wonder if we have a bad storm to-night, Master Bart," said Joses, as the sun set in a band of curious coppery-coloured clouds, while others began to form rapidly all over the face of the heavens, with a strangely weird effect. "You won't go if the weather's bad, I s'pose, my lad?"

"Indeed but I shall," said Bart excitedly. "If I am to go, I shall go."

The Doctor came up then and seemed torn by two opinions, speaking out frankly to the lad upon the point.

"I don't want to send you, Bart, and yet I do," he said, rather excitedly. "It seems an act of cruelty to send you forth on such a mission, but it is my only hope."

"I'll go, sir," cried Bart, earnestly. "I'll go for your sake and Maude's."

"Thank you, my brave lad," cried the Doctor with emotion, "but it is going to be a terrible night."

"The safer for our purpose, sir," replied Bart. "There, sir, I won't tell a lie, and say I do not feel timid, because I do; but I mean to mount and ride off boldly, and you'll see I'll bring back plenty of help, and as quickly as I can."

"But wait another night, my lad; it will be finer perhaps. There is no moon, and if it clouds over, you will never find your way to the lake."

"Black Boy will, sir, I know," said Bart laughing. "I am keeping him without water on purpose."

"A clever idea, Bart," said the Doctor.

"Yes, sir," said Bart, "but it is not mine. It was the Beaver's notion. Those dismounted Indians are coming right in, sir, I think," he said.

"Yes, without doubt, Bart," exclaimed the Doctor, watching them. "Yes, they mean to get somewhere close up. There will be an attack to-night."

"Then I shall gallop away from it," said Bart laughing, "for I am afraid of fighting."

Two hours later, Black Boy, already saddled and bridled, a good blanket rolled up on his saddle-bow, and a bag of meal and some dried bison-flesh attached to his pad behind, was led down the rugged way to the gate, which had been opened out ready. Joses and the Indians were on either side ready with their rifles as the lad mounted in the outer darkness and silence; a few farewell words were uttered, and he made his plans as to the direction in which he meant to ride, which was pretty close in to the side of the mountain for about a quarter of a mile, and then away at right angles for the end of the lake.

"Good-bye, my boy, and God be with you," whispered the Doctor, pressing one hand.

"Take care of yourself, dear lad," whispered Joses, pressing the other, and then giving way to the chief, who bent forward, saying, in his low, grave voice—

"The Beaver-with-Sharp-Teeth would like to ride beside the brave young chief, but the Great Spirit says it must not be. Go; you can laugh at the Apaché dogs."

Bart could not answer, but pressed his steed's sides, and the brave little animal would have gone off through the intense darkness at a gallop; but this was not what Bart wished, and checking him, Black Boy ambled over the soft ground, avoiding the rocks and tall prickly cacti with wonderful skill, while Bart sat there, his ears attent and nostrils distended, listening for the slightest sound of danger, as the Indians might be swarming round him for aught he knew; and as he thought it possible that one of the dismounted bodies might be creeping up towards the gateway close beneath the rocks, he found himself hoping that the party had gone in and were blocking up the entrance well with stones.

The darkness was terrible, and still there was a strange lurid aspect above him, showing dimly the edge of the top of the mountain. That there was going to be a storm he felt sure—everything was so still, the heat was so great, and the strange oppression of the air foretold its coming; but he hoped to be far on his way and beyond the Indians ere it came, for the flashes of lightning might betray him to the watchful eyes of the enemy, and then he knew it meant a ride for life, as it would not take the Apachés long to mount.

All at once, as he was riding cautiously along, his rifle slung behind him, and his head bent forward to peer into the darkness, there was a sharp flash, and what seemed to be a great star of fire struck the rock, shedding a brilliant light which revealed all around for a short distance, as if a light had suddenly appeared from an opening in the mountain; and then, close in beneath where the electric bolt had struck, he could see a knot of about a dozen Indians, who uttered a tremendous yell as they caught sight of him, making Black Boy tear off at full speed, while the next moment there was a deafening crash, and it seemed to Bart that a huge mass of the mountain-side had fallen crumbling down.

That one flash which struck the mountain seemed as if it had been the signal for the elements to commence their strife, for directly after the heavens were in a blaze. Forked lightning darted here and there; the dense clouds opened and shut, as if to reveal the wondrously vivid glories beyond, and the thunder kept up a series of deafening peals that nearly drove the little steed frantic.

As to his direction, Bart was ignorant. All he knew was that he ought to have ridden some distance farther before turning off, but that awful flash had made the cob turn and bound away at once; and as far as the rider could make out, they were going straight for the lake with the dismounted Indians running and yelling madly behind.

At least that was what he fancied, for, as he listened, all he could hear was the deafening roar of the thunder, and the sharp crackling sound of the lightning as it descended in rugged streaks, or ran along the ground, one flash showing him the lake right ahead, and enabling him to turn a little off to the left, so as to pass its end.

He knew now that the pealing thunder would effectually prevent the Indians from hearing him, but the lightning was a terrible danger when it lit up the plains; and as he peered ahead, he fully expected to see a body of horsemen riding to cut him off. But no; he went on through the storm at a good swinging gallop, having his steed well now in hand, a few pats on its arching neck and some encouraging words chasing away its dread of the lightning, which grew more vivid and the thunder more awful as he rode on.

After a time he heard a low rushing, murmuring sound in the intervals when the thunder was not bellowing, so that it seemed to rock the very foundations of the earth. It was a strange low murmur, that sounded like the galloping of horsemen at a great distance; and hearing this, Bart went off at a stretching gallop, crashing through bushes and tall fleshy plants, some of which pierced the stout leggings that he wore, giving him painful thrusts from their thorns, till, all at once, the rushing sound as of horsemen ceased, and he realised the fact that it was the noise of a storm of rain sweeping across the plain, borne upon the wind to fall almost in sheets of water, though he passed quite upon its outskirts, and felt only a few heavy pattering drops.

He had passed the end of the lake in safety, and was beginning to be hopeful that he would escape the Indians altogether, but still he could not understand how it was that the little dismounted body of men had not spread the alarm, for he knew that they must have seen him, the ball of light that struck the rock having lit up everything, and he knew that he seemed to be standing out in the middle of a regular glare of light; but after the deafening crash that followed he had heard no more—no distant shouts—no war-whoop. They would be sure to communicate with their nearest scouts, and their bodies of mounted men would have begun to scour the plain in spite of the storm; for he could not think that the Apachés, who were constantly exposed to the warfare of the elements, would be too much alarmed to attempt the pursuit.

"They would not be more cowardly than I am," he said with a half laugh, as he galloped on, with Black Boy going easily, and with a long swinging stride that carried him well over the plain, but whether into safety or danger he could not tell.

All he knew was that chance must to a great extent direct his steps, and so he galloped on with the rain left behind and a soft sweet breeze playing upon his face, the oppression of the storm seeming to pass away, while it was plain enough that the thunder and lightning were momentarily growing more distant, as if he were riding right out of it towards where the air and sky were clearer. Before long, he felt sure, the stars would be out, and he could see his way, instead of galloping on in this reckless chance manner, leaving everything to his horse.

"I can't quite understand it," said Bart; "there must have been some mistake. Of course, I see now. I was riding straight along under the mountain-side when Black Boy swerved almost right round and went off in another direction: that and the darkness threw them off the track, but they will be sure to strike my trail in the morning. Black Boy's hoof-prints will be plain enough in the soft earth where the rain has not washed them away, and they'll come on after me like a pack of hungry wolves. How I wish I knew whether I was going right! It would be so valuable now to get right away before morning."

Bart was getting well ahead, but not in the best direction. He had, however, no occasion to fear present pursuit, for the knot of dismounted Indians whom he had seen close under the rock when the lightning fell lay crushed and mangled amongst a pile of shattered rocks which the electric discharge had sent thundering down, while as Bart was cantering on, full of surmises, where not a drop of rain was falling, the storm seemed to have chosen the mountain as its gathering point, around which the lightning was playing, the thunder crashing, and the water streaming down, so that in places regular cascades swept over the sides of the rock, and tore away like little rivers over the plain.

For the time being, then, Bart had nothing to fear from these unfortunate Apachés; but, as the storm lulled, and another little body of dismounted Indians crept cautiously up to the fallen rocks, their object being to surprise the guards at the gateway, they learned from one of their dying friends of the appearance of the young chief upon his little black horse, and that he had gone right off over the plain.

The sequel to this was that the dead and dying soon were borne away, and a party was formed at daybreak to take steps that would have made Bart had he known, feel terribly uncomfortable, instead of growing hour by hour more confident and at his ease.

Chapter Thirty Eight.: Hunted by Indians.

There's something wonderfully inspiriting in sunshine—something that makes the heart leap and the blood course through the veins, raising the spirits, and sending trouble along with darkness far away into the background.

As the sun rose, flooding the wild plains with heat, and Bart drew rein and looked about after his long night-ride to see that there was hardly a cloud in sight, and, better still, no sign of Indians, he uttered a cry of joy, and bent down and smoothed and patted his brave little steed, which had carried him so far and so well.

Then he had a good look round, to see if he could make out his position, and, after a while, came to the conclusion that he was not so very far out of his way, and that by turning off a little more to the west he would soon be in the direct route.

In patting and making much of Black Boy, Bart found that the little horse was dripping with perspiration, many, many miles running having been got over in the night; and if the journey was to be satisfactorily performed, he knew that there must be some time for rest.

With this idea, then, Bart turned a little to the east, and rode straight for a clump of trees about a couple of miles away, a spot that promised ample herbage and shade, perhaps water, while, unseen, he could keep a good look-out over the open plain.

The patch Bart reached was only of a few acres in extent, and it offered more than he had bargained for, there being a pleasantly clear pool of water in an open spot, while the grass was so tempting that he had hardly time to remove Black Boy's bit, so eager was he to begin. He was soon tethered to a stout sapling, however, feeding away to his heart's content, while, pretty well wearied out by his long night-ride, Bart sat down beneath a tree where he could have a good view of the plain over which he had ridden, and began to refresh himself, after a good draught of pure cool water, with one of the long dry strips of bison-meat that formed his store.

Nature will have her own way. Take away from her the night's rest that she has ordained for man's use and refreshment, and she is sure to try and get it back. And so it was here; for as Bart sat munching there in the delicious restfulness of his position, with the soft warm breeze just playing through the leaves, the golden sunshine raining down amongst the leaves and branches in dazzling streams, while the pleasant whirr and hum of insects was mingled with the gentle crop, crop, crop of Black Boy's teeth as he feasted on the succulent growth around, all tended to produce drowsiness, and in a short time he found himself nodding.

Then he roused himself very angrily, telling himself that he must watch; and he swept the plain with his eyes. But, directly after, as he thought that he must hurry on, as it was a case of life and death, he was obliged to own that the more haste he exercised the less speed there would be, for his horse could not do the journey without food and rest.

That word rest seemed to have a strange effect upon him, and he repeated it two or three times over, his hand dropping wearily at his side as he did so, and his eyes half closing while he listened to the pleasant hum of the insects all around.

Then he started into wakefulness again, determined to watch and wait until a better time for sleep; but as he came to this determination, the sound of the insects, the soft cropping and munching noise made by Black Boy, and the pleasant breath of the morning as it came through the trees, were too sweet to be resisted, and before poor Bart could realise the fact that he was ready to doze, he was fast asleep with his head upon his breast.

The sun grew higher and hotter, and Black Boy, who did not seem to require sleep, cropped away at the grass till he had finished all that was good within his reach, after which he made a dessert of green leaves and twigs, and then, having eaten as much as he possibly could, he stood at the end of his tether, with his head hanging down as if thinking about the past night's storm or some other object of interest, ending by propping his legs out a little farther, and, imitating his master, going off fast asleep.

Then the sun grew higher still, and reached the highest point before beginning to descend, and then down, down, down, all through the hot afternoon, till its light began to grow softer and more mellow, and the shadows cast by the tree-trunks went out in a different direction to that which they had taken when Bart dropped asleep.

All at once he awoke in a fright, for something hard was thumping and pawing at his chest, and on looking up, there was Black Boy right over him, scraping and pawing at him as if impatient to go on.

"Why, I must have been asleep," cried Bart, catching at the horse's head-stall and thrusting him away. "Gently, old boy; your hoofs are not very soft. You hurt."

He raised himself up, stretching the while.

"How tiresome to sleep like that!" he muttered. "Why, I had not finished my breakfast, and—"

Bart said no more, but stood there motionless staring straight before him, where the plain was now ruddy and glowing with the rays of the evening sun.

For there, about a mile away, he could see a body of some twenty or thirty Indians coming over the plain at an easy rate, guided evidently by one on foot who ran before them with bended head, and Bart knew as well as if he had heard the words shouted in his ear that they were following him by his trail.

There was not a moment to lose, and with trembling hands he secured the buckles of his saddle-girths, and strapped on the various little articles that formed his luggage, slung his rifle, and then leading the cob to the other side of the patch of woodland, where he would be out of sight of the Indians, he mounted, marked a spot on the horizon which would keep him in a direct line and the woodland clump as long as possible between him and his enemies, and rode swiftly off.

The inclination was upon him to gaze back, but he knew in doing so he might swerve from the bee-line he had marked out, and he resisted the temptation, riding on as swiftly as his cob could go, and wondering all the while why it was that he had not been seen.

If he had been with the Apachés he would have ceased to wonder, for while Bart was galloping off on the other side, his well-rested and refreshed horse going faster and faster each minute as he got into swing, the Indians began to slacken their pace. There was no doubt about the trail, they knew: it led straight into the patch of woodland; and as this afforded ample cover, they might at any moment find themselves the objects of some able rifle-firing; and as they had suffered a good deal lately in their ranks, they were extra cautious.

The trail showed that only one fugitive was on the way, him of whom their dying comrade had spoken; but then the fugitive had made straight for this clump of trees, and how were they to know but that he expected to meet friends there, whose first volley would empty half the saddles of the little troop?

Indians can be brave at times, but for the most part they are cowardly and extremely cautious. Naturally enough an Indian, no matter to what tribe he belongs, has a great objection to being shot at, and a greater objection to being hit. So instead of riding boldly up, and finding out that Bart had just galloped away, the Apachés approached by means of three or four dismounted men, who crept slowly from clump of brush to patch of long grass, and so on and on, till first one and then another reached the edge of the woody place, where they rested for a time, eagerly scanning each leaf and tree-trunk for an enemy at whom to fire, or who would fire at them.

Then they crept on a little farther, and found Bart's halting-place and the feeding-ground of the horse. Then they came by degrees upon his trail through the wood, all very fresh, and still they went on cautiously, and like men to whom a false step meant a fatal bullet-wound, while all the time their companions sat there upon the plain, keen and watchful, ready for action at a moment's notice, and waiting the signal to come on.

At last this came, for the advanced dismounted scouts had traced the trail to the farther edge of the wood, and seen even the deep impression made by Bart's foot as he sprang upon his steed.

Then the mounted Apachés came on at a great rate, dashed through the wood and came up to their friends, who triumphantly pointed to the emerging trail, and on they all went once more, one man only remaining dismounted to lead the party, while the rest followed close behind.

This little piece of caution had given poor Bart two hours' start, and when the Indians came out of the wood, he had been a long time out of sight; but there was his plainly marked trail, and that they could follow, and meant to follow to the end.

Chapter Thirty Nine.: The End of the Race.

Bart had the advantage of his enemies in this, that as long as he could keep well out of sight across the plains, he could go on as fast as his horse could gallop, while they had to cautiously track his every step. Then, too, when he came to dry, rocky, or stony portions, he took advantage thereof, for he knew that his horse's hoof-prints would be indistinct, and sometimes disappear altogether. These portions of the trail gave the Apachés endless difficulty, but they kept on tracking him step by step, and one slip on the lad's part would have been fatal.

Fortune favoured him, though, and he pressed on, hitting the backward route pretty accurately, and recognising the various mountains and hills they had passed under the Beaver's guidance; and every stride taken by the untiring little horse had its effect upon the lad, for it was one nearer to safety.

Still it was a terrible ride, for it was only after traversing some stony plain or patch of rock that he dared draw rein and take a few hours' rest, while his steed fed and recruited its energies as well.

He would lie down merely meaning to rest, and then drop off fast asleep, to awake in an agony of dread, tighten his saddle-girths, and go on again at speed, gazing fearfully behind him, expecting to see the Apachés ready to spring upon him and end his career.

But they were still, though he knew it not, far behind. All the same, though, they kept up their untiring tracking of the trail day after day till it was too dark to see, and the moment it was light enough to distinguish a footprint they were after him again.

Such a pertinacious quest could apparently have but one result—that of the quarry of these wolves being hunted down at last.

The days glided by, and Bart's store of provisions held out, for he could hardly eat, only drink with avidity whenever he reached water. The terrible strain had made his face thin and haggard, his eyes bloodshot, and his hands trembled as he grasped the rein—not from fear, but from nervous excitement consequent upon the little sleep he obtained, his want of regular food, and the feeling of certainty that he was being dogged by his untiring foes.

Sometimes to rest himself—a strange kind of rest, it may be said, and yet it did give him great relief—he would spring from Black Boy's back, and walk by his side as he toiled up some rough slope, talking to him and encouraging him with pats of the hand, when the willing little creature strove again with all its might on being mounted; in fact, instead of having to whip and spur, Bart found more occasion to hold in his patient little steed.

And so the time went on, till it was as in a dream that Bart recognised the various halting-places they had stayed at in the journey out, while the distance seemed to have become indefinitely prolonged. All the while, too, there was that terrible nightmare-like dread haunting him that the enemy were close behind, and scores of times some deer or other animal was magnified into a mounted Indian in full war-paint ready to bound upon his prey.

It was a terrible journey—terrible in its loneliness as well as in its real and imaginary dangers; for there was a good deal of fancied dread towards the latter part of the time, when Bart had reached a point where the Apachés gave up their chase, civilisation being too near at hand for them to venture farther.

On two occasions, though, the lad was in deadly peril; once when, growing impatient, the Apachés, in hunting fashion, had made a cast or two to recover the trail they had lost, galloping on some miles, and taking it up again pretty close to where Bart had been resting again somewhat too long for safety, though far from being long enough to recoup the losses he had sustained.

The next time was under similar circumstances, the Apachés picking up the sign of his having passed over the plain close beside a patch of rising ground, where he had been tempted into shooting a prong-horn antelope, lighting a fire, and making a hearty meal, of which he stood sadly in need.

The meal ended, a feeling of drowsiness came over the feaster, and this time Bart did not yield to it, for he felt that he must place many more miles behind him before it grew dark; so, rolling up the horse-hair lariat by which Black Boy had been tethered, once again he tightened the girths, and was just giving his final look round before mounting, congratulating himself with the thought that he had enough good roasted venison to last him for a couple more days, when his horse pricked his ears and uttered an impatient snort.

Just at the same moment there was the heavy thud, thud, thud, of horses' hoofs, and, without stopping to look, Bart swung himself up on his horse's back and urged him forward with hand, heel, and voice.

The plain before him was as level as a meadow, not a stone being in sight for miles, so that unless the cob should put his foot in some burrow, there was nothing to hinder his racing off and escaping by sheer speed.

There was this advantage too: Black Boy had been having a good rest and feed, while the pursuers had doubtless been making a long effort to overtake him.

The Apachés set up a furious yell as they caught sight of their prey, and urged on their horses, drawing so near before Bart could get anything like a good speed on, that they were not more than fifty yards behind, and thundering along as fast as they could urge their ponies.

This went on for half a mile, Bart feeling as if his heart was in his mouth, and that the chances of escape were all over; but somehow, in spite of the terrible peril he was in, he thought more about the Doctor and the fate of his expedition than he did of his own. For it seemed so terrible that his old friend and guardian—one who had behaved to him almost as a father should be waiting there day after day expecting help in vain, and perhaps thinking that his messenger had failed to do his duty.

"No, he won't, nor Joses neither, think that of me," muttered Bart. "I wish the Beaver were here to cheer one up a bit, as he did that other time when these bloodthirsty demons were after us."

"How their ponies can go!" he panted, as he turned his head to gaze back at the fierce savages, who tore along with feathers and long hair streaming behind them, as wild and rugged as the manes and tails of their ponies.

As they saw him look round, the Apachés uttered a tremendous yell, intended to intimidate him. It was just as he had begun to fancy that Black Boy was flagging, and that, though no faster, the Indians' ponies were harder and more enduring; but, at the sound of that yell and the following shouts of the insatiate demons who tore on in his wake, the little black cob gathered itself together, gave three or four tremendous bounds, stretched out racing fashion, and went away at a speed that astonished his rider as much as it did the savages, who began to fire at them now, bullet after bullet whizzing by as they continued their headlong flight.

The sound of the firing, too, had its effect on Black Boy, whose ear was still sore from the effect of the bullet that had passed through it, and he tore away more furiously than ever, till, finding that the Indians were losing ground, Bart eased up a little, but only to let the cob go again, for he was fretting at being held in, and two or three times a bullet came in pretty close proximity to their heads.

When night fell, the Apachés were on the other side of a long low ridge, down whose near slope the cob had come at a tremendous rate; and now that the Indians would not be able to follow him for some hours to come either by sight or trail, Bart altered his course, feeling sure that he could save ground by going to the right instead of to the left of the mountain-clump before him; and for the next few hours he breathed more freely, though he dared not stop to rest.

The next day he saw nothing of his pursuers, and the next they were pursuers no longer, but Bart knew it not, flying still for his life, though he was now in the region that would be swept by the lancers of the Government.

He did not draw rein till the light-coloured houses of the town were well within sight, and then he was too much excited to do more than ease up into a canter, for his nerves were all on the strain, his cheeks sunken, and his eyes starting and dull from exhaustion.

But there was the town at last, looking indistinct, though, and misty. All seemed to be like a dream now, and the crowd of swarthy, ragged Mexicans in their blankets, sombreros, and rugs were all part of his dream, too, as with his last effort he thrust his hand into his breast, and took out the letter of which he was the bearer. Then it seemed to him that, as he cantered through the crowd, with his cob throwing up the dust of the plaza, it was some one else who waved a letter over his head, shouting, "The governor! the governor!" to the swarthy staring mob; and, lastly, that it was somebody else who, worn out with exhaustion now that the task was done, felt as if everything had gone from him, every nerve and fibre had become relaxed, and fell heavily from the cob he rode into the dust.

Chapter Forty.: Bart tries Civilisation for a Change.

For some hours all was blank to the brave young fellow, and then he seemed to struggle back into half-consciousness sufficient to enable him to drink from a glass held to his lips, and then once more all was blank for many hours.

When Bart awoke from the long sleep, it was to find Maude seated by his bedside looking very anxious and pale; and as soon as she saw his eyes open, she rose and glided from the room, when in a few minutes the governor and a tall quiet-looking fair-haired man, whom Bart had never before seen, entered the apartment.

"Ah! my young friend," exclaimed the governor, "how are you now?"

"Did you get the letter?" cried Bart excitedly.

"Yes; and I have given orders for a strong relief party to be mustered ready for going to our friend's help," replied the governor, "but we must get you strong first."

"I am strong enough, sir," cried Bart, sitting up. "I will guide them to the place. We must start at once."

"Really, my young friend," said the governor, "I don't think you could manage to sit a horse just yet."

"Indeed I can, sir," cried Bart. "I was only tired out, and hungry and sleepy. The Apachés have been hard upon my trail ever since I started a week—ten days—I'm afraid I don't know how many days ago."

"Here! you must not get excited," said the tall pale man, taking Bart's hand and feeling his pulse, and then laying his hand upon his forehead.

"Are you a doctor?" said Bart eagerly.

"Yes," said the governor, "this is Doctor Maclane."

"Yes, I am Doctor Maclane," said the tall fair man; "and Miss Maude, yonder, said I was to be sure and cure you."

"But I'm not ill," cried Bart, flushing.

"No," said Doctor Maclane, "you are not ill. No fever, my lad, nothing but exhaustion."

"I'll tell you what to prescribe for that," cried Bart excitedly.

"Well, tell me," said the Doctor, smiling.

"The same as Doctor Lascelles does, and used to when Joses and he and I had been hunting up cattle and were overdone."

"Well, what did he prescribe?" said Doctor Maclane.

"Plenty of the strongest soup that could be made," said Bart. "And now, please sir, when may we start—to-night?"

"No, no—impossible."

"But the Doctor is surrounded by enemies, sir, and hard pushed; every hour will be like so much suffering to him till he is relieved."

"To-morrow night, my lad, is the very earliest time we can be ready. The men could set out at once, but we must have store waggons prepared, and a sufficiency of things to enable the Doctor to hold his own when these savage beasts have been tamed down. They do not deserve to be called men."

"But you will lose no time, sir?" cried Bart.

"Not a minute, my lad; and so you had better eat and sleep all you can till we are quite ready to start."

"But you will not let them go without me, sir?" cried Bart imploringly.

"Not likely, my lad, that I should send my men out into the desert without a guide. There! I think he may get up, Doctor, eh?"

"Get up! yes," said the Doctor, laughing. "He has a constitution like a horse. Feed well and sleep well, my lad, and lie down a good deal in one of the waggons on your way back."

"Oh, no, sir, I must ride."

"No, my lad, you must do as the Doctor advises you," said the governor, sternly. "Besides, your horse will want all the rest it can have after so terrible a ride as you seem to have had."

"Yes, sir," said Bart, who saw how much reason there was in the advice, "I will do what you wish."

"That's right, my lad," said the governor. "Now then we will leave you, and you may dress and join us in the next room, where Donna Maude is, like me, very anxious to learn all about the Doctor's adventures and your own. You can tell us and rest as well."

Bart was not long in dressing, and as he did so, he began to realise how terribly worn and travel-stained his rough hunting costume had become. It was a subject that he had never thought of out in the plains, for what did dress matter so long as it was a stout covering that would protect his body from the thorns? But now that he was to appear before the governor's lady and Maude, he felt a curious kind of shame that made him at last sit down in a chair, asking himself whether he had not better go off and hide somewhere—anywhere, so as to be out of his present quandary.

Sitting down in a chair too! How strange it seemed! He had not seated himself in a chair now for a very, very long time, and it seemed almost tiresome and awkward; but all the same it did nothing to help him out of his dilemma.

"Whatever shall I do?" thought Bart. "And how wretched it is for me to be waiting here when the Doctor is perhaps in a terrible state, expecting help!"

"He is in safety, though," he mused the next minute, "for nothing but neglect would make the place unsafe. How glad I am that I ran that risk, and went all round to make sure that there was no other way up to the mountain-top!"

Just then there was a soft tapping at the door, and a voice said—

"Are you ready to come, Bart? The governor is waiting."

"Yes—no, yes—no," cried Bart, in confusion, as he ran and opened the door. "I cannot come, Maude. Tell them I cannot come."

"You cannot come!" she cried, wonderingly. "And why not, pray?"

"Why not! Just look at my miserable clothes. I'm only fit to go and have dinner with the greasers."

Maude laughed and took hold of his hand.

"You don't know what our friends are like," she said, merrily. "They know how bravely you rode over the plains with dear father's message, and they don't expect you to be dressed in velvet and silver like a Mexican Don. Come along, sir, at once."

"Must I?" said Bart, shrinkingly.

"Must you! Why, of course, you foolish fellow! What does it matter about your clothes?"

Bart thought that it mattered a great deal, but he said no more, only ruefully followed Maude into the next room, where he met with so pleasantly cordial a reception that he forgot all his troubles about garments, and thoroughly enjoyed the meal spread before him whenever he could drag his mind away from thoughts of the Doctor in the desert waiting for help.

Then he had to relate all his adventures to the governor's lady, who, being childless, seemed to have made Maude fill the vacancy in her affections.

And so the time faded away, there being so much in Bart's modest narrative of his adventures that evening arrived before he could believe the fact, and this was succeeded by so long and deep a sleep, that it was several hours after sunrise before the lad awoke, feeling grieved and ashamed that he should have slept so calmly there while his friends were in such distress.

Springing from his couch, and having a good bath, he found to his great delight that all the weary stiffness had passed away, that he was bright and vigorous as ever, and ready to spring upon his horse at any time.

This made him think of Black Boy, to whose stable he hurried, the brave little animal greeting him with a snort that sounded full of welcome, while he rattled and tugged at his halter, and seemed eager to get out once more into the open.

The cob had been well groomed and fed, and to his master's great joy seemed to be no worse than when he started for his long journey to Lerisco. In fact, when Bart began to examine him attentively, so far from being exhausted or strained, the cob was full of play, pawing gently at his master and playfully pretending to bite, neighing loudly his disgust afterwards when he turned to leave the stables.

"There! be patient, old lad," he said, turning back to pat the little nag's glossy arched neck once more; "I'll soon be back. Eat away and rest, for you've got another long journey before you."

Whither Black Boy understood his master's words or not, it is impossible to say.

What! Is it ridiculous to suppose such a thing?

Perhaps so, most worthy disputant; but you cannot prove that the nag did not understand.

At all events, he thrust his velvety nose into the Indian-corn that had been placed for his meal, and went on contentedly crunching up the flinty grain, while Bart hurried away now to see how the preparations for starting were going on; for he felt, he could not explain why, neglectful of his friend's interests.

To his great delight, he found that great progress had been made: a dozen waggons had been filled with stores, thirty horses had been provided with drivers and caretakers, and a troop of fifty lancers, with their baggage-waggons and an ample supply of ammunition, were being prepared for their march, their captain carefully inspecting his men's accoutrements the while.

A finer body of bronzed and active men it would have been impossible to select. Every one was armed with a short heavy bore rifle, a keen sabre, and a long sharply pointed lance; while their horses were the very perfection of chargers, swift, full of bone and sinew, and looking as if, could their riders but get a chance, four times the number of Indians would go down before them like dry reeds in a furious gale.

"Are you only going to take fifty?" said Bart to the captain.

"That's all, my lad," was the reply. "Is it not enough?"

"There must have been five hundred Indians before the camp," replied Bart.

"Well, that's only ten times as many," said the captain laughingly, "Fifty are more than enough for such an attack, for we have discipline on our side, while they are only a mob. Don't you be afraid, my boy. I daresay we shall prove too many for them."

"I am not afraid," said Bart, stoutly; "but I don't want to see your party overwhelmed."

"And you shall not see it overwhelmed, my boy," replied the captain. "Do you see this sabre?"

"Yes," said Bart, gazing with interest at the keen weapon the officer held out for his inspection. "It looks very sharp."

"Well," said the captain, smiling, "experience has taught that this is a more dangerous weapon than the great heavy two-handed swords men used to wield. Do you know why?"

"Oh! yes," cried Bart; "while a man was swinging round a great two-handed sword, you could jump in and cut him down, or run him through with that."

"Exactly," said the captain, "and that's why I only take fifty men with me into the desert instead of two hundred. My troop of fifty represent this keen sharp sword, with which blade I can strike and thrust at the Indians again and again, when a larger one would be awkward and slow. Do you see?"

"Ye–e–es!" said Bart, hesitating.

"You forget, my boy, how difficult it is to carry stores over the plain. All these waggons have to go as it is, and my experience teaches me that the lighter an attacking party is the better, especially when it has to deal with Indians."

"And have these men ever fought with Indians?"

"A dozen—a score of times," replied the captain. "Ah! here is our friend the governor. Why, he is dressed up as if he meant to ride part of the way with us."

"Ah! captain! Well, my young Indian runner," said the governor, laughing, "are you ready for another skirmish?"

"Yes, sir, I'm ready now," said Bart promptly. "I can saddle up in five minutes."

"I shall be ready at sunset," said the captain. "My men are ready now."

"I've made up my mind to go with you," said the governor.

"You, sir?" cried Bart.

"Yes, my lad. I want to see the silver canyon and your mountain fortress. And besides, it seems to me that a brush with the Indians will do me good. I want them to have a severe lesson, for they are getting more daring in their encroachments every day. Can you make room for me?"

The captain expressed his delight, and Bart's eyes flashed as he felt that it was one more well-armed, active, fighting man; and when evening came, after an affectionate farewell, and amidst plenty of cheers from the swarthy mob of idlers, the well-mounted little party rode out along the road leading to the plains, with the lancers' accoutrements jingling, their lance-points gilded by the setting sun, and their black-and-yellow pennons fluttering in the pleasant evening breeze.

"At last," said Bart to himself, as he reined up and drew aside to see the gallant little array pass. "Oh! if we can only get one good chance at the cowardly demons! They won't hunt me now."

And in imagination he saw himself riding in the line of horsemen, going at full speed for a body of bloodthirsty Indians, and driving them helter-skelter like chaff before a storm.

Chapter Forty One.: The Lancers' Lessons.

With Bart for a guide, the relief party made good progress, but they were, of course, kept back a great deal by the waggons, well horsed as they were. Alone the lancer troop could have gone rapidly over the ground, but the sight of hovering knots of Apachés appearing to right and left and in their rear, told that they were well watched, and that if the baggage was left for a few hours, a descent would be certain to follow.

In fact, several attempts were made as they got farther out into the plains to lure the lancers away from their stores, but Captain Miguel was too well versed in plain-fighting to be led astray.

"No," he said, "I have been bitten once. They'd get us miles away feigning attacks and leading us on, and at last, when we made ready for a charge, they'd break up and gallop in all directions, while, when we came back, tired out and savage, the waggons would have been rifled and their guards all slain. I think we'll get our stores safe at the silver canyon fort, and then, if the Apachés will show fight, why, we shall be there."

The days glided on, with plenty of alarms, for, from being harassed by the presence of about a dozen Indians, these increased and grew till there would be nearly a hundred hovering around and constantly on the watch to cut off any stragglers from the little camp.

They never succeeded, however, for the captain was too watchful. He never attempted any charges; but when the savages grew too daring, he gave a few short sharp orders, and half a dozen of the best marksmen dismounted and made such practice with their short rifles, that pony after pony went galloping riderless over the plain.

This checked the enemy, but after a few hours they would come on again, and it seemed as if messengers were sent far and wide, for the Indians grew in numbers, till at the time when half the distance was covered, it seemed as if at least four hundred were always hovering around in bands of twenty or forty, making dashes down as if they meant to ride through the camp or cut the body of lancers in two. For they would come on yelling and uttering derisive cries till pretty close, and then wheel round like a flock of birds and gallop off again into the plain.

"I'm saving it all up for them," said Captain Miguel, laughingly, as a low murmur of impatience under so much insult ran through his men. "Wait a bit, and they will not find us such cowards as they think."

"I should like your lancers to make one dash at them though, captain," said Bart one evening when, evidently growing more confident as their numbers increased, the Apachés had been more daring than usual, swooping down, riding round and round as if a ring of riderless horses were circling about the camp, for the savages hung along their horses so that only a leg and arm would be visible, while they kept up a desultory fire from beneath their horses' necks.

"Bah! let the miserable mosquitoes be," said the captain, contemptuously. "We have not much farther to go, I suppose."

"I hope to show you the mountain to-morrow," replied Bart.

"Then they can wait for their chastisement for another day or two. Come now, my excitable young friend, you think I have been rather quiet and tame with these wretches, don't you?"

Bart's face grew scarlet.

"Well, sir, yes, I do," he said, frankly.

"Well spoken," said the governor, clapping him on the shoulder.

"Yes," said Captain Miguel, "well spoken; but you are wrong, my boy. I have longed for days past to lead my men in a good dashing charge, and drive these savage animals back to their dens; but I am a soldier in command, and I have to think of my men as well as my own feelings. These fifty men are to me worth all the Indian nations, and I cannot spare one life, no, not one drop of blood, unless it is to give these creatures such a blow as will cow them and teach them to respect a civilised people, who ask nothing of them but to be left alone. Wait a little longer, my lad; the time has not yet come."

That night strong outposts were formed, for the Indians were about in great force; but no attack was made, and at daybreak, on a lovely morning, they were once more in motion, while, to Bart's great surprise, though he swept the plain in every direction, not an Indian was to be seen.

"What does that mean, think you?" said the governor, smiling.

"An ambush," replied Bart. "They are waiting for us somewhere."

"Right," exclaimed the Captain, carefully inspecting the plain; "but there is little chance of ambush here, the ground is too open, unless they await us on the other side of that rolling range of hills. You are right though, my lad; it is to take effect later on. This is to lull us into security; they have not gone far."

A couple of hours brought them to the foot of the low ridge, when scouts were sent forward; but they signalled with their lances that the coast was clear, and the party rode on till the top was reached, and spurring a little in advance of the troop in company with the captain and the governor, Bart reined up and pointed right away over the gleaming lake to where the mountain stood up like some huge keep built in the middle of the plain.

"There is the rock fortress," he cried.

"And where is the silver canyon?" said the governor, looking eagerly over the plain.

"Running east and west, sir, quite out of sight till you are at its edge, and passing close behind the mountain yonder."

"Forward, then," cried the captain; "we must be there to-night. Keep up well with the waggons, and—halt! Yes, I expected so; there are our friends away there in the distance. They will be down upon us before long, like so many swarms of bees."

The greatest caution was now observed, and they rode steadily on for a few miles farther, when Bart joyfully pointed out that the occupants of the rock fortress were still safe.

"How can you tell that?" said the governor, eagerly.

"By the flag, sir," said Bart. "There it is out upon the extreme right of the mountain. If the Indians had got the better of the Doctor's party, they would have torn it down."

"Or perhaps kept it up as a lure to entrap us," said the captain, smiling; "but I think you are right about that."

"What a splendid position for a city!" exclaimed the Governor, as they rode on towards where the waters of the lake gleamed brightly in the sun.

"Yes; a great town might be placed there," said the captain, thoughtfully; "but you would want some large barracks and a little army," he added with a smile, "to keep our friends there at a distance."

For, as they neared the mountain, it seemed ominously like a certainty that the savages now meant to make a tremendous onslaught upon the band, for they were steadily coming on in large numbers, as if to meet the new-comers before they could form a junction with the holders of the rock.

"I don't want to fight them if I can help it," said Captain Miguel, scanning the approaching Indians carefully as they advanced—"not until the waggons are in safety. If we do have to charge them, you drivers are all to make for the rock, so as to get under the cover of our friends' fire. That is, if it comes to a serious attack, but I do not think it will."

The watchfulness and care now exercised by their leader showed how well worthy he was of being placed in such a position, and the men, even to the governor, obeyed him without a word, though at times his orders seemed to run in opposition to their own ideas. For he seemed to be almost skirmishing from the Indians, instead of making a bold stand, and the result was that when, after a couple of hours, they came on in strength, their insolence increased with the seeming timidity of the relieving force.

"You underrated the numbers, young gentleman," said Captain Miguel at last, when the Apachés were in full force. "You said five hundred. I should say there are quite six, and as fine a body of well-mounted warriors as I have seen upon the plains."

"Well, Miguel," said the governor, "it seems to me that, unless you attack them, we shall all be swept into the lake."

"I don't think you will, sir," replied the captain, calmly; "they are only bragging now, many as they are; they do not mean to attack us yet."

Captain Miguel was right, for though the Apachés came yelling on, threatening first one flank and then the other, their object was only to goad the lancers into a charge before which they would have scattered, and then gone on leading the troops away. But the captain was not to be tricked in that manner; and calmly ignoring the badly aimed rifle-bullets, he made Bart lead, and getting the waggon-horses into a sharp trot, they made straight now for the fortress-gate.

"Steady, steady!" shouted the captain; "no stampeding. Every man in his place, and ready to turn when I cry Halt!—to fire, if needs be. Steady there!"

His words were needed, for once set in motion like this, and seeing safety so near, the waggon-drivers were eager to push on faster, and made gaps in the waggon-train; but they were checked by the lancers, who rode on either side, till at last faces began to appear on the various ledges and the zigzag path up the mountain, and a loud cheer was heard, telling that all was right.

Then came the fierce yelling of the Indians, who suddenly awoke to the fact that they had put off their attack too long, and that the waggon-train would escape them if they delayed much more.

Captain Miguel read the signs of their movements as if they were part of an open book, and with a cry of satisfaction he shouted out, "At last!"

Then to the waggon-drivers, "Forward there, forward, and wheel to your right under the rock. Then behind your waggons and horses for an earth-work, and fire when it is necessary. You, my lad, see to that, and get your friends to help."

This was shouted amidst the tramp of horses and the rattle and bumping of the waggons, while the Indians were coming on in force not half a mile away.

"Steady, steady!" shouted the captain, and then, almost imperceptibly, he drew his men away from the sides of the waggon-train, which passed thundering on towards the rock, while the lancers, as if by magic, formed into a compact body, and cantered off by fours towards the canyon.

"They've run; they've left us," yelled some of the drivers, in their Spanish patois. "Forward, or we shall be killed."

But they were wrong; for all at once the little body of lancers swung round and formed into a line, which came back over the same ground like a wall, that kept on increasing in speed till the horses literally raced over the level plain.

The Indians were at full gallop now, coming on like a cloud of horse, yelling furiously as they stood up in their stirrups and waved their lances, their course being such that the lancers would strike them, if they charged home, at an angle.

All at once there was a fluttering of pennons, and the lances of the little Mexican force dropped from the perpendicular to the level, the spear-points glistening like lightning in the evening sun.

This evolution startled the Apachés, some of whom began to draw rein, others rode over them, and the great cloud of horsemen began to exhibit signs of confusion. Some, however, charged on towards the waggons, and thus escaped the impact, as, with a hearty cheer and their horses at racing pace, the lancers dashed at, into, and over the swarm of Indians, driving their way right through, and seeming to take flight on the other side as if meaning to go right away.

Their course was strewed with Apachés and their ponies, but not a Mexican was left behind; and then, before the savages could recover from their astonishment, the gallant little band had wheeled round, and were coming back, trot—canter—gallop, once more at racing speed.

There was another tremendous impact, for there were so many of the savages that they could not avoid the charge, and once more the lancers rode right through them, leaving the ground strewn with dead and wounded men and ponies. Their riderless steeds added to the confusion, while no sooner were the lancers clear, and forming up once more a couple of hundred yards away, than a tremendous fire was opened from the rock fortress and the waggon-train, making men fall fast.

The lancers were soon in motion once more for their third charge, but this was only a feint, for the firing would have been fatal to friend as well as foe, there being no one to signal a stay. Still the Apachés did not know this, and having had two experiences—their first—of the charge of a body of heavily mounted, well-disciplined men, they were satisfied, and as the lancers began to canter, were in full flight over the plain, men and ponies dropping beneath the fire and from previously received lance-wounds, while the ground for a broad space was literally spotted with the injured and the dead.

"Oh, if I could have been with you!" cried Bart, riding up to the captain rifle in hand.

"Let soldiers do soldiers' work, my young friend," said the captain, bluntly. "You are excited now; perhaps you will think differently another time."

Chapter Forty Two.: The Silver City in the Plains.

Bart did think differently when he cooled down, and, after a warm greeting from the Doctor, who praised his bravery and thanked him for bringing help, saw the dreary business of burying the fallen in those fierce charges; for he shuddered and thought of the horrors of such an occupation, even when the fights were in thorough self-defence.

Joses was full of excitement, and kept on shaking hands with the Beaver instead of with Bart.

"I knew he'd do it. I knew he'd do it," he kept on saying. "There arn't a braver lad nowhere, that I will say."

There was but little time for talking and congratulations, however, for the waggons had to be unloaded and camp formed for the lancers and Mexicans, the former being out in the plains driving in the Indian ponies that had not gone off with the Apachés, the result being that thirty were enclosed in the corral before dark, being some little compensation for the former loss.

Bart learned that night, when the captain and the governor were the guests of the Doctor, that beyond occasional alarms but little had gone on during his absence. The Indians had been there all the time, and his friends had always been in full expectation of an attack, night or day, but none had come.

The most serious threatening had been on the night when Bart set off, but the terrible storm had evidently stopped it, and the Doctor related how the rock had been struck by lightning, a large portion shattered, and the bodies of several Indians found there the next morning.

There was good watch set that night, not that there was much likelihood of the Indians returning, but to make sure; and then many hours were spent in rejoicing, for several of the adventurers had been giving way to despair, feeling that they had done wrong in coming, and were asking in dismay what was to become of them when the stores were exhausted.

"We can't eat silver," they had reproachfully said to the Doctor; and when he had reminded them how he had sent for help, they laughed him to scorn.

All murmurers were now silenced, and, light-hearted and joyous, the future of the silver canyon became the principal topic of conversation with all.

The next morning, as it was found that the Indians were still hovering about, Captain Miguel showed himself ready for any emergency. The Beaver and his men were at once mounted on the pick of the Indian ponies, and a start was made to meet the enemy.

So well was this expedition carried out, that, after a good deal of feinting and manoeuvring, the captain was enabled to charge home once more, scattering the Indians like chaff, and this time pursuing them to their temporary camp, with the result that the Apachés, thoroughly cowed by the attacks of these horsemen, who fought altogether like one man, continued their flight, and the whole of the horses and cattle, with many Indian ponies as well, were taken and driven back in triumph to the corral by the rocks.

This encounter with the Indians proved most effectual, for the portion of the nation to which they belonged had never before encountered disciplined troops; and so stern was the lesson they received, that, though predatory parties were seen from time to time, it was quite a year before any other serious encounter took place.

In the meantime, the governor had been so impressed with the value of the Doctor's discovery, that, without interfering in the slightest degree with his prospects, communications were at once opened up with Lerisco; more people were invited to come out, smelting furnaces were erected, the silver purified, and in less than six months a regular traffic had been established across the plains, over which mules laden with the precious metal, escorted by troops, were constantly going, and returning with stores for use in the mining town.

A town began to spring up rapidly, with warehouses and stores; for the mountain was no longer standing in solitary silence in the middle of the great plain. The hum of industry was ever to be heard; the picks of the miners were constantly at work; the great stamps that had been erected loudly pounded up the ore; and the nights that had been dark and lonely out there in the plains were now illumined, and watched with wonder by the roving Apachés, when the great silver furnaces glowed and roared as the precious metal was heated in the crucibles before being poured into the ingot-making moulds.

The growth of the place was marvellous, the canyon proving to be so rich in the finest kinds of silver, that the ore had but to be roughly torn out of the great rift that was first shown by the chief, and the profits were so enormous that Doctor Lascelles became as great a man in his way as the governor, while Bart, as his head officer and superintendent of the mine, had rule over quite a host.

Houses rose rapidly, many of them being of a most substantial kind, and in addition a large barrack was built for the accommodation of fifty men, who worked as miners, but had certain privileges besides for forming the troop of well-mounted lancers, whose duty it was to protect the mining town and the silver canyon from predatory bands of Apachés.

These lancers were raised and drilled by Captain Miguel, Bart being appointed their leader when he had grown to years of discretion—that is to say, of greater discretion than of old, and that was soon after Doctor Lascelles had said to him one day:

"Well, yes, Bart; you always have seemed to be like my son. I think it will be as well;" and, as a matter of course, that conversation related to Bart's marriage with Maude.

But, in spite of his prosperity and the constant demand for his services in connection with the mines and the increase of the town, Bart never forgot his delight in a ramble in the wilds; and whenever time allowed, and the Beaver and some of his followers had come in from some hunting expedition, there was just a hint to Joses, when before daybreak next morning a start was made either to hunt bison and prong-horn, the black-tailed deer in the woods at the foot of the mountain, or to fish in some part of the canyon. Unfortunately, though, the sparkling river became spoiled by degrees, owing to the enormous quantities of mine-refuse that ran in, poisoning the fish, and preventing them from coming anywhere near the mountain.

Still there were plenty to be had by those daring enough to risk an encounter with the Indians, and many were the excursions Bart enjoyed with Joses and the Beaver, both remaining his attached followers, though the latter used to look sadly at the change that had come over the land.

And truly it was a wondrous change; for, as years passed on, the town grew enormously—works sprang up with towering chimneys and furnaces, the former ever belching out their smoke; while of such importance did Silver Canyon City grow, and so great was the traffic, that mules and waggons could no longer do the work.

The result is easy to guess. There was a vast range of rolling plain to cross, a few deviations enabling the engineer, who surveyed the country with Apachés watching him, to avoid the mountains; and this being done, and capital abundant, a railway soon crept, like a sinuous serpent, from Lerisco to the mountain foot, along which panted and raced the heavily laden trains.

The Apachés scouted, and there was some little trouble with them at first, but they were punished pretty severely, though they took no lesson so deeply to heart as the one read their chief upon seeing the first train run along the rails.

Poor wretch! he had not much more sense than a bison; for he galloped his little pony right on to the line, and pressed forward to meet the engine after firing his rifle—he rode no more!

"Well, I dare say it's all right, Master Bart," said Joses one day; "everybody's getting rich and happy, and all the rest of it; but somehow I liked the good old times."

"Why, Joses?" said Bart.

"Because, you see, Master Bart, we seem to be so horrid safe now."

"Safe, Joses?"

"Yes, Master Bart," grumbled the old fellow; "there arn't no risks, no keeping watch o' nights, no feeling as it arn't likely that you'll ever see another morning, and it isn't exciting enough for me."

But then the Beaver came up with some news that made Joses' eyes sparkle.

"There's buffalo out on the far plain, captain," he said; "and I've seen sign of mountain sheep three days' journey up the canyon. Will the young chief Bart go?"

"That I will, Beaver," cried Bart. "To-morrow at daybreak."

"No; to-night," said the Beaver.

"That's the way," growled Joses. "Say yes, Master Bart."

Bart did say yes, as he generally would upon hearing such news as this—these excursions carrying him back to the old adventurous days, when, quite a lad, he joined in a hunt to find provision for the little camp.

Then Black Boy would be saddled, for the sturdy little cob never seemed to grow old, except that there were a few grey hairs in his black coat; provisions were prepared, ammunition packed, good-byes said, and for a few days Bart and his friends would be off into the wilderness, away from the bustle and toil always in progress now at the silver canyon.

22279977R00106

Printed in Great Britain
by Amazon